T...
INVITATION

To, Dove

Patrick

THE
INVITATION

PATRICK MACDONALD

For my wife, Mary.

PROLOGUE

As she came to the bend above the Forty Foot Drain she slowed down. Also known as the Black Sluice Navigation, the road running alongside it had a fifty mile an hour speed limit and was notoriously dangerous. She peered ahead through the gloom. Mist rose from the flat Fenland fields around her giving the landscape an otherworldly feel, the sun smeared across the horizon.

Until the age of nine she had lived with her parents near Inverness in the village of Drumnadrochit on the shores of Loch Ness, and she had spent some of the happiest years of her childhood there, a magical landscape of soft rounded hills and forest folded around the forbidding vastness of Loch Ness. Then her father had been offered a teaching post in marine biology at Cambridge, moving her mother, younger sister and her to a modest house in the small town of Godmanchester. In contrast to her father's fascination, she had always been repelled by the Fens: a watery marshland of drains and dikes clawed from the sea, a monotonous land of hedgeless fields, of feathery reeds and bulrushes, of uneven lanes and tilted houses, the black peaty soil pulling them earthwards, water oozing upwards to drown them.

Having scarcely slept the previous night, she was fighting to stay awake. She turned off the heating and moved to press the switch to open the window, hoping a blast of cold air might help. As she reached, the window still shut, there was a loud bang, the car juddering and swerving violently across the road. Her heart exploded in her chest. She drove down the brake pedal. The car spun and tipped forward. There was a brief sensation of weightlessness, of time suspended, then a hard upward shove as the car hit water.

She stared in horror as ice-cold water welled up from the footwell, rising quickly to her waist, her breath choked off in her throat. She reached again for the switch on the door panel to open the window. There was no response. She tried again, and then again, a frantic jabbing. Nothing. She drew her arm back and punched the glass as hard as she could. Pain shot up through her hand into her arm. The glass was still intact. Ignoring the pain, she rammed her elbow against it. There was a new jolt of agony as it bounced off to add to the symphony of agony she was already feeling. The water was now at chest level. She tore off her seat belt, and eased herself up, moving across, and then scrabbling backwards between the front seats into the rear of the car. Because of the angle of the car, nose down in the ditch, the water was at a lower level there and she could still lift her head and neck above it.

Her breathing was coming in short panicky bursts, her heart pounding furiously. She knew that barely three months earlier, a mother and her toddler had drowned here. The water still rising, she craned her neck upwards to keep her mouth and nose above it.

She stared at the windscreen, a thin sliver of light at the top. Then darkness. The front of the car was now entirely immersed. She knew she had seconds to live.

*

Kings Cross, London, the same day

Eighty miles away another woman stepped onto a tube escalator. She was smartly dressed, professional, her brown hair immaculately styled. Fifteen years had elapsed since a carelessly dropped match on the same stairs ignited a fire which killed thirty-one people. Then wooden, now they were gleaming steel. Where once they shuddered and squealed, now they slid silently into the bowels of the station. A nervous traveller, she had more in common with the tourists who stood, bewildered, staring at the tube maps displayed in bright primary colours on the walls than the seasoned commuters who pushed against them.

The convention was that people stood on the right on the down escalators to allow those either braver or less patient to walk down on the left. The woman stood on the right. The immediate two steps below her were empty but below that was a tourist with a suitcase propped on the stair below. The tourist was small, elderly, with untidy grey hair and her frailty was to prove fatal to the woman above her who was suddenly and violently shoved in the back. She fell forward, lost her grip on the rail and pushed hard into the woman in front. The elderly woman crumpled, and she toppled over her, tumbling helplessly to the bottom. She hit the ground as screams erupted around her and lay there, a broken marionette, her knickers flashing white beneath her blue dress.

CHAPTER ONE

As she pulled into the drive the rain increased in intensity; it was as though a wall of water had suddenly descended on her. Claire sat exhausted as it roared outside, pounding against the car's roof. She would have to wait until the rain relented a little before she dared make a dash for her front door.

She could feel the tension in her shoulders and neck; it had been a difficult day with two autopsies, the first for a ten-year-old girl and the second a man in his late twenties who had been crushed under the wheels of a lorry whilst cycling to work. The girl was particularly upsetting; she had died suddenly at school; the autopsy CTI uncovered a cerebral AVM, a tangle of abnormal blood vessels in her brain which had suddenly ruptured causing a catastrophic bleed. She had died almost instantly. The knot was congenital; the poor girl had been carrying a time bomb from birth. It was rare that such a genetic abnormality was passed down among families but, nonetheless, Claire had recommended that CTIs should also be carried out for her two brothers. If they were affected, they would probably need immediate surgery. It would also depend, of course, on the precise location of the AVMs – it might well be decided that such surgery was too risky.

Claire peered through the windscreen. She was feeling anxious; ten months previously there had been an almost biblical fall of rain over a three-day period. The Great Ouse was less than half a mile from their house but, ironically, it was not the river which had caused the problem. The drains choked on the rain and spewed it back onto the streets; a number of houses on the Causeway had flooded and the floodwaters had run in torrents down the street.

Some of the residents had access to sandbags. Others, less fortunate, filled black bin bags with sand, or wedged old bits of carpet or plastic sheeting against their doors. The floodwater was relentless; it punched through front doors, oozed through air bricks, came up through floorboards, laid waste to gardens.

At last, the rain eased. She twisted round to grab her coat from the rear seat, slid herself out and ran. The post was piled up against the front door inside and she bent to pick it up. As she did this, she noticed a letter still wedged in the metal flap of the letterbox. She frowned, tugged it out. There was no postmark or stamp and it had obviously been hand delivered. Curious, she tore it open. Inside was a single card, edged in black.

There was a photograph of her, passport sized, at the top of the card, and underneath, in an elaborate copperplate black script:

You are respectfully invited to the funeral of Claire Evans, much beloved, on 13th June 2012 at 9 AM at St Mary the Virgin Church, Chadley Lane, Godmanchester, Huntingdon.

No floral tributes. The family's wish is that, instead, donations should be made to the Bradbury Oaks Hospice in Brampton

Her brain scrambled to do the maths. 13th June. A month away. No, less: twenty-eight days.

She stared again at the photograph. Looking back at her was a younger version of herself: mid-twenties, blonde straight hair parted in the middle, blue-grey eyes.

She could feel her breathing becoming shallow as her heartbeat quickened. Who could have sent this? She opened the door and peered out into the darkness. There was a car parked a little way down the street, its headlights on. From the shape she was sure it was a Ford, either a Focus or a Fiesta. She could just make out the hunched figure of the driver, but it was impossible to see whether it was a man or a woman. For a moment she thought about walking down to the car and challenging the person inside. No, that was ridiculous. Whoever had delivered the card was hardly likely to have stuck around. It could have been delivered hours ago. She closed the door and forced herself to breathe more slowly. Putting the card and envelope down on the glass-topped hallway table, she shrugged off her wet raincoat, hanging it on the coat stand.

Claire looked again at the envelope and noticed to her annoyance that the handwriting was now smeared with water. Pulling a tissue from her pocket she hurriedly blotted it. Neat cursive penmanship. Female? She needed to calm down. This was just some horrible, twisted joke; a spiteful hoax but no more serious than that.

Her professional instincts kicked in. Paper had a porous surface so it would be a simple task to lift fingerprints off it. If she kept both the envelope and card, she could arrange to do that back in the lab. The problem, of course, was then finding a match. If whoever had sent this had never been required to provide prints to the police, then the prints themselves wouldn't get her very far. Both paper and card might have been handled by others before it arrived at her door so there could be multiple prints. Whoever had sent the card though, had made one crucial mistake – they had provided a sample of their handwriting and she knew courts accepted the testimony of handwriting experts.

She took both the card and envelope and walked into the kitchen; granite worktops, a central island, gleaming white cupboards and mid-grey walls. Elephant's breath, her husband had told her, or some such nonsense. Clearly an elephant with very bad halitosis. Bi-folding doors took up the entire front of the kitchen opening out onto cream composite decking, a seating area and an expensively landscaped garden. There was still a faint smell of the takeaway curry from the previous evening. I need to empty the waste bin she thought. Not now though.

Claire grabbed a bottle of Chablis from the fridge. It was half full. Every night now, the first thing she did on arriving back home was to treat herself to a large glass of wine. If it had been a particularly stressful day there would be a second, and sometimes a third. Sean had given her a hard time about her supposedly excessive drinking, but he wasn't here was he? Yet another week with his mates playing golf in the Algarve, so to hell with it. He was probably getting tanked up himself every night so who was he to preach? If he was home, he would have asked her whether she'd taken her medication that day. He was quite scrupulous in that respect, almost as though he feared she would slip into madness if she missed even a single day. She tried to remember if she had taken it that morning, gave up, and turned instead to pick up the card again. She stared hard at it, as though she could force it to give up its secret with the intensity of her glare.

Taking the bottle from the fridge again, she refilled her glass to the brim, shaking the last drops from the bottle. So, who? Who could have sent it? Could it be Alan's wife, Rachel? Could his wife have found out? Claire had persuaded Alan to buy a separate mobile phone in addition to his work one. She told him to tell Rachel that he was fed up getting work calls during his hard-earned downtime, so he'd decided to get a second one for his personal use. Claire said she would do the same. They had agreed they would only communicate with each other via WhatsApp. No phone calls.

Alan, being Alan, of course had initially suggested they should just get two burners, pay-as-you-go mobiles, where the only calls and texts would be between them. Claire thought this was too obvious, a suspicious partner could still find the phone. Its very existence would lead someone to wonder. Burners. He'd been watching too many episodes of *The Wire*.

There were other possible suspects, though, the ones she had encountered through her work. Some singularly unpleasant people. Claire felt a tight knot of fear in her stomach and her hands were still shaking as she reached for her glass of wine.

She remembered Toby and glanced at the clock. It was just after six. Her friend Jessica would be bringing him home around now. She stuffed the card back into the envelope and pushed it into one of the overstuffed drawers in the central island, tucked away under a pile of receipts and bank statements. Taking her wine with her, she went upstairs to the master bedroom and changed into leggings and a loose top. She took another mouthful. It was beginning to work its magic, a slow drifting of her mind from its moorings, her thoughts becoming fuzzy and indistinct.

Then the chime of the doorbell. She left the wine on the bedside table and walked down. She could hear Toby's excited chatter through the door as she reached for the latch. Jessica and Toby tumbled through, laughing, coats and lunchboxes spilling onto the floor, Toby's pink rabbit with buttons for eyes clutched tightly to his chest.

"Mummy!" he cried, launching himself into Claire's arms.

"And how are you, light of my life?"

"We played pirates at nursery; I had a sword."

"Not a real one, I hope," Claire said in mock horror, "I hope you didn't hurt anybody with it?"

"I stuck it in Amy – she screamed, but it was only a pretend scream. It didn't hurt – look"

She was crouching down in front of him and he pushed the sword into her upper shoulder; it was plastic, the blade retracting back into the handle as it hit her arm. She laughed and pretended to be upset. "You monster, you could have killed me."

"Only a little kill, Mummy, not a big one."

"Good to know. Let me know when you're planning your big kill and I'll try to arrange to be somewhere else that evening."

"Me too," said Jessica, laughing. Claire looked up at her.

"Jess, there's something I need to talk to you about."

"Yes, no problem. I need to learn a part for some rehearsals starting next week but it can wait. Can't say it's much of a part anyway."

"What's the play?"

"Merchant of Venice – and no, before you ask, I haven't been cast as Portia. I'm Nerissa, her lady-in-waiting and confidante."

"Oh, well, never mind – who knows where it could lead?

11

Perhaps, some Hollywood producer might be in the audience."

"Doubt it, since it's in Kilburn. But enough about me, what did you want to talk about?"

"Pour yourself a glass of wine, Jess, and I'll take this monster up to bed and see how well I can frighten him with a strong dose of Roald Dahl. Then we can have a proper talk."

Jessica had already fed Toby, who was going through a phase of only eating chicken nuggets and baked beans. Claire was worried about this, but Jessica said it was just a phase they all went through. Then they become foodies as adults, acquire a taste for garlic bread and olives, and complain bitterly that they were force-fed rubbish as children. Jessica had an older daughter, about to take her GCSEs, and a younger son who had just started secondary school.

Claire bundled Toby into his pyjamas, searched for the Roald Dahl book they had been reading, failed to locate it, and settled instead on a Winnie-the-Pooh book. She was struggling to focus, her thoughts circling in a tight loop. Who? Who could be so nasty as to—

"That's not Mr Twit," cried Toby.

"No, Mr Twit's gone missing, so we'll have to look for him tomorrow. I found Winnie though. Is that alright?" she said, nestling in beside him.

"But I want Mr Twit."

"Perhaps tomorrow, Toby, but tonight, for one night only, we'll have Pooh Bear."

"Does Pooh smell?"

"What? I don't think so… well, if he does, he smells of honey – honey and possibly bees."

"George smells."

"George, Elaine's son?"

"He smells," Toby giggled. "He had to be taken out of the class – he did a poop in his trousers." He repeated the word, relishing the sound of it on his lips, the soft explosion of sound. "A poopy pooh."

Now Claire was giggling herself and pulled him closer to her, his body exuding an intoxicating perfume of its own, a complex mix of milk, shampoo and his own body odours. She inhaled deeply and for a moment felt calmer. She read aloud to him for a little, curled up beside him, and despite her unease, found herself starting to nod off. She awoke with a start. She wondered how long she had been asleep. She glanced at the bedroom clock which emitted a soft green digital glow: 7:05 PM. Twenty minutes? Longer? Toby was asleep. She eased herself out of the bed, taking care not to wake him. She gazed down at his prone form and kissed him gently on his forehead. The guilt of what she had done during her pregnancy never left her.

She remembered Jessica was still waiting downstairs. Stretching upwards like a cat, she smoothed her top down and crept out of the door, pushing it shut behind her.

Jessica was sitting on the cream sofa in the living room, her shoes off, her legs tucked under her. Claire observed her for a moment through the glass-panelled doors before she entered.

Jessica had always been the sensible one in their friendship, the one able to switch off her emotions, bringing a coolly analytical approach to a problem. It was odd; Claire was all of these things in her work, but her personal life was something else again.

Claire was also a little envious of her looks. Jessica had auburn hair, an expensive layered cut, with blonde and gold highlights. She had a flawless complexion, and the sort of pert nose Audrey Hepburn would have been proud of. She was pretty – in some lights, beautiful. Claire's own nose was a more patrician affair, one which people said gave her face a strong, almost masculine look. Claire was holding the funeral card down at her side as though to hide it, but when she sat down beside Jessica she handed her the card.

Jessica looked at it blankly for a moment, comprehension slowly dawning, a look of horror finally emerging. "When did you get this?"

"It was hand-delivered today. I can't tell when."

"Have you rung the church?"

"No, I meant to, but then you two came back and—"

"You must phone them now. It's obviously a hoax and they should be able to confirm that Look, I'll google their number."

Jessica fished out her phone from her shoulder bag, which had been dumped on the floor. It was black, with an ornate gold chain strap. New, Claire thought, and she could tell from the etched logo of a tree on the tag that it was a Mulberry bag, very expensive. It would have cost far more money than Claire was prepared to spend on a bag. She thought about commenting on it but then decided against. Jessica had been at university with her, studying English and drama. She had become an actor, but her career had never flourished and now she combined temp work as a waitress or barmaid with the odd stint in provincial theatre. It was a precarious existence and money was often tight. Realising this, Claire had asked her to help out with childcare, taking and collecting Toby from nursery three days a week. She insisted on paying and Jessica had reluctantly accepted. Brenda, Claire's aunt, did the nursery runs on the remaining two days of the week.

Jessica found the number and handed the phone to Claire. Claire pressed the small telephone icon. The call went to voicemail. She pressed cancel, sighed, and handed the phone back.

"And?" said Jessica.

"Voicemail."

"Well, call them back – leave a message, explain it's urgent."

"Yes, sorry, of course, give it back to me."

She rang again. Voicemail. Waited for the monotonous greeting to finish, inviting her to leave a message, and took a deep breath. "I'm calling about a funeral service which is supposedly taking place at your church on the 13th of June. I believe it's for a Claire Evans. Could you call me back, please? It's very important I speak to you. My number is 07700 334208. I'll repeat that: 07700 334208. Thank you."

Jessica leaned towards her, covering one of her hands with her own.

"I'm so sorry, Claire, this must be so frightening. Are you okay?"

"No, not really."

"Have you thought about who might have sent this?"

Claire gave a bitter laugh. "I've thought of nothing else. But I can't… my mind's in a complete… I can't think straight. I'm sorry, I just—"

Tears pricked her eyes.

"It's just someone playing a very nasty trick. I think they stopped burials there anyway in the 1970s."

"They stopped using the graveyard, but they still hold funeral services there. I'll try and ring them again in the morning, but if I can't get through I'll visit the church and see what I can find out. I might find something, a clue, something that helps me find out who did this. Even the most careful person will leave something behind, my job has at least taught me that."

"Not if they didn't go there in the first place. The person sending that card wouldn't have needed to visit the church. They probably don't even live locally, just looked up your address on Google Maps and worked out where the nearest church was."

"The card was hand-delivered."

"Oh, of course, it was. Sorry, I'm sure I'd make a lousy detective. Do you want me to stay over? I could come to the church with you tomorrow."

"No, Jess, it's fine. I think I have to do this on my own."

CHAPTER TWO

The oak doors to the church were open but there was no sound from inside. It had been raining steadily all night, the morning sky shrouded by dense grey clouds. She stepped through the doors and gazed around. The church was deserted. A faint smell of damp and incense. She went back outside. The rain had increased in intensity but she scarcely noticed. The vicarage. There must be someone there who could help even if the vicar himself was absent. If not his wife then a housekeeper perhaps. However, when she got there she found that too was empty. There was no response when she rang the bell. Frustrated, she turned away, If she had been fearful and anxious before, now she was angry. Her car was parked in one of the quiet side streets and she decided to walk back through the cemetery surrounding the church. It was a longer route, but she needed time to think.

Claire looked around at the ancient headstones: some sunk into the ground, others leaning over. Even though the cemetery was closed to new burials, it still had to be maintained and she could see the grass must have been cut within the last day or two. It had rained almost constantly over the previous week, and the mower had torn up the wet grass, spilling it in green gobbets across its surface. She had tried phoning the church again before leaving but had got the same voicemail message. No-one had rung her back. Jessica had offered to take Toby to the nursery and to pick him up again in the evening, which was a godsend because she knew she wouldn't be able to drop him off and drive to the church in time for the funeral.

Near the exit stood one of the largest headstones in the cemetery, white marble, edged in black. She had never had cause to visit this church or its graveyard before, but so striking was its appearance that she stopped to read the inscription. In ornate black lettering it stated that the headstone had been erected by public subscription. A woman called Mary Ann Weems had been buried there, following her murder by her husband in 1819. He had been executed, and although the headstone didn't say, she presumed he had been hanged.

She moved closer to read the final lines of the inscription which were in a fainter and smaller font.

> *Ere crime you perpetrate survey this stone.*
> *Learn hence the God of justice sleeps not on his*
> *throne but marks the sinner with unerring eye.*
> *The suffering victim hears and makes the guilty die.*

A rook swept noisily into the air behind her and, startled, she turned around. She spotted what appeared to be a freshly dug grave which, of course, was impossible because—

There was a temporary marker at the head, a simple

wooden cross. She gazed transfixed at the inscription on the small metal plaque mounted on the cross.

Claire Evans

3rd September 1979 – 13th June 2012

The suffering victim hears and makes the guilty die.

She could feel her heart pounding, her breath choked off in her throat. The air around her felt heavy and dense, a spider's web vibrating with tension. She sensed a movement behind her and, turning, she saw a grey-bearded man watching her keenly. He was standing just in front of some iron gates close to the exit. She started to walk towards him. He suddenly bent down, gingerly scooping dog shit into a small plastic bag. Now, she could see his dog, a brown cocker spaniel, head down in the grass just ahead of him. He stood and smiled at her. She didn't return the smile and, edging past him, walked out of the cemetery.

It was just as she reached her car that she realised she should have taken a photograph of the temporary grave marker. She hurried back. The car was parked five minutes' walk from the church so at worst she would have lost ten minutes. When she arrived back at the grave, though, she had another shock. The marker had gone.

CHAPTER THREE

2010

"**D**id you remember the milk?"

This from Kate, the department's secretary, a mischievous nineteen-year-old with an untidy mop of curly brown hair.

Claire grimaced.

"Sorry, Kate, I forgot."

"Well, there's still some left but the sell-by date's yesterday. Never mind, we'll just have to risk it. I'm sure none of us are going to—"

"Don't say you were going to use the word 'die,'" groaned Mark.

Mark Simmons was a trainee pathologist, late twenties, his pale skin marked with red blotches from psoriasis.

"Go down with a bad case of the runs," grinned Kate. "Your turn to make it anyway, Mark. And remember, don't make it too strong for me. I like strong blokes but weak tea."

She winked at Claire, who hid a smile. Mark had a crush on Kate but lacked the self-confidence to do anything about it.

Kate knew this and enjoyed teasing him mercilessly.

"So, what delights await us this morning?" said Claire.

"It's the SIDS baby, I'm afraid," grimaced Mark. She had been brought in last night. "Doctor Madison rang to say she should be here by ten – her train got cancelled so she's had to catch a later one."

Claire's heart sank. Not only the dubious death of a baby to investigate, but she would be working with someone she found less than congenial. Joan Madison was a paediatric pathologist, Claire a forensic one. The unexplained death of a child was really her territory and Claire would simply be her assistant.

Claire had dealt with only two previous instances of Sudden Infant Death Syndrome, but both had been stressful. It was always important to arrive at the right diagnosis, but particularly so for SIDS cases, which could have devastating consequences for families who were already traumatised, and now she had Madison to contend with as well. Madison looked to be in her late forties but was in fact much older. One of her colleagues had told Claire in confidence she was fifty-eight – not far off drawing her pension, although Claire suspected she was the sort who would want to go on until she dropped. Madison had never married and appeared to have no interest in men. Claire suspected she was gay. There had been a rumour that she had once had an affair with a female work colleague, that they even lived together for a while, until her friend's promiscuity had driven Madison away. Now she lived alone, a cat her only companion. She was obviously besotted with it. Uncharacteristically, she had shown photographs of the cat to Claire on her phone. Claire had to confess it was gorgeous, a Persian, with a wash of black and white fur.

Claire looked at her watch; it was nine-thirty, so they had half an hour before Madison's arrival. "Right," she said, "we might as well have a cup of tea while we wait for her. Will anyone from the police be in attendance?"

"Yep. We've got a DS coming in," said Kate. "Your old mucker, Pete Hamlin, and a trainee detective apparently. Don't know his name – just hope he's porkable."

Kate was an outrageous flirt and "porking" was her favourite slang expression as far as men were concerned, as in "I wouldn't mind giving him a good porking." Mark, needless to say, wasn't considered suitable porking material. A bit too green for Kate, who preferred her men well-seasoned.

"So, when can we expect the pleasure of their company?" said Claire.

"Any time now. I took a call from them fifteen minutes ago saying they were on their way."

Mark handed Claire a cup of tea. The mug was chipped and had a hairline crack down one side.

"Mark, I can't possibly drink out of this."

"Why? What's wrong with it?"

She turned the mug round to show him.

"See the crack? If this broke, I'd be soaked in hot tea."

"Ah," he said. "Sorry, I'll start again."

Ten minutes later, the door entry system buzzed.

"That should be them now," said Kate, pressing the switch to unlock the door. A tall, barrel-chested man in his early fifties entered, followed by a young police officer, bearded, with neatly trimmed hair. Trailing behind them was a man who towered above his colleagues, with sunken cheeks and a deeply lined face. Claire guessed that he was a smoker. He was carrying a large camera and had a black canvas bag slung over his shoulder. It was the barrel-chested man who spoke first.

"Hi, Claire – good to see you again," said Hamlin. For once he wasn't smiling, looking both pale and anxious.

"I'm pleased to see you too," said Claire. "This is going to be a difficult case, unfortunately."

"Yeah, I know," said Hamlin. "Can I first introduce you to my colleague, Tony Foster? He's the SOCO on this job. Tony, this is Claire, the forensic pathologist, Kate, her secretary and… ?" He looked at Mark quizzically. "Sorry, I don't think we've met—"

"Mark, Mark Patterson – sorry, I'm new here. Started a couple of months ago – trainee pathologist."

Hamlin gave a brief smile. Foster nodded but didn't speak. The taciturn, watchful sort. No bad thing in his profession.

"Oh, I almost forgot," said Hamlin, nodding towards the young police officer. "I do apologise – this is Michael Adams, a trainee detective. I brought him down to show him the ropes, so to speak. Treat him gently, because this is his first post-mortem. He'll part of the younger generation taking over when I retire, God help them."

"I didn't know you were retiring," said Claire. "When are you going?"

"Eighteen months, nine days and five hours. Not that I'm counting, of course."

"Well, I'm not going to pretend you won't be missed."

"That's very kind of you. If only my colleagues felt the same."

Claire gave a brief smile and looked away to hide her sadness. She was very fond of Hamlin and would miss him.

"Unfortunately, we're still waiting for the paediatric consultant pathologist. She's had a problem with her train, but she should be here in the next ten minutes or so. You might as well join us for a tea or coffee first. Pete, I know you're a tea with one sugar. Tony, what would you like?"

"A black coffee, if that's alright – no sugar."

She had already forgotten the trainee detective's name so, to avoid embarrassment, she simply turned to him and said, "And what's your poison of choice?"

"Tea would be great, no sugar," said the trainee.

"Kate, can you do the honours?" said Claire.

"Yep, will do." Kate glanced at Hamlin. "We've only got instant I'm afraid – is that okay?"

"Yeah, that's fine, thanks," said Hamlin.

At that moment the door burst open. Standing in the

25

doorway was Madison, leaning forward as she tried to catch her breath, still holding her pass card. She had clearly been running to get there. She looked soaked through, her hair hanging down in limp strands around her face.

"Sorry I'm late," said Madison. "Sodding train – they're always cancelling them. They should bloody privatise the lot. Oh, wait – they already have."

So, she was in a bad mood already. Claire forced a smile. She had only worked once before with Madison but had taken an immediate dislike to her. She had been both arrogant and condescending.

Madison grimaced. "Forgot my umbrella as well this morning. I always have one in my bag, but I used it yesterday and forgot to put it back. I'll need five minutes to sort myself out. Where are the toilets? You can introduce me to everyone afterwards."

"Out that door there," Claire said, pointing. "They're shared, I'm afraid, unisex. Just an excuse to only provide the one really. It also doubles up as the disabled toilet, although, if you did get a wheelchair in there, you'd probably never get it out again. Oh, and we've run out of toilet paper, so we're making do with tissues. Still, at least that's better than newspaper." She nodded towards Kate. "Kate was going to get some last night but forgot."

Kate cheerfully acknowledged this with a bow, bending low and sweeping one arm across her chest. "One of my finer moments, of which I've had many."

"Kate will make you a cup of tea while we wait – unless, of course, you'd prefer coffee?"

"Black coffee, no sugar, please."

"Yes, of course. Chocolate biscuit with it? We've only got McVities, I'm afraid."

"I don't eat biscuits. Or cake for that matter. I won't be long."

She disappeared through the door, leaving a wet puddle on the floor behind her.

Hamlin glanced at Claire, raising an eyebrow.

Claire hesitated. "She's a very good paediatric pathologist: one of the best." She was tempted to say more but that would have been unprofessional.

When Madison returned Claire hurried through the introductions. She and Madison then changed into scrubs, masks and plastic clogs in the cramped changing area next to the post-mortem room. When they had emerged, the three police officers and Mark went in and once everyone had changed Claire led them into the brightly lit dissecting area. They were immediately assailed by the pungent smell of formalin. A bank of tall stainless-steel fridges lined the connected body storage area, a row of trolleys arranged in front of them.

The mortuary staff had already laid out the small corpse ready for examination, sheathed in plastic and dwarfed by the immense dissecting table.

This wasn't the first time Claire had taken part in the post-mortem of a baby, but they were never easy. The death of a baby swept aside her normal professional and emotional barriers, more so since the stillborn death of her first child. A girl, Elizabeth. The tiny kicks and flutters in her stomach had stopped, and the scan confirmed the worst. She was in her third trimester and was told it was best if she gave birth naturally. So, they induced her, an unnatural process in itself, and then the even more unnatural process of hugging her own dead child.

Looking down at the tiny lifeless form in front of her, also a girl, she felt lightheaded, a sense of dread welling up inside her. She briefly shut her eyes, forced herself to breathe deeply. The feeling passed. The others hadn't noticed but Hamlin was eyeing her keenly.

"Photographs first," said Madison.

The SOCO, Foster, edged forward. Madison lifted the shroud.

"So, what's the story on this?" Madison asked, turning towards Hamlin.

"The mother was killed in a road traffic accident. Lorry went into the back of her. The driver was both sending and receiving texts at the time. She was eight months pregnant, and they managed to save the baby at least. The father works in the City, no idea doing what, but he couldn't afford to give up his job to look after the baby, so he got his mum to look after it. Four months in, the baby dies. Now, the interesting thing about this case is that I did some digging and found out that twenty-five years ago, his mother had another supposed SID. In those days, of course, it wouldn't have been diagnosed as SIDS so the cause of death was given as unascertained."

"Alright," said Madison, "so, possibly two strikes against her, but the first death could have been as a result of a number of causes. Are you thinking shaken baby syndrome?"

"Perhaps," said Hamlin. "I need to trace the pathologist's report for the first death."

"But you're thinking the same thing might have happened here?" interrupted Claire.

"Again, I don't know – it's your job to tell me what you think might have happened. Once I get hold of the pathology report, I'll send you both copies. One other thing I did find out, though – she never had another kid. The father for this baby," he said, pointing at the baby lying on the table, "grew up as an only child. There was a gap of five years before he turned up but, in the meantime, there was another pregnancy, and she had the foetus aborted at sixteen weeks. Intriguing, don't you think?"

"Maybe," said Claire, cautiously. "On the other hand, this may still be a simple case of SIDS." She glanced at the SOCO, who had been busy taking photographs of the baby.

"With shaken baby syndrome," said Madison, "there's a classic triad of symptoms which we need to check for: a subdural haemorrhage, retinal bleeding and hypoxaemic encephalopathy."

"I'm up to speed on that," said Hamlin. "Useful for young Adams, though," and he gave a nod towards the trainee. "Can you turn it into English for him? God knows how you even managed to spell this stuff when you two sat your medical exams, never mind knowing what it all meant."

"Multiple choice," grinned Claire, "didn't need to spell it."

"I never had a problem spelling medical terms," said Madison. "Most of them are derived from the Latin or Greek and I studied both at grammar school."

Behind Madison's back, Claire winked at Hamlin.

"So, for Michael's benefit," said Hamlin. "What does it boil down to?"

"Joan, do you want me to cover this?" asked Claire.

"No, it's fine," said Madison, already in full flow. "A subdural haemorrhage is a bleed between the dura mater and the surface of the brain. Retinal bleeding is a rupture of the blood vessels in the eyes, and hypoxaemic encephalopathy is a lack of oxygen to the brain. Now, looking at this baby's retinas, I can see there is damage to the blood vessels, to the retinas in both eyes, in fact."

Claire turned to the SOCO. "Did you get some photos of this, Tony?"

"Yeah, I did. Might take some more, though – need to do some close-ups to pick up the burst blood vessels."

Foster moved nearer for the rapid-fire close-ups.

"Retinal haemorrhaging can occur at a baby's birth," said Madison, "but in most cases, these haemorrhages usually resolve within four to six weeks. This baby died at ten weeks, so I think we can rule out the possibility that the haemorrhaging happened when she was born. Haemorrhaging in both retinas also points towards SBS, although, obviously, this isn't conclusive, not on its own, anyway."

Madison did a visual examination of the body to check whether there was anything unusual that merited closer attention. "What do you think, Claire? Do you think this bruising to the mouth and the tissue split on the lips could be the result of abuse?"

Hamlin interrupted. "A neighbour attempted CPR on the baby, which might explain the cut to the lips."

"May I?" said Claire.

"Of course," said Madison and she stepped back a little to allow Claire better access to the body.

Claire carefully felt around the baby's ribs. "I think two of the ribs are broken. We can confirm it when we open up the body, but I'm pretty sure this is what we'll find. So, the bruising to the lips and the cracked ribs were probably the result of CPR."

"I think you're right," said Madison. "I can't see any other bruising or marks. Still, I'm sure the truth will emerge once we have a closer look at the brain and internal organs."

Out of the corner of her eye, Claire saw that the young trainee was shifting uncomfortably, moving nervously from foot to foot. There was a sheen of sweat on his face.

"Okay," said Madison, "let's start with measuring the body's length and then we'll weigh her. Claire, are you okay with recording our findings?"

"Yes – give me a second." She'd left her bag on a table which stood nearby and moved across to retrieve a dictaphone from one of its many pockets. "Right – all set."

"Can you do the body diagram as well?"

"It might be easier if you do. I need to concentrate on making sure my notes are accurate," said Claire.

Madison gave an exasperated sigh. "Okay, I'll do the diagram. Once your notes are typed up, I'd like to see them before they go to anyone else; we both need to be in complete agreement on the cause of death. If this goes to court – and I have a feeling it may well do that – we'll need to be bulletproof."

Unseen by the self-absorbed Madison, Claire rolled her eyes at Hamlin. Unable to help himself and, perhaps, because he was feeling nervous, Mark giggled.

Madison glanced around. "Are you finding something amusing?"

Mark flushed a deep crimson. Claire almost had to suppress a laugh herself. Kate called Mark's blushes "grimsons", an inspired mash-up of grim and crimson which perfectly described a blush marred by psoriasis. Unkind but funny.

"Sorry," muttered Mark, "I laugh when I get nervous."

"Good, because this is serious stuff," glared Madison. "If we get it wrong, it will mean a prison sentence for a woman who might well have been innocent."

Madison bent over the body, gently prodding the ribcage with her fingers.

"There appear to be possible fractures and trauma on a

number of this poor child's ribs but we'll need radiographs to confirm this. I'm going to leave this for the moment, though, because I think we need to take a look at the brain."

Cradling the baby's head, she swiftly drew her scalpel across the crown. Then, using a bone saw, she carefully cut through the skull, exposing the brain underneath.

At this point, the young detective suddenly retched and, holding his hand over his mouth, rushed from the room. As he departed, Hamlin yelled after him, "There's a toilet immediately to your right."

The door banged shut.

"Oh, for God's sake," muttered Madison.

"Don't be too hard on him," said Hamlin. "This is his first autopsy. I didn't fare that well on my first one either. Fainted clean away. Very embarrassing, to say the least."

"Do you think he'll be back?" said Claire.

"Not sure – he looked pretty green around the gills," said Hamlin.

"Well, I for one don't want him back," said Madison. "The last thing I need is the smell of vomit in here. Can someone go and have a word with him? Put him in the office, get him a cup of tea. Just keep him out of here."

Hamlin looked at Foster, who had an air of resignation. "Alright, I'll do it. If he really can't stomach this, perhaps he should go back to traffic."

"RTAs?" whispered Hamlin, his eyebrows raised.

"God, forgot about those. A desk job then – maybe

cybercrime. That would suit him down to the ground, especially if he can bring his PlayStation in."

Hamlin noticed Madison's look of exasperation and shot Foster a warning look. It was too late.

"Can you please stay quiet? It's difficult enough to concentrate as it is."

Visibly chastened, Foster walked out.

Madison exhaled slowly. "I'm now convinced as to the cause of death. What do you think, Claire?"

Claire moved closer. "There are blood clots on the surface of the brain, and I can also see how much paler the frontal area is." She was standing beside Madison, close enough to be mildly repelled by the smell of her breath. Garlic? Bad enough anyway to cut through the smell of formalin.

"It looks like oxygen starvation accompanied by a bleed," she said.

"Yes, I think so too," said Madison quietly. "SBS."

CHAPTER FOUR

2012

Claire sat in her car. She turned the key in the ignition to start it, but her hands trembled as she gripped the steering wheel. She turned off the engine. She had frantically scanned her surroundings in the cemetery when she had found the marker gone. There was no-one around. Even so, she felt that someone was watching her. Now she sat in the car staring blankly out, her mind whirling. This was no hoax; someone was targeting her, taunting her with the fact that they intended to kill her.

She eased her phone from her pocket. Pete Hamlin answered on the third ring.

"Hi, Claire. How are you? Strange you should phone now. I was literally just thinking about you."

"Nice thoughts, I hope." Her voice sounded strange to her, pitched too high, the stress she was feeling obvious in her tone. Hamlin sensed it immediately.

"Claire, are you alright? You sound—"

"Not really, Pete, no, not really. I need to see you urgently

– are you around at all today?"

"I should be free around lunchtime if that works for you. I've just finished dropping the grandchildren off at school and Margaret has asked me to pop into town to collect some dry cleaning. What's wrong? Are you okay?"

Claire went to speak but the words caught in her throat. Her breathing was shallow. She was taking panicky quick breaths, and she covered the phone's mouthpiece to try and conceal this from Hamlin. Calm down. Take a deep breath. She resumed speaking.

"Can you meet me in the Black Bull, say at half-twelve?"

"Yes, should be alright. Do you want to tell me anything now in case I need to speak to someone or—"

She could tell his curiosity was piqued and he was anxious to know immediately what the problem was, but she needed some space to process what had happened first, to get off Planet Hysteria and come up with a plan.

"No, better if I tell you face to face."

"Okay – you realise though I'll now be completely distracted wondering what the problem is until I see you?"

Claire forced a laugh.

"Yeah, I do. See you then. I've got to go. I need to ring the office—"

"Okay, see you at half-twelve. Look after yourself."

"Don't I always?"

"No, actually, you—"

She didn't hear the rest of the sentence because she had

already ended the call. She rang the office and told Kate she was taking a day's leave. The boiler had broken down again, she said, and she needed to get someone out to fix it. Kate started to tell her about her a problem that had arisen on a recent post-mortem, but Claire cut her short. They could discuss it tomorrow, she said, and rang off.

*

Apart from an old, unshaven man nursing a pint of Guinness at the bar and a young couple huddled at a table near a window, the pub was empty. There was a smell of woodsmoke from the fire, the logs making a soft cracking sound as they settled lower in the flames. Scanning the room, she chose to sit at a small oak table in a quiet corner, wincing with pain as she bumped her knee against it as she sat down. She hesitated as to whether she should have a glass of wine, but, as tempting as it was, for the moment at least she needed to focus. Instead, she ordered some mineral water and asked for the bar menu. Hamlin arrived shortly afterwards and she rose to hug him. He was wearing a heavy black jacket, zipped at the front, and Claire immediately regretted hugging him, drops of rain from the jacket spotting her own dress. The jacket smelled of rain and damp grass, undercut by a smell of newly dug earth.

"Good to see you again," she said. "You look well – retirement obviously suits you. People always say that once you retire, you lose ten years. Can I get you a drink?"

"You're looking good as well. I love your new hairstyle –

really suits you. Let me get the drinks, my treat. What would you like?"

"Don't worry," she said, gesturing at her glass, "I've got a drink already."

"Well, there's not much of that left. Can I get you another? Or something else? Glass of wine? We could share a bottle."

Claire hesitated but then gave in. "Yeah, sounds great."

Once they were settled, she quickly took him through what had happened.

"So," she said, "what do you think? Can the police help?"

"At this point, I don't think they would want to investigate. If you were simply to phone the police you would just end up talking to a civilian call handler who would suggest it's probably a hoax and, as yet, there's no real evidence of a crime. So, you were right to come to me. I've obviously still got contacts in the police force. I could talk to a former colleague, a DI, Andrews. He's a very good detective and, given who you are, I think I could persuade him to treat it as a potential threat to kill. At the very least he could make some calls, see what he could dig up."

Claire winced at the phrase "threat to kill", which Hamlin noticed.

"It must have been very frightening," he said gently.

"It was and it is," she said grimly. "Twenty-eight days, Pete. Less than a month. Whoever did this is threatening to kill me—"

She could feel a note of hysteria entering her voice. Once

again, she had to force herself to calm down.

"There's the invitation card – could your DI check it for fingerprints? I've brought it with me, hang on a second." She bent to rummage through her handbag. "Here, give him this – I've put it one of those plastic freezer bags to prevent further cross-contamination. The envelope's in there as well."

Hamlin studied it for a moment before slipping it into the inside pocket of his jacket. "Where do you think they might have got your photograph from?"

"I'm not sure – initially I thought Facebook, but I've gone through my Facebook gallery and I'm fairly certain it hasn't been lifted from there. I also restrict access to Friends Only, so if it had come from there that would have definitely narrowed it down."

"What to around a million you mean?" laughed Hamlin.

"Maybe on your site," Claire smiled, "but I try to be a little more discerning than you. You're not on it, for a start."

Hamlin grinned. "I'll send you a friend request."

"Fine, I'll ignore it."

"Seriously, though, I probably do need access. I might find something you've missed."

"Sorry, you're right," said Claire. "In fact, I'll do it right now, whilst you're sat in front of me – otherwise I'll forget."

"What about your other social media sites? LinkedIn? Instagram? Twitter?"

"Definitely not the LinkedIn profile but it could have come from Instagram or Twitter, I suppose, although I can't pretend to use either of those much. I'll have a look this evening. I've just had another thought as well; they could have scraped the photo from one of my friends' Facebook pages. If I appeared on their site, say in a group shot—"

"Exactly," said Hamlin.

"There's also the possibility they could have copied it off the web from a conference I attended or talk I might have given."

"True. If we can trace the photograph it might help us find whoever sent this but that's obviously not going to be easy. I'll drop into the station tomorrow so I can brief Andrews and give him a copy of the invitation and envelope. He can check them against the Interpol database and see if there's a match for fingerprints. The problem is that card will probably have been handled by a number of people including you. So, that will muddy the waters for a start. The truth is, there's a very low chance there will be a match."

"I thought as much. Still, it must be worth doing – you never know," said Claire.

"They'll need to take your fingerprints to eliminate you from the results."

"I don't have a problem with that. The handwriting on the envelope might help as well."

"Have you kept your own copy of the card and envelope?" said Hamlin.

"Yes, why?"

"If the person is local, and they could well be, it might be worth showing it around, see if anyone recognises it."

"Thanks, Pete, that makes a lot of sense. As long as I don't end up unwittingly showing it to whoever sent it in the first place—" She gave a nervous laugh.

"I can also make my own enquiries," mused Hamlin, "talk to the vicar – see if he's aware of anything."

"The cemetery's a cut-through for local people – someone passing through might have seen someone digging that grave," said Claire. "It would have taken a while to do it, even if all they did was mound up the earth. I suspect that's exactly what they did do. I can't believe someone didn't notice."

"Unless they did it at night or very early in the morning – not many people around at four or five, first thing. It wouldn't take that long, either. I reckon I could do it in fifteen or twenty minutes, or even quicker, and I'm not that fit anymore."

Claire smiled. "Still playing golf?"

"Trying to – I'm not that good. To be honest, I do it more for the social side. I go round with a couple of mates. Hack our way round, then have a pint afterwards. There are worse ways of spending a day."

"Tell me about it."

"You've got a tough job, Claire. I don't envy you, and you've got Toby to worry about as well."

"All true – I love the job, though. It's what I always wanted to do."

"Too much time spent watching CSI."

"Not really – I just conceived a passion for it when I started my medical degree."

"Pathologists – my opinion?"

There was a glint in his eye and Claire knew what was coming.

"Doctors like their patients, anaesthetists are indifferent to them and pathologists actively hate them." He grinned at her.

Claire laughed. "You do realise you told me this last time we were together?'

His face fell. "Did I? Good grief – I'm definitely on the slippery slope. Who are you again?"

"Don't joke, Pete. My grandad had dementia."

"Sorry, I didn't realise." He fingered the stem of his glass and stared out of the window. It was still raining. He turned back to her.

"Did you know, by the way, that this place is haunted?"

"How so?"

"Mary Ann Weems, the woman who was murdered; she's said to haunt this pub. Can't say as I've ever seen her behind the bar though."

Claire was startled. She felt a shiver. Before today, she had no idea who this woman was. Now, it was as if she was following her around. She drained her glass of wine and stood up.

"I've got to go, I'm afraid. I've got to pick Toby up from nursery. I was going to let a friend pick him up, but that was before my day got blown up by all this rubbish."

Hamlin also rose and gave her a hug.

"You'll let me know what you find out?" she asked him.

"Yeah, let me see what I can do, and I'll give you a ring. If you find anything useful on social media or the web let me know as well. Take care, Claire, and if anything else happens call me immediately."

"Thanks, Pete. I really appreciate this."

"No problem – it will give me something to do when I'm not playing golf."

As she left the pub, she saw the man who had been in the cemetery that morning. Another odd coincidence. He was stood a short distance away gazing at the town cenotaph, a finger of granite pointing into the sky, surrounded by a neat lawn, traffic humming past. This time he didn't have a dog with him. As she stared, he turned and looked at her. This time there was no smile and there seemed to be an air of challenge in his gaze. She studied him more closely. He looked to be in his fifties, similar in age to Hamlin. He was tall and gaunt, his frame a scarecrow, his clothes hanging loosely on him. He seemed familiar somehow, but she couldn't place him. He turned and walked away, carefully picking his way through the oily puddles which lined the road.

CHAPTER FIVE

The meeting with Hamlin had been reassuring but she still needed to speak to Alan to rule out Rachel as a possible suspect. She sent him a WhatsApp message asking him to contact her urgently. Two hours passed before he responded.

Sorry, I was in a meeting. Only just picked this up. You said it was urgent?

I need to see you – something has come up and we need to talk.

I have to work late – is tomorrow okay?

Are you sure you can't do tonight?

No, I can't. What about tomorrow evening?

She made a quick mental calculation. Sean was flying back from his golfing trip that day; she was supposed to pick him up around 7 pm. It was an hour's drive to Stansted, which meant she would have to leave at 6.

> *Tomorrow evening's difficult – Sean's flying back, and I have to pick him up from the airport. Are you sure you can't do tonight?*

> *No – what about lunchtime tomorrow? Meet at the Eagle at one?*

> *Yes, that would work. See you then. xx*

Alan was based in the centre of Cambridge so getting there was relatively simple for him, a ten-minute walk. Claire, though, was based at Addenbrookes; she would need a longer break to manage it.

She had first met Alan, ironically enough, through her own husband. They had been invited to a dinner party Alan and his wife had organised. Sean and Alan had themselves met through a local squash league where they had struck up a friendship. Alan was a partner at the accountancy firm, Cliffords; she had expected someone both arrogant and dull, but he had surprised her. He was engaging, with a subtle but incisive wit, a keen interest in the arts, and a seemingly bottomless fund of anecdotes. Although not obviously handsome, he had an animal magnetism: piercing blue eyes, dark hair swept carelessly back from his forehead and, most winning of all, a nose which would have been perfect if it hadn't veered slightly from the vertical, the legacy of a break playing rugby that had been badly reset.

The only sour note to the evening was that Alan seemed to have a mildly combative edge to his relationship with his wife. Claire had seen something similar in other couples they had known, and it was usually the precursor to a divorce. Alan had been fascinated with her job. Claire was always a little reticent about saying too much about what she did because she had found it usually led to long and sometimes tedious enquiries as to its precise nature, but on this occasion, she indulged him, and as she did so, she noticed a subtle shift in their relationship, as though both had begun to sense there were two conversations taking place, the first a gentle banter and the second a subtle probing as to whether this might lead to something more.

She had gone outside for a smoke. He had left the table almost immediately. Sorry, he said to the others, weak bladder or too much wine – one of the two. Claire stood in the porch, the front door partially closed behind her. He joined her, was silent for a moment, but then asked for her mobile number. He didn't explain why, as though it had somehow already been agreed between them. She hesitated and then gave it to him. She had crossed a threshold and she had known this even as she had tried to pass it off as the most natural thing in the world.

Two weeks passed before he contacted her, a long enough period for her to have dismissed what had taken place as mere foolish flirtation, and to dismiss it from her thoughts. Then she received a voicemail message:

Hi, it's Alan. Sorry I haven't been in touch. I've been dealing with the fallout from one of our audits – lots of late nights and quite stressful to boot. Bloody FRC's got involved as well – last thing we need. Give me a ring.

She waited what she felt was a suitable length of time (he had after all left her on tenterhooks for a fortnight) and rang him the following day. He picked up straight away and suggested they meet for a coffee at the weekend. He said he had tickets for the Hockney exhibition at the Royal Academy and wondered whether she'd like to come. She'd said yes, of course, even though she knew what he was proposing wasn't entirely innocent. By a stroke of luck, Sean was himself away on a conference in Birmingham so she was free but then, perhaps, Alan knew that already.

The exhibition was stunning. Room after room of huge paintings by Hockney of his beloved Yorkshire landscape: woodland scenes of towering trees in a rich wash of almost blinding colours, the same scene captured at different times of the year, the woodland floor carpeted with leaves of fiery reds and oranges in the autumn and leaves of luminescent green in the spring.

"So, do you like it?" he had murmured.

"They're amazing. Thank you so much for inviting me."

"It's an absolute pleasure. Hockney is one of my favourite painters. Well, besides Rembrandt."

"Slightly different styles," said Claire.

"Completely, but I don't see why I can't admire stuff from

different ends of the spectrum. I love Beethoven, for example, but I'm also quite fond of the Sex Pistols."

"Funnily enough, me too. Beethoven's Third is one of my favourite pieces of music."

"Especially the second movement," said Alan.

Claire felt a frisson of pleasure. It was rare to find someone who shared her own passions. Sean was more prosaic in that regard; he didn't really warm to music at all. It was like a foreign language to him. He could just about tolerate the Foo Fighters but loathed classical music. Jazz was completely beyond the pale.

"Rachel likes ballet and opera but hates pop music. She probably thinks the Rolling Stones are part of Stonehenge. As for the Sex Pistols…"

Claire laughed. Interesting, she thought. It was almost as though he was deliberately distancing himself from her at the same time as he was inviting Claire to step into a closer intimacy. The point was, did she go there?

"So, shall we meet again?" Alan said.

"Some sunny day, some sunny place," laughed Claire.

"Well, hopefully, not after five years at war."

She hesitated. Should she play hard to get? No, she was too old for playing games.

"Yes, I'd love to."

"Tomorrow?"

"You don't waste much time, do you?"

"Had we but world enough and time…"

It was a reference to the Andrew Marvell poem, "To His Coy Mistress". And also, something else; an invitation to become his lover.

"Yes, why not?" she smiled, a knowing smile which he returned.

*

He was both a skilful and considerate lover. So much so, she wondered whether, at some point in the past, a more worldly lover had taken great care in showing him precisely what a woman wanted during lovemaking. She started to look forward to their stolen moments together, imagined his face and body when she made love to Sean. Her husband seemed surprised by the new vigour in their lovemaking, as well as her daring in suggesting what she wanted him to do. She was both flattered and excited by Alan's interest in her. Was it any more than that, though? Was it in fact an act of revenge on her part? Payback for what Sean had done to her. Certainly, lust was a part of it. Perhaps, it was a combination of all these things, a potent cocktail she was unable to resist. And where did he stand? How did he feel towards her? Was it simply a fling or was he looking for a possible exit from his own fraying marriage? Best not go there; it was complicated enough as it was.

They took risks, meeting in hotels and sometimes in each other's homes when they knew their respective spouses would be absent. Somehow this heightened the piquancy of their lovemaking, giving it an element of danger. They were constantly on the brink of discovery, almost seeming to invite it. Now, as she sat waiting for him in the pub, she wondered again whether Rachel might have found out. In a way, it would be a relief if this had happened and it emerged she was responsible for the hoax. That would be so much easier to deal with than an unknown antagonist. It was unlikely, if it was Rachel, that this would then be anything other than a nasty hoax. The alternative might be much more sinister, and she would also be no wiser as to who it might be. She thought again about the dinner party where she had first met Alan. His wife had seemed a brittle, nervous woman. Alan had told Claire that when they rowed her words could cut like glass, vicious and wounding. She threw things too: books, framed photographs, a Venetian glass sculpture of two entwined lovers smashed against a wall. Then, on one particularly nasty occasion, a kitchen knife plucked from the drawer. Luckily, it had bounced off him, handle side up, but even Rachel had looked shaken afterwards by what she had done. Yes, it was possible, she thought. Anything was possible with that woman.

Her thoughts were interrupted by the sudden appearance of Alan.

"Hi, sorry I'm late – there was an idiot on the phone I just couldn't get rid of. Shall I get a bar menu? Do you want anything more to drink? Glass of wine, another one of those?" he said, pointing at her glass.

"No," she said. "I've got to drive back, remember. I don't

have the luxury of walking back to the office."

"Sorry, yes, of course. I'll have a pint anyway. I'll get the menus."

She stared after him. As he stood at the bar, she noticed he was already glancing surreptitiously at his watch. He came back, placed his lager on the table and, still standing, presented her with a menu.

"I'll have the fish and chips," he said. "They're pretty good here."

She studied the menu. "I'll have the Caesar salad. Stay off the big fish and chip meal, get the standard – you need to watch your waistline."

"God, you're as bad as Rachel," he grinned. "I thought you liked my love handles."

"Don't flatter yourself."

He picked up his glass, gulped down a large mouthful, and went back to the bar. When he returned, she quickly told him about the hoax.

"God, that's awful," he said. "Do you think it's serious?"

"Serious enough for me to have gone to the police."

"But surely—"

"Surely what? Until proven otherwise I have to take this seriously. Or do you think it might be better for me to wait until I'm attacked?"

"Sorry, no, of course, I don't mean that—"

He was interrupted by the arrival of their food. She noted that he had ordered the big fish and chip meal after all. The waitress was pretty, and she noticed Alan staring after her retreating form. She glanced upwards. The pub was famous because it was there, pints of ale spilling in their excitement, that Watson and Crick had announced their discovery of the spiral helix for DNA. The Eagle was famous for something else as well, though. It had been a hangout for the American and British flight crews during the Second World War. The ceiling was covered with their graffiti, a smoky black against the blood red of the plaster. Claire imagined a man lifted on another's shoulders, drunk, a candle held unsteadily aloft, hot wax dripping onto his wrists and hand, his friends roaring with laughter, shouting encouragement. *Ben's boys, 59th squadron.* Had he survived the war, she wondered, or had his life been snuffed out in a matter of days by a very different flame? Her eyes turned back to Alan.

"Are you alright?" he said. "Looks like you drifted off there for a moment."

Claire blinked, her eyes adjusting again to the light from the window.

"Does Rachel know about us?"

"What? No, of course she doesn't."

"How can you be so sure? Is it possible she sent me the invitation?"

He gave an awkward laugh.

"No way on God's earth – she'd skin me alive if she did find out, but I think you're safe. Even if she did want to have a go at you, she definitely wouldn't have had either the imagination or the inclination to do anything like this. The worst that would happen is she would give you a mouthful of abuse down the phone."

Reaching into her bag, Claire placed the photocopy of the invitation and envelope on the table. "I'm sure it isn't her, but humour me for a second. Is the handwriting on this envelope anything like Rachel's?"

He pulled the two documents across the table and stared at them for a moment.

"No, that isn't Rachel's handwriting – it's nothing like it. Her handwriting's a disaster, looks like a spider has fallen into a pot of ink."

"She could have disguised it, though—"

Alan gave a snort of laughter. "There's no way she could have written this; if she spent the rest of eternity on it, she wouldn't get even close to anything as neat or impressive as this."

"Yeah, you're probably right – I'm just scared; scared and paranoid."

He put his hand on top of hers.

"It is horrible, and I'd be scared and paranoid in your position as well. Is there anything I can do?"

"No, no – just be there for me."

"Look, I could take Friday off; we could spend the day together, perhaps walk over the meadows to Grantchester. We could have a pub lunch and I'll book a room – what do you think?"

"I don't have any PMs booked that day, so, yeah, that would be great."

"Fantastic." He glanced at his watch. "Look, I've got to get back – partners' meeting. Is that okay?"

"Well, I've got to get back as well so it's fine." As they both got to their feet, he kissed her lightly on the lips.

"Love you," he murmured.

"Love you more."

"I certainly hope so," he laughed. In return she gave him a playful punch in the ribs.

They left together and she stared after him as he walked away. So, not Rachel then. But if not her, then who? Could it be connected to that trial? She stared, unseeing, at the street scene in front of her, her mind elsewhere.

CHAPTER SIX

2010

Claire was sitting at her desk in the office when her mobile phone rang. She looked at the number: Joan Madison.

"Hi, Joan – how are you?"

"I'm fine, Claire. How are you?"

"Good. Well, I'm not sleeping terribly well, but apart from that I'm fine."

"That's one thing I've never had a problem with, strangely enough. I'm asleep immediately my head hits the pillow – sometimes before my head hits the pillow. Anyway, I've just received the lung tissue results for the SBS baby, Alice Turner. I think she may well have been smothered – there's evidence of intra-alveolar siderorphages."

Claire's heart sank; this was not good news. "When's the inquest?"

"Friday – I've been called as a witness," said Madison.

"So, probably a CPS referral, then."

"Yes, quite possibly. We still haven't received copies of the autopsy for the first child, though – the findings from that will be important and we'll need that for the inquest as well, so I'll chase Hamlin up."

"Okay. Thanks for the update anyway – not the best start to the day, is it?"

"No, it's not. If there is a referral and, following the police investigation, the CPS agree to prosecute, this is likely to attract a lot of media attention, so hang on to your hat."

"Great – can't wait. Can you let me know the results of the inquest?"

"Yes, of course, I will."

Immediately Madison had rung off Claire phoned Hamlin. She was too stressed to wait for Madison to come back to her; she needed to find out for herself where all of this might be leading, and she needed to know now. She quickly told him the results of the test on the lung tissue samples.

"Have you had the pathology report back for the first child?"

"Funnily enough," said Hamlin, "it came in this morning. I'll ping it over to you. Having read it, though, it says her own child died from natural causes."

"So, a cot death then?" asked Claire.

"Looks very much like it, yeah."

"Which in turn might throw some doubt on the PM conclusion for Alice?"

"Yeah, it could but then there's the pathologist's note. There were ALTEs for both children."

Claire held her breath. An acute life threatening event, or ALTE, prior to a baby's death was a possible telltale for SBS.

"The first child; was it a boy or a girl?" she asked.

"Another girl, Amanda. She was only eight weeks when she died. You know, the more I look into this, the more I'm convinced this woman did kill both of them."

"Okay, send me the report and I'll have a look at it. Joan will need a copy as well, obviously. Once I've had a chance to study it, I'll ring you back – probably tomorrow, I'm afraid, because I'm in meetings all afternoon."

"No problem – speak to you tomorrow."

*

Claire decided she couldn't wait until the following day to look at the report, so she took it home with her. Once she'd settled Toby down, she poured herself some wine, perched on the sofa in the living room with her legs tucked under her and started to read.

She scanned the autopsy report first. The death was unexplained, and its cause or causes, although natural, were unknown. Then she turned to the pathologist's separate note. Claire knew that when it came to a sudden infant death or shaken baby syndrome, it was vitally important to gather as much information as possible about the family's circumstances leading up to the death. A PM was a powerful tool in ascertaining the true cause of death, but the circumstances surrounding it were just as critical, if not more so. The presence of an ALTE prior to a baby's death was worrying and possibly significant, and there had been such an incident with Amanda; she had been admitted to hospital, her small body limp, with a bluish colouration or cyanosis indicating a lack of oxygen. Alice had also had a similar ALTE incident at six weeks old.

Claire realised her hands were trembling a little. She felt both uneasy and alarmed. She knew ALTEs, although very frightening for the parents, were relatively common in infancy, and often subsequent investigation failed to identify the cause. In infant murder trials, though, they were frequently cited as early evidence of abuse. She was concerned Madison would jump to exactly that conclusion, and if the case did go to trial, emphasise it in any evidence she gave. Madison already seemed convinced Alice's death had been as a result of smothering and would probably suspect the same was true for Amanda. Claire had often envied the confidence in their own abilities shown by her peers in the profession. She herself was far more uncertain in her diagnoses. Sometimes it felt miraculous to her that she had managed to qualify as a doctor at all, never mind going on to undertake the specialist training needed to become a pathologist. She felt a fraud, a child masquerading in an adult's clothes, an imposter who was forever on the brink of being unmasked as unworthy or incompetent.

CHAPTER SEVEN

Claire glanced at her iPhone on the bedside table. 5.25 AM. Not good; she felt exhausted, but it seemed there was little chance of her going back to sleep before her alarm went off at seven. Reflecting on the conversations with Madison and Hamlin earlier in the week, Claire felt both uneasy and anxious. Worse still, she realised she had tipped again into a deep depression.

Sean was still asleep, turned away from her, lying on his side. She eased herself out of bed and crept downstairs. Toby slept in the bedroom adjoining the stairs and she was anxious not to wake him too early. She made some tea for herself and a strong black coffee for her husband and crept upstairs again. Sean was now awake, glancing through the day's news headlines on his iPad.

"Thanks, love," he said, taking the cup from her. She put her own cup down on her bedside table and got back into bed. This was unusual; her normal routine would have been to start to wash and dress immediately, but she felt she needed a few extra minutes in bed to arm herself against what she knew would be a difficult day, now made much worse by her depression. Sean looked over. He knew from her expression and the change in her routine what was happening and gently rested his hand on hers.

"Are you alright?"

"No, not really."

"Do you have to go to work today?"

"Don't have a choice. Anyway, I need to get Toby up and take him to nursery and once I'm up then I might as well go to work."

"I thought Jess was doing that."

"She's got an audition."

"Ah, right." He paused. "I could take him."

"Then you'll be late for work. No, don't worry, it's the weekend tomorrow. Just need to grit my teeth and get through today."

"Are you sure? I can get away with being late. I can just say my train got cancelled, had to catch the next one."

"No, honestly, I need to go in, especially today."

"Difficult case?" he asked.

"You could say that."

"Want to talk about it?"

"Maybe tonight, it would take too long now."

*

She spent a tedious morning going through her email backlog. Just before twelve, Kate suddenly looked up from a file she had been studying on her desk. "Oh, I almost forgot," she said.

"Madison phoned earlier wanting to speak to you. She asked if you could phone her back."

Claire stared at Kate. The last thing she needed was to have to speak to Madison, particularly since she knew precisely what she would want to discuss.

"What time did she phone?"

Kate looked embarrassed.

"First thing this morning, around eight-thirty. It was literally ten minutes before you arrived. I'm sorry, Claire. I got the call from Mark saying he was sick and wouldn't be coming in immediately afterwards, and after that, my solicitor rang about the house I'm buying. Madison's call just went clean out of my head."

"Don't worry about it – I'll ring her now. How's it going on the house?"

"The solicitor said the local authority searches had come back and they seemed okay. He wanted to make me aware, though, that the house was on a flood plain, which might be a concern."

"Didn't you know that already?"

"Course I did; it's only a couple of hundred yards from the river, but there's never been a problem before with flooding."

"Still, with climate warming..." said Claire.

"I honestly don't see it as a problem."

"So, when are you hoping to exchange?"

Kate rolled her eyes. "God knows, apparently the people I'm buying from are still looking – they'd found somewhere but that fell through, so they had to start again."

"The joys of moving house – they say the stress involved is right up there with losing your job or getting a divorce."

"So, am I forgiven on the Madison thing?"

"Yeah, don't worry. I wasn't looking forward to speaking to her anyway."

Kate looked at Claire. "Are you okay, Claire? You seemed a bit down when you came in."

"I'm fine. Looking forward to the weekend. Tough week, really."

"That poor baby?"

"Yeah, exactly. I'm going to go for a walk, see if I can pick up a sandwich. I'll ring Madison when I get back. Can you hold the fort whilst I'm away?"

"*Ce n'est pas un problème, mon capitaine.*"

"*Merci beaucoup.* Do you want me to get you anything whilst I'm out?"

"A new boyfriend would be great, Brad Pitt if you can manage it. Otherwise, I'll settle for Beckham."

*

Claire rang Madison on leaving the office. She knew it was likely to be a tense conversation and it wasn't one she therefore wanted Kate to overhear.

"Hi, Joan – you wanted to speak to me? Sorry, I would have phoned earlier but Kate has only just told me you rang."

"That's fine – I was in a meeting for the rest of the morning anyway. Only just got out. Have you read the report Hamlin sent on the first death?"

"Yeah, I did. Not good."

"Claire, although I'm the lead pathologist on this, if it does go to trial, then we'll both be asked to give testimony. It's very important, therefore, that we're on the same page. My report on Alice points to SBS with smothering as the cause of death; you need to back me up on this. So, in short, can I rely on you?"

Claire felt her stomach flip over and her hands trembled as she tried to focus.

"Yeah – assuming the coroner refers it."

"He won't have a choice," said Madison grimly. "So, you'll back me up?"

Claire's mouth felt dry, and she hesitated. Did she really have a choice, though? Madison was the lead, a paediatric pathologist with twenty years' experience under her belt. Claire was still very much a novice, nor was she the specialist in this area.

"Claire, are you still there?"

"Sorry, yeah, I am, yeah."

"Good – I thought the line had gone dead for a moment. You'll support me, then?"

"Yes, of course."

"Great – I'll talk to you again following the hearing on Friday. Look after yourself."

"You take care as well."

Claire took a deep breath to try and calm herself. One of the features of her depression, she knew, was that her thinking slowed almost to a stop. Making a decision about the simplest things became almost impossible; in this state she also knew that it was all too easy for others to decide for her and sometimes to actively bully her. She had an uneasy feeling that was precisely what had happened during her conversation with Madison. She found it difficult to tease out whether Madison was right in deciding SBS was the cause of death, and whether her own doubts were coloured by her depression rather than having any real basis in fact. The nameless anxiety she always felt when low now gripped her even more fiercely. She was at the bottom of a deep well and there was no light above, only darkness.

CHAPTER EIGHT

2012

Twenty-Six Days Left

Claire sat staring through the rain-smeared glass. The plane would have arrived half an hour ago so Sean should be out by now, she thought. Then, she saw him, hunched over against the rain, his rain-spattered suitcase dragged behind him, a heavy bag of golf clubs hoisted over one shoulder. She flicked her headlamps and a moment later, he wrenched open one of the rear passenger doors and hefted his golf clubs down onto the seats, wedging his suitcase down into the well behind the passenger seat.

As he sat down beside her, slamming the door shut, the stale smell of cigarette smoke filled the car. He was supposed to have given up smoking but had obviously relapsed whilst he'd been away. She wanted to say something but bit her tongue. Now was not the time.

"How was it?" she said brightly.

"Rough; we were only there five days and it rained solidly for four of them. We managed one decent round of golf; the rest of the time was taken up sat round the hotel drinking. Lots of boozing."

"Poor you."

"Yeah, poor me. Oh well, there's always next year. How's your week been? How's Toby? Is your aunt looking after him?"

"Yeah, Brenda's there now. Toby's fine." She hesitated. "Something's happened by the way; something quite scary, actually."

"Scary, how so, scary? What's the matter? Is it work?"

"No, no, nothing like that – two days ago someone sent me a funeral invitation."

"Really? Who—"

"I don't know who sent it." She hesitated. "But worse than that, the invitation was to my own funeral."

"Sorry – your own funeral? What the fuck? What did it say?"

"It was hand-delivered – apparently I'm supposed to die in just under a month's time. 13th June to be precise. It even had a photograph of me."

"Christ. You should have rung me. What did you do?"

"Well, I went to the church the following day to see what I could find out. Tried ringing first but no-one was picking up. Anyway, the church was locked. I tried the vicarage as well but no luck there either. Then I found something really horrible. As I was walking away from the church through the graveyard

I came across this grave, freshly dug. There was a temporary marker on it - a crude wooden one - with my name and the date I was supposed to die. 13th June, less than a month away."

Despite herself, she could feel her eyes starting to well up. Until now, despite the fear she had felt, it had all seemed unreal, a bad dream. Talking about it to Sean was like waking up to find the nightmare had actually happened, a body whose outline had appeared only murky and indistinct beneath the water now revealed in all its bloated horror, as it burst to the surface. Sean noticed her tears and reached across and gently squeezed her shoulder.

"Oh, Claire, I'm so sorry I wasn't here – you should have rung, told me, I could have come back early."

"No, no, it's fine. I didn't want to worry you. Anyway, it's probably just some nasty hoax. Some horrible little shit getting his kicks tormenting others."

"Still, he must be some sick fuck."

"The world's full of them, sick fucks spewing out filth in their sordid fucking bedrooms and then wanking themselves off because that's what they get off on."

They were both quiet for a moment. Claire squinted against the glaring light of the oncoming traffic on the opposite carriageway.

"Look, have you spoken to the police about all of this?"

"I have – they were a complete waste of space; said it was probably just a hoax and there wasn't enough to act on. So, I rang Pete Hamlin – you know, the DS I used to work with on some of the PMs I've done. He's retired now but he's said he'll look into it for me. He's also going to ask someone who's still serving to do some digging. Probably won't go anywhere but it's worth a try."

"Okay, well, that's something at least. Do you want me to speak to the police? See if I can get them to take it seriously?"

"What? Because you're a bloke you mean? Because why would the police ever take a woman seriously? Anyway, Pete was the police, and his mate is in the police, so it's covered."

"Yeah, sorry, I didn't mean to—" He trailed off.

"No, I'm sorry, I've just been so wound up, even talking about it now is just making it worse. I think I'm starting a headache."

"Well, at least we're nearly back. You can have an early night. I should have just taken my own car, saved you all this."

"No, it's fine. Anyway, I very much doubt I'll get an early night – Brenda's going to want to stay and chat."

"Yeah, I suppose she will. She can talk for England, that woman."

*

In bed that night, exhausted, she had fallen asleep straightaway. Now, barely two hours later, she was wide awake. She could feel her mind racing and knew immediately she had tipped into mania. She had learned to read the signs: a new restless energy and focus, the quickening of her thoughts, a bubbling euphoria – a river released from its prison of ice after a long winter. The truth was she both looked forward to and dreaded this; she welcomed the surge in confidence it gave her, the feeling of wellbeing, the fluidity and ease with which she could now deal with what had previously seemed intractable or impossible.

But what it brought with it too was an almost unendurable insomnia. She knew it would be impossible to get back to sleep. She got up and crept downstairs. Having made herself some tea, she flipped her laptop open, glancing at the kitchen clock as she did so. It was an antique railway clock with Roman numerals, the letters LNER emblazoned in black; another Sean purchase she had never cared for that he thought added a whimsical touch to their decor. Nearly four o'clock.

She blinked at the screen. She had already bought several books from Amazon. Now her cursor hovered over the "Buy" button on the Ticketmaster website: two platinum tickets for a Coldplay concert at £495 each. Claire had promised Sean that she wouldn't make any big purchases during her manic phases which both would subsequently come to regret, but this was different, surely? Sean loved Coldplay and this could be an early birthday present for him. So, why not? Everything else had gone anyway. She clicked "Buy".

She propped the funeral invitation card against her now empty coffee cup and looked again at it: donations to be given to the Bradbury Oaks Hospice. Perhaps this was a clue. But if so, how? She googled the hospice and did a skim read of their website. Clicking on an "About Us" tab, she found a second tab labelled "Patient Stories". There were several photographs of patients who had been cared for by the charity with links to their personal experiences of illness and end of life care. For a while she simply became engrossed in their stories, forgetting why she had decided to look at the site in the first place.

Life was so fragile: a mother diagnosed with breast cancer, with surgery, and then gruelling chemotherapy, followed by an all-clear diagnosis, only for her youngest son to then die of a brain tumour. *Another blow to the family*, she'd written in her blog.

A second story: a baby diagnosed whilst in the womb with hyperplastic left heart syndrome; the literal absence of a heart on the left-hand side. Did the mother want to terminate the pregnancy now or opt for surgery or palliative care once it had been born? An impossible choice. She had chosen surgery following the birth. Despite the operation, the baby had died at just three weeks old.

There was so much misery in the world. How did people endure it? And yet they did.

She glanced again at the clock; it was now close to six. Christ, where had the time gone? And she was still no nearer to identifying who had sent the card. What possible connection could the hospice have with all of this? Was it a warning? Was she meant to end up there, confined to a bed, in constant pain and dosed up on morphine?

She gave up, snapping the laptop shut and drumming her fingers impatiently against the table. It was summer and already light. Standing up, she walked into the hallway, shrugged off her dressing gown, and lifted her coat from the hatstand. Her pyjamas were a two piece from Jigsaw, embroidered with pale peach roses; not warm enough really for a walk outside but then it was a mild day, so why not? Anxious not to disturb Sean and Toby, she eased the door open and closed it gently behind her.

*

As she neared the grave of Mary Ann Weems, she slowed down. What was she hoping to find? She could see even from this distance, though, that the mound of earth for the hoax grave had disappeared and in its place was a neat rectangle of newly laid turf. She moved closer to look at it and as she did so, saw another mound of earth, this one on the far side of the Weems gravestone. Puzzled, she turned to look at it. Had the grave been moved? This mound was much smaller, though; there also seemed to be something red at one end of it. She walked slowly across and stared down. At the head someone had laid a bouquet of red roses, the waxed white paper holding them still damp with condensation and smeared with dirt from the grave. A new grave, much smaller. She started to tremble, her vision blurring, her blood pumping in her ears. She felt a choking acid bile rise up in her throat. She bent double and vomited.

Claire stood and shakily looked round at her surroundings, wiping her mouth with the back of her hand. No-one had seen her. Toby. She had to get home.

CHAPTER NINE

Walking back to the house, she rang Hamlin.

"Hi, Claire. What's up? Not like you to ring me so early. I've only just got up; crept downstairs to make myself a cup of tea. Sheila's still in bed."

"I'm really sorry to ring you so early, Pete – it's the grave, there's a new one. I—"

"Sorry, what do you mean a new one?"

"The other grave's gone, but there's a new much smaller one – someone's left some flowers on it, roses."

"Sorry, Claire, I'm not following. I'm still half asleep, I'm afraid."

"There's a new grave and it looks like a child's – I think he's – or it could be a woman, Christ, I don't know – whoever it is, they're sending me some sort of horrible message. Bastard, fucking bastard. Who would—"

"Could the grave be perfectly innocent? Perhaps it's a pet's grave."

"What, in a church graveyard? No, no, it's not, I just know. I need to see you. I can't do today; I'm going to stay home with Toby. But I can't stay home all the time; I've taken too much time off as it is, I'll end up getting the sack. I'm going to ask my aunt to look after him for a few days. Can you come to the house today, say around nine? Sean will have left for work by then so…"

"I'm really sorry, Claire, I can't do today. It's a friend's wedding anniversary, their fiftieth – they're having a celebration down in Kent. I can't get out of it; they're close friends anyway, it wouldn't—"

"No, it's fine, I understand. Look, tomorrow's Saturday. Sean will be at home to look after Toby, I'll tell him I'm seeing Jess for coffee. Could we meet up then?"

"You've not told him, then?"

"No, I've only just seen the grave. But I won't be telling him anyway. I don't want to worry him. He was upset enough about the first grave."

"Are you sure? I think I'd want to tell him."

"No, no, I can't. I might be being paranoid anyway and this would be his worst nightmare. I can't tell him."

"It's a lot to carry on your own."

"I might tell him later, I don't know. Look, can we meet up?"

"Yes, that should be okay – where do you want to meet?"

Claire thought for a moment. "There's a café on Cambridge Street."

"Yes, I know the one – tomorrow at nine? Does that work for you?"

"Yes, that works. See you then."

*

Sean was up when she returned, busying himself in the kitchen making coffee and toast.

"There you are – I was starting to worry," he said, as she entered the kitchen.

"Sorry, couldn't sleep again, so I went for a walk."

He looked at her. "You're manic again, aren't you?" he said, exasperation in his voice.

Claire was annoyed. Yes, she was manic, but she had it under control. She hated the way he reduced her to a set of symptoms, a problem to be managed, rather than a real person. It was one of the things she loathed most about her illness; what she had thought was unique to her turned out to be something she shared with millions of others, her personality the product of her brain chemistry. A gift for those who thought free will was a sodding illusion.

"Where's Toby?'

"He's asleep in our bed. Came in at six but, of course, you weren't there.'

She could hear the suppressed anger in his voice. Avoiding his gaze, she pushed past him and went upstairs. Toby was sprawled across the bed, lying on his back, his legs and arms spread wide, a splayed starfish in sandy coloured pyjamas, the Little Mermaid emblazoned on his chest with flame-red hair and an emerald-green tail. She knelt down beside him, her reluctance to wake him struggling with her need to hold him tight, pressed against her. She hesitated, her hand moving uncertainly towards him, to stroke his brow. His eyes opened.

"Mummy!" he squealed in delight, as he lifted his arms towards her. Claire held him to her chest and hugged him, his hair damp with sweat around his neck. He recoiled a little, as he lifted his head to gaze at her.

"You smell."

Claire cupped her hand around her mouth and nose. The sour smell of vomit.

"Oh, I'm so sorry, darling, Mummy's been naughty and needs to clean her teeth. Naughty Mummy."

Toby giggled. "Naughty Mummy," he repeated. "I'm not naughty, am I?"

"No, you could never be naughty; only mummies and daddies are naughty."

Toby looked perplexed. "Does Daddy smell too?"

She laughed and hugged him tighter, taking care to turn her head to the side. "No, Daddy doesn't smell."

"He does sometimes."

"When does he smell?"

"When he drinks beer," said Toby triumphantly.

Claire gave an involuntary snort of amusement. "Well, perhaps, a little. You're a little rascal, aren't you?" She stood up, still cradling him. "Come on, little man. We need to get you dressed. You and I are going to have a special day together. Mummy's not going to go to work today, I'm going to stay home with you."

"Can we have Haribo? Jessica gives me Haribo."

"Does she now? Well, we might have to talk to her about that." She relented. "Well, just this once then, but you mustn't tell Daddy. It'll be our secret."

*

"So, what do you think?" said Claire.

"I'm not sure," said Hamlin.

He said nothing for a moment, gazing out of the window at the passing traffic. The café was empty apart from two women sitting at a table in a far corner, but they looked too self-absorbed to want to listen in on anyone else's conversation. Hamlin had ordered himself and Claire coffee, and a bacon sandwich. Claire passed; she felt too wound up to eat.

"I'm worried Pete, really worried. This is looking more and more serious, and now this other grave..." She trailed off, fiddling nervously with a sugar sachet which she twisted between her fingers. Glancing towards the serving counter, she noticed a black upright piano standing to one side of it, a life-size model of a white bulldog placed incongruously in front, as though guarding it from undesirables. It stared mournfully back at her.

"Andrews couldn't find a match on the fingerprints, I'm afraid. I did speak to the vicar, but he hasn't seen anything and nor apparently has his gardener; there's a bloke cuts the grass once a week. The vicar was pretty worked up about the whole thing – furious actually – but it hasn't moved us on very far. The Facebook search was also a waste of time. Did you turn up anything on the other social media sites?"

"No, nothing," sighed Claire. "What about dog walkers or locals crossing through there? There was a man with a dog that time I saw the first grave. I saw him again last time we met at the Black Bull."

"How's that then?" said Hamlin.

"He was near the war memorial when I came out."

"Do you suspect him?"

She thought for a moment. "No, not really, if I'm honest."

"Okay, this is what I'm going to do; I'm going to spend tomorrow morning in the graveyard. I'll try and be discreet, but I'm going to talk to anyone using the footpath through it and ask whether they might have seen anything over the last couple of weeks. I can't believe someone could have dug two graves without at least one person having seen them."

"Unless he did it in the middle of the night," said Claire. "Not many people around at three in the morning."

"Yes, but if you remember they did duck back into the cemetery to retrieve the grave marker whilst you were sat in your car; that was in broad daylight and perhaps at least some of what they've done also happened during the day. It's worth a shot, anyway."

"No, you're right – it's worth doing." She reached out and touched his arm. "I can't thank you enough, Pete."

"That's alright – what are friends for? You'd do the same for me if I had a problem. I've also done some research on Mary Ann Weems, by the way; I wanted to explore whether there might be anything in the choice of location near that gravestone – apart from a taste for the macabre. I turned up some interesting stuff."

"Really? Like what?"

"Well, the bloke who murdered her, Thomas Weems, was used in experiments after his death; they passed electricity through his body to see if it could be revived. You know, Frankenstein stuff. Now, the author of *Frankenstein*, Mary Shelley – though I imagine you knew that already – like you, she was bipolar."

"I didn't know she was bipolar."

"I don't know whether it's just a coincidence, but you've got two things linking you – the pathology stuff with the dissection and the fact that Mary Shelley was bipolar. It might not mean anything, but if there is a connection, whoever's behind this seems to know an awful lot about you. How many people know you're bipolar?"

Claire felt her heart pounding faster in her chest, a feeling of nausea welling up in her stomach.

"Claire, are you alright? You look really pale. I'm sorry, I didn't mean to upset you—"

"No, it's fine. I needed to know, so thank you for telling me. Hardly anyone knows I'm bipolar – I haven't told anyone at work. I've only told a few close friends like you."

"So, whoever did this must know you quite well – very well, in fact." He hesitated. "Can you think of anyone close who hates you or dislikes you enough to have done this?"

"No, no, I can't – I can't think of anyone who would do such a horrible thing."

"No, okay – well, let's just tuck that away for now. It might be important, it might not. I might just be overreaching. If you think of anything, though, let me know. I also found something else, by the way, although I'm certain this doesn't have anything to do with it – they used some of Thomas Weems' skin to cover a book. It's in the Wren Library in Cambridge."

"You're kidding?"

"No, it's true – weird, I know, but then everything about that murder is weird."

"I wonder what sort of book it was?" said Claire.

"Dunno – just thought it was interesting."

Two men stumbled through the café door, laughing. Claire glanced across but she didn't recognise them.

"Might be an idea if we left," murmured Claire. "I have to get back to work anyway. I'll pay – least I can do."

"Are you sure? I don't mind paying. I think my pension can run to two cups of coffee and a bacon sandwich."

"No, I'll get this."

She stood and hugged him. Pete hesitated. "I hope you don't mind me saying this, but you look exhausted."

"I've not been sleeping well."

"Well, hardly surprising."

"No, I suppose not. Thanks. I don't know what I'd do without you."

"I haven't really done anything yet—"

"Just knowing you're there for me is enough, to be honest."

She felt depression fold itself round her. The rush of euphoria she normally felt when she was manic was missing. Now she seemed to have the worst of all worlds; she was suffering the insomnia which also accompanied mania, but instead of euphoria, she had tipped into depression. The insomnia would also make the depression worse, until she was barely able to function.

As she walked away, she thought again about whether someone close to her might have been involved. Alan knew she was bipolar, of course. Was it possible he had told Rachel? She resolved to ask him next time they were together.

There was a florist quite close to the café and as she passed, she suddenly remembered the flowers on the grave. They were fresh and must have been bought only a day or two previously. Could they have been bought here? If so, the florist might remember who bought them and even be able to provide a description. She stopped and turned back.

CHAPTER TEN

2010

As Claire was driving to work, her phone rang, the sound muffled by her handbag which she had placed on the seat next to her. Careful not to take her eyes off the road, she fumbled in the bag, lifted the phone out and brought it to her ear.

It was Hamlin. "Hi, Claire, can you talk? You sound as though you're in the car—"

"Yes, I am. Look, I'll find somewhere to stop and ring you back. Is that okay?"

"Should be alright. I've got a meeting at nine this morning, so don't leave it too long. I need to bring you up to date on the Alice case."

"Next ten minutes – talk to you then."

She was still twenty minutes from Addenbrookes. There was a turning off the road just ahead of her. She swung into it and coasted to a stop in a small residential cul de sac. It was a new housing estate with a few garages and even fewer driveways. Cars sat on the road or squatted on pavements, jostling with each other in a fight for space. Frustrated, she swung the car around, eventually finding a space where she could park on another road close to a primary school. She rang Hamlin back.

"Hi, Pete. How are you? What's happened on the Alice case?"

"Not too clever for a Monday morning, but I'm sure it'll get better once I've managed to get more coffee down me. Are you okay?"

"I'm fine – what's happening then?"

"Well, following the inquest we decided we had enough to arrest the grandmother. We took her in that same afternoon and spent most the weekend interviewing her. To cut a long story short, we've made a recommendation to CPS to prosecute."

"And do you think they'll go for it?"

"I'll be amazed if they don't. As soon as I hear back from them I'll ring you – is that okay?"

"Yes, fine. Look after yourself, Pete."

"Don't I always? You too, Claire."

Claire rang off. Mothers were busy dragging their reluctant children to school, one child, a girl with plaited chestnut hair, carelessly scraping her green satchel against the side of a car as she eased her way past. A man stood opposite, near a patch of waste ground, whilst his dog, a Jack Russell, squatted down to do its business. The expression it wore, one of seeming embarrassment and shame, seemed identical to that a human being would display in such circumstances. She smiled to herself, and for a moment forgot the gnawing tension in her stomach. Get a grip, she told herself, this is what you signed up for, so get on with it.

CHAPTER ELEVEN

2010

"So, we've got the Sarah Davis autopsy this morning, then?" asked Mark.

"Yep, that's the plan," said Kate. "Strangulation. Boyfriend claims she got off on being strangled during sex. Says it was an accident; was enjoying himself so much he failed to notice she'd gone a bit blue and no longer seemed interested in conversation. God, I'm knackered, who would have thought watching *Gardener's World* with a cup of cocoa could be so tiring?" She stretched her arms above her head, arched her back, and yawned. She was wearing a loose-fitting green jumper, but the stretching motion pulled the material tight over her breasts, making it obvious she wasn't wearing a bra. Mark blushed, and Kate grinned back at him.

Claire smiled. "Hamlin's doing this one. Oh, and I think that tall bloke, the photographer – can't remember his name – is joining us as well."

"Oh, I know who you mean," said Kate, "the bloke from the Harlem Globetrotters, whassisface."

"Foster," said Mark.

"Yep, Foster," said Kate. "I knew I'd remember his name."

"You didn't—"

Kate ignored him. "At least today, you won't have to worry about that witch, Madison, looking over your shoulder. She gives me the creeps."

Claire sighed. "At least there's that, I suppose. Mark, will you be joining us for this one?"

Mark lifted his head from the report he had been studying. "Yeah, I wouldn't mind sitting in on this one if that's alright?"

"Yeah, I bet you would. Always had you down as someone who enjoyed a bit of a kink in their sex," laughed Kate.

Another grimson. "No, I just thought it sounded like an interesting case."

"In fairness, it is an interesting case," said Claire, coming to his rescue. "Asphyxiation robs the brain of oxygen and that supposedly heightens sexual arousal. If you do indulge, though, you're supposed to have some sort of non-verbal clue between you to make sure it doesn't go too far."

"Would a knee in the bollocks do the trick?" said Kate. "I use it as a form of contraceptive. Hasty withdrawal one hundred per cent guaranteed."

"That's actually bloody painful," said Mark."

"Can't be as bad as childbirth though, can it?" said Kate.

"Yes, but at least with childbirth you've got something positive at the end."

"What? Oh, you mean a fag and a chance to hit the gin

again. Yes, I see what you mean. Anyway, you could end up with something positive as well; you could become sterile. I'm sure a lot of women would welcome that."

"Thanks a bunch, Kate. That's what I love about you; you've always got my best interests at heart."

"Abso-bloody-lutely, Mark. I'll always have your back, although that's probably because I prefer it to your front." She imitated a crusty Northern comedian. "Thanking you, thanking you all very kindly. Playing all week, with matinees on a Wednesday and Saturday for the pensioners, so they can have a good kip in the afternoon."

Kate dissolved into cackles of laughter. Mark was about to say something else but then thought better of it.

"One day, Kate, that tongue of yours will either make you famous or put you in a prison cell," said Claire, smiling.

"High praise indeed," grinned Kate. "By the way, Mark, if you think a knee in your crown jewels is a bit excessive as a non-verbal clue, you could always take your cue from the Tony Orlando song."

"What Tony Orlando song?"

"You know the one. I'll sing it for you. 'Knock three times on the ceiling, if you want me? Twice on the pipe, if the answer is no-oh-wohh' – personally, I think I would go for the pipe."

"You've got quite a good voice, Kate; never heard you sing before," smiled Claire. "I also didn't realise you were a Tony Orlando fan."

"I'm not, but my mum liked him. Used to drive me mad singing that song all the time."

Their banter was suddenly interrupted by the sound of the entry buzzer.

"Whoops, that will be them now," said Kate, hitting the switch to release the door lock.

"Well, how are we all?" said Hamlin, sweeping through the door, Foster hanging back a little behind him.

"Well, I'm fine. Can't really speak for these two, though," said Claire.

"No, I'm pretty good," said Kate. Mark's not, though. Peterborough lost again."

"We should have won that game, and that was never a penalty, anyway. Still reckon we'll get promotion this year."

"Well, I doubt I will," said Hamlin. "Had another set-to yesterday with the chief inspector. Bloody idiot. Well, you know what they say, scum always rises to the top. Ah, well, not long now and I'm out."

"So, how old will you be once you go?"

"Fifty-three – still young enough to enjoy life, and I intend to take full advantage. Might even take up golf."

"Well, that'll ruin your retirement. I thought you played already?"

"No, I never had the time, too busy holding down a job and bringing up two kids."

"Yeah, I know what you mean," laughed Claire. "The amount of golf Sean plays, I might as well be single. I see the postman more often than I do Sean."

"Well, golf should be ideal for me, then; Liz is already making noises about not wanting me under her feet all day."

"Sounds a very sensible woman to me," said Claire.

"Hark at you two," said Kate. "Love's young dream – not exactly the poster children for marriage and happy ever after, are you?"

Foster grunted. "I'm divorced – never been happier."

"God, kill me now," groaned Kate.

"Do you want to discuss the case, Pete?" said Claire.

"Certainly do. Tea first, though; had to leave the house in a rush this morning so this will be the first. Suffering withdrawal symptoms already."

"Slice of toast with it?" said Kate.

"Kate, one day you'll make someone very happy. That would be great."

"Tony, black coffee, no sugar, wasn't it?" enquired Claire.

Foster raised his eyebrows. "You've got a good memory."

Claire shrugged. "Anyone else want toast since Kate's making it anyway?"

"No, I'm fine," said Foster.

"I wouldn't mind some," said Mark.

Kate looked at Claire. "Do you want some, Claire?"

"You know, I think I will. Thanks, Kate. Do you want any help with all this?"

"Probably. Might be quicker."

"I'm happy to do the toast," said Mark.

"Okay. As long as you don't burn it," said Kate. "Mum always burnt it and hid the burnt side underneath. Ended up with a mouthful of ash. Said it was good for me."

"Whereas it's actually carcinogenic," said Claire. She turned to Hamlin. "Pete, I know we went over all this when I saw the body with you on Monday, but Mark's going to be joining us, so for his benefit, can you just run through it again?"

"Yes, of course. Young woman, Sarah Davis, twenty-two, found dead in a flat on the Oxmoor estate. Neighbour called it in, said she'd popped round to ask if Sarah could do some babysitting for them. Couldn't get a response when she knocked. She noticed the *Hunts Post* was still jammed in the letterbox, which was odd because the delivery had been three days earlier. Thought she must have gone away – she had family in London so often went down to see them. Then, she heard a whining sound through the door. Sarah's dog. She knew Sarah would never have left the dog on its own – joined at the hip apparently, took it everywhere, even to work – so she got suspicious, rang the police, we broke in, found her in the bedroom strangled."

"Interesting," said Mark.

"An innocent man would have gone to the police straightaway," said Hamlin. "He took himself off to Scotland. Had to drag him off an oil rig in the Shetland Isles. Not the easiest of arrests. We also spoke to a previous boyfriend; he said she had wanted him to choke her during sex, but he wanted nothing to do with it."

"Which at least in part backs up his story," said Claire.

"Yeah, he got lucky with that one. Still doesn't explain why he ran though, does it? My gut's telling me this is a murder; I just hope you find something this morning that proves it."

Claire grimaced. "No pressure, then?"

"No, no pressure," smiled Hamlin.

*

Attending the scene had been a singularly squalid and depressing experience. Discarded plastic milk containers, beer cans, and polystyrene fast-food containers littered the long grass, forming a buffer zone between the road and long monotonous rows of cheaply built terraced housing. Some of the windows in the houses had been boarded over; newspapers or rags had been wedged into the cracked and broken windows of others. A black faux-leather sofa sat on one corner of the grass, its inner yellow foam billowing out from where it had been slashed on one side.

Hamlin was waiting for her inside the flat. He nodded and, without speaking, led her upstairs. There was a faecal smell of decay, urine and damp, sweat and cheap perfume. The girl's body was in the larger of the two upstairs bedrooms and was wedged against the inside of the half open door, a blue silk scarf taut around the neck, tied onto the brass door handle. Her long dark hair hung in fronds around her face and throat.

"Unfortunately, one of those occasions when trying not to move the body proved impossible," he said drily.

Claire frowned and knelt to examine the girl's corpse.

"Foster's already taken photographs. Just waiting on forensics," said Hamlin.

The woman was young, early to mid-twenties, attractive. She was also naked, apart, incongruously, from a pair of heavy black Doc Martens. A deep-sea diver, tethered to the ocean floor, unable to break free. Her eyes were still open, rolled back into her head. Claire bent forward and gently closed them.

CHAPTER TWELVE

Claire opened her eyes. For a moment, she had felt she was about to faint. She stared down at the girl on the dissecting table again. She took a deep breath and started by snipping the plastic ties she had used to secure the polythene bags she had placed on the girl's hands and head when she had first seen her.

"Why did you put…?" asked Mark.

"You often find evidence helpful to the case at these sites and the bags make sure it's protected and isn't lost," said Claire. "Mark, would you mind taking some cuttings from the fingernails? There are sample bags over on the table there. When you've done that, take samples of both plucked and combed hair."

Gently, she removed the girl's heavy boots and then began a careful examination of the external appearance of the body.

"Well, I think we can agree there is evidence of asphyxia. There are petechial haemorrhages over the face and neck, and again in the conjunctiva. There are also signs of swelling or oedema and cyanosis of the face and lips." She raised one of the body's hands, carefully examining the fingertips. "And evidence of cyanosis here as well."

"The defence will claim the strangulation was consensual, of course," said Hamlin.

"Someone being asphyxiated can lose consciousness very quickly, sometimes within seconds, and from there it's a short road to death," said Claire. "So, a very strong argument could be made that it was consensual, that her death was an accident."

She prised the victim's mouth open and peered in. There was a sticky residue on the girl's teeth. She took a thin blade and carefully scraped some of it away so she could examine it more closely. "This looks like blood. Were there any bite marks on this bloke?"

"I don't think so – no, wait, he had a T-shirt on. If the bite was on his upper arm or his chest, perhaps, it could have been concealed by the sleeves of the T. I'm not sure that was looked at; I'll need to speak to the SOCO to confirm."

"Okay, let me know what you find. My expectation, though, is that you will find a bite mark and it looks as though the victim would have drawn blood. We'll take some swabs and have them analysed in the laboratory. There may well be some of the boyfriend's skin and tissue in addition to the blood."

Hamlin stared at her. "So, this might indicate possible violence during the assault; I mean, other than the strangling?"

"Possibly," said Claire cautiously. "However, he could claim the bite mark occurred because they were having rough sex. It would be plausible if she had an appetite for asphyxiation."

She bent down, and gently pushed one of the ears forward so she could inspect behind it. There was clear evidence of a crescent-shaped bruise. She looked behind the other ear and found similar bruising.

"I can't be a hundred per cent sure, but these symptoms – the periorbital ecchymosis and the bruising behind the ears – may be signs of a basilar fracture."

"Sorry, you've lost me."

"Periorbital ecchymosis is bruising around the eyes," said Mark.

"Sorry, Pete, the technical stuff is really for Mark's benefit so we can record it in the notes."

"Yes, of course, but what does it all mean?"

"Well, in layman's terms she may have sustained a fracture at the base of the skull. If you look, the crescent-shaped bruises behind the ears are known as the Battle sign – I won't bore you as to why it's called that, the important thing is her skull has suffered a fracture."

"And that could have killed her?"

"Well, it's certainly a contributory factor. It requires considerable force to inflict this type of injury."

"Wait a minute, could it have been caused by her head striking the door frame?"

"Possibly, but I would then have expected the fracture to occur higher up. I'm also not sure whether that would generate enough force."

Foster had remained silent to this point but now he jumped

in. "What about if her head struck the door handle, I mean at the base of her skull?"

"Yes, that's it," said Hamlin, "he must have struck her head on the door handle. That would work, wouldn't it, Claire?"

"It might," said Claire cautiously.

"I'll talk to Forensics – they may have found traces of her blood and hair fibres on the handle. Would the fracture have occurred prior to the asphyxiation or afterwards?"

"Impossible to tell, but it's certainly an indication of a possible struggle and violence on his part. I doubt she could have inflicted that injury on herself. Either way, it's hardly indicative of an accidental sexual asphyxiation. We'll need a CTI scan, incidentally, to confirm it is a basal break."

"If the CTI's positive – and I'm sure it will be – then taken with the other evidence and his flight from the scene I think we've probably got enough to go for a conviction."

"Don't count your chickens," said Claire. "Even if the CTI is positive, a defence barrister could still possibly pick holes in all of this. They'll also have their own expert witnesses."

"No, I'm sure we've got enough, especially with your expert testimony, Claire. Juries love you."

Claire sighed. "I wish I had your confidence, Pete. What's he like, this bloke?"

"Nasty piece of work. Bit of a drifter – variety of dead-end jobs when he left school. Worked as a mechanic with his brother at one point. By the way, I've been meaning to tell you, we've got a trial date for the Alice murder – 8th November."

Claire felt her stomach flip, the anxiety she had pushed down bubbling up again. "Okay, thanks for letting me know."

"Best put it in your diary; Joan will be the key expert witness, but we'll have to call you as well."

"How long do you think the trial will last?"

"Dunno, should be a couple of weeks at least. One thing I do know, there'll be a lot of media interest. It was bad enough when we arrested Granny; now it'll go into the stratosphere."

"Yes, I suppose it will. We had booked a holiday in Hawaii the last two weeks in November – wedding anniversary – so that's great. Our anniversary is cursed; every year something crops up to spoil it. Sean broke his arm last year; tripped walking up some steps outside the hotel."

"Oh dear, perhaps you should just stop celebrating it. Me and the wife did that years ago. Don't even bother with a card now, and Liz hates flowers – says she doesn't want dead things cluttering up the house."

"Chocolates?" said Mark.

"Diabetic," said Hamlin.

Claire laughed. "Sounds like a cheap date."

"That's why I picked her – if she could knock the champagne on the head, she'd be perfect. Which reminds me, Joan wants you to ring her about the trial; said she's got something important she needs to share."

"She didn't say what at all?"

"No, 'fraid not. Not sure why she couldn't tell me, mind; not as though we're not all on the same side."

"If it's a problem affecting the trial I'll ring you, Pete."

"Great. Better not be, mind. I need a failed prosecution in front of the world's media like a hole in the head."

CHAPTER THIRTEEN

2012

Claire stared through the window. The only occupant was a woman busy with a flower arrangement in one corner of the shop. She pushed the door open, the woman glancing up as she entered. How was she supposed to phrase this?

"Hi," she said. "This is going to sound a little strange, but did you sell a bouquet of roses recently… I mean, in the last, say, two days – for a funeral. Sorry, I know this sounds odd, but it's important—"

The woman stared at her. She looked both puzzled and suspicious. "Sorry, love, why do you need to know?"

Claire's mouth was now dry. She glanced nervously at the flower arrangement on the counter, a heavily scented mixture of roses, lilacs and delphiniums. The flowers sat in a dark blue foam block, pink wrapping paper and cellophane lying in sheets next to them, freshly cut green stems scattered across the counter.

"I'm sorry, I can't explain, but it is important."

The florist picked up a wand of purple lisianthus, her hand reaching for a pair of scissors lying nearby. She carefully snipped off part of the stem and then pushed the flower into the foam block. Claire noticed the tips of her fingers had been stained green by the cut stems.

"What colour were they? The roses , I mean."

"Sorry, I should have said; they were red," said Claire anxiously.

"I sold a bouquet of red roses on Tuesday, I think, might have been Wednesday, I'm not sure, my memory's shocking these days."

"Do you remember anything about the person who bought them? Was it a man? A woman?"

"A woman, I think, no, wait, a man. I'm sorry, love, I really can't remember, my memory see… and I'm hopeless at remembering faces."

Claire tried to hide her disappointment. "Are you sure? Are you sure you can't remember? It's very important—"

"I'm sorry, I really am, I just can't remember. I think it was a man, but I'm not a hundred per cent sure. We sell a lot of flowers and unless someone's a regular, I don't tend to remember much about who bought them. Unless they act up, of course. Some customers can be incredibly rude, they seem to think—"

Claire cut across her. "Is there anything else you can remember about them… what they were wearing, how tall… ?

"No, I'm sorry, I can't. Sorry."

CHAPTER FOURTEEN

It was the third time that morning; her mobile would ring, but when she went to answer it, there was only dead air. She had looked at the call log; it was a mobile number and the same one each time. If it was a scammer, they usually had a sequence of numbers they used, each one slightly different, an automatic dialler diligently searching out the next victim. The number given wasn't one she was familiar with, though; otherwise it would have been in her contacts list and a name would have come up.

Was someone trying to frighten or intimidate her? She thought about phoning Hamlin but then changed her mind. She rang Alan. The rule was that they always WhatsApped each other, but this was different; her life, and possibly that of her child, was being threatened and she needed to speak to him. Some instinct told her it was him she needed to speak to. Initially, there was no response. The phone rang and rang, and she was just about to give up when he answered. "Claire, why on earth are you ringing me on this number? Took me an age to find the bloody thing. I thought we agreed—"

Claire cut him off. "Never mind what we agreed. Does Rachel know about us?"

"No, of course she doesn't. I've told you, I'd be the first to know if she did. I'd be out on my bloody ear."

"Well, someone is targeting me, and you might as well know. Toby, too."

She quickly told him about finding the new, smaller grave. Alan was horrified, but repeated that Rachel couldn't have found out about them. Claire suddenly had a thought, something she should have grasped immediately. "Rachel's mobile number – what is it?"

"What? Oh alright," he sighed. "If it'll put your mind at rest: 07700 919644."

"Hang on, let me look at my phone." She pulled up Recent Calls. It was the same number. "Alan, that's the number that called me. It's the same."

"What – are you sure?"

"Of course I'm bloody sure. She knows, Alan."

"If that's the case, why hasn't she given me a hard time?"

"Think about it – you're on a fat partner's salary. Why would she give that up?"

"Don't be ridiculous – she would destroy me if she found out, absolutely skewer me."

"Well, she certainly seems to be trying to do that to me. Maybe she'll start in on you afterwards."

"You're being paranoid."

"And don't I have good cause to be? Someone sends me

an invitation to my own funeral and then threatens my son and you're accusing me of being paranoid? You bastard, you fucking bastard."

"Claire, please, I'm sorry, please, I didn't mean to—"

"Yes, you fucking did." She ended the call, pounding the desk with her fist in frustration. For a moment she sat, closing her eyes, covering her face with her hands. There was a tentative knock on the door. The door opened, Kate anxiously peering through.

"Are you alright? I heard—"

Claire waved her away. "I'm fine, well, no, I'm not fine, I'm a mess." Tears filled her eyes. Embarrassed, she hastily wiped them away with the heel of her hand, reaching blindly at the same time down into her handbag to grope for a tissue.

"Can I help? Is there anything I can do?"

"No, I'm fine, honestly. Period, always go a bit mental when – you must have noticed." She grimaced, an awkward attempt at a smile which didn't reach her eyes.

"It's not your period, is it?" said Kate gently. "I've been watching you the last few days – something is very wrong, isn't it? I can tell. I'm worried about you; I've never seen you like this."

Claire stared at her for a moment, trying to decide whether she should tell her. "Pub," she said. "It's lunchtime anyway and I need a drink. Come on, let's get out of here."

Kate smiled. "Great idea, give me a second to sort myself

out. I need to tell Mark as well, make sure he's okay to cover. Unless—"

"No, just us. We need to talk."

*

Once they'd got their drinks, she told her, told her everything; about the hoax, the threats to both her and Toby, her affair with Alan, all of it, the whole sorry mess. Claire had driven them to a small pub tucked away in a quiet backstreet; there were few people inside, an old couple nursing their drinks in one corner and a man, badly dressed, sitting near the door. Despite herself and her own agitation Claire could not help glancing up at him occasionally. She could see long grey hairs spiralling up from his thinning scalp, and in the sunlight from a window, they formed a ragged halo. The pub itself wore the same air of neglect, the pale timber floor sticky beneath their feet, the blue embroidered fabric covering their seats faded and worn.

"God, Claire, I can't believe what you've been through. It's so awful. Do you really think Rachel might be at the bottom of this? You've met her – what's she like?"

"Attractive, slim – thinner than me, anyway – good figure, dresses well. Seemed pleasant enough on the surface but Alan told me they've had some shocking rows. She's thrown stuff at him, even threw a knife at him once."

"God, was he hurt?"

"No, luckily it was just the handle that hit him. He was pretty shaken by it, though."

"So, it could have been her."

"Possibly. I just don't know. People are never what they seem. Do you remember that civil servant who butchered all those men – what was his name? – well, everyone at his office thought he was a normal bloke, quiet, unassuming, good at his job. Can't remember his name – Nelson? No, not that. Something… oh, it doesn't matter, you get the drift."

"I can try and google it if you like," said Kate, reaching for her phone.

"No, don't worry, it's not important. The thing is, you can never really know what someone's like or what they're capable of. There was a book I read recently by a forensic psychologist. She said that, depending on the circumstances, we're all capable of evil."

"God, that's deep. I think you're safe with me, though; my idea of evil is wolfing down a tub of Häagen-Dazs whilst watching *Friends*."

"Actually, that's my idea of evil as well," smiled Claire.

"So, what now? How can I help?'

Claire shrugged. "Kate, I love you to bits, but I honestly can't see how you can help. Pete's helping me; you remember Pete, he was a DS—"

"Course I remember Pete – very funny man. Did either of you have any luck tracking down the source of the photograph on the invitation card?"

"No, unfortunately. Another dead end."

"Have you heard of a reverse image search?"

"No, I haven't – what is it?"

"It's a feature on Google: if you put in an image or photo, it will try and either find similar images or the source of the image you've used. We could try it on that photo, if you like. Might be another dead end but still worth a try I would have thought."

"Well, nothing else has worked so why not? Pete's still got the card, though, so I'll have to retrieve it off him first."

"Okay. Let me have it once you've got it back and I'll give it a go." She hesitated, then: "How are you getting on with Sean now?"

"Not great, hasn't been good for a while. He's such a moody sod – well, yes, alright, I can talk, I know – but his sulks can go on for days. He went three days once without speaking to me."

"I'd be delighted if a bloke did that to me. Most of them just keep banging on about themselves; I did this, I did that. Who sodding cares? What about asking me what I've done?"

"I must admit, sometimes I think it's one of those 'be careful what you wish for' things. Sometimes I think I might be happier on my own – well, just me and Toby."

"Blokes, eh? said Kate. "Only good for one thing and most of them are not very good at that either. Sometimes I think I should give being a lesbian a try."

Claire giggled. "God, you're funny. You're the only thing keeping me sane at the moment. Did you have anyone in mind for your lesbian frolics?"

Kate's fingers pulled at a loose thread in the seam of her

dress. Then she lifted her head, staring unseeing into the middle distance.

"Yes… you, actually."

For a moment Claire sat stunned, unable to look at Kate, who was blushing furiously.

"I'm sorry, I really shouldn't, I don't know why I—"

"No, no, it's alright, I'm glad you told me," said Claire, now looking directly at her. "I'm sorry, Kate, I'm so sorry, I can't – I just don't—"

Kate cut across her. "No, it's fine, I understand, I was stupid to even think… Please don't let this spoil our friendship. I couldn't bear it if—"

Claire rested a hand on Kate's. "Kate, nothing will spoil our friendship, certainly not this. And if I was gay, I would definitely be attracted to you. To be frank, I think you're beautiful, always have done. You light up a room when you walk into it."

Tears appeared in Kate's eyes. "You're sure? God, I feel so embarrassed. How could I be so stupid?"

"You're far from stupid. I'm flattered you would think of me as a possible partner, I really am. Look, let me get us another drink…"

"No, no, I'm okay, don't really want another one. Should be getting back anyway, I've got a shedload of work to get through—"

"Are you sure? Are you sure you're alright?"

"Yes, of course," Kate said brightly. She stood up, almost

knocking her chair over, catching hold of one of its arms just in time. The barmaid, a young woman with blonde hair scraped back in a ponytail, looked up at the noise.

"God, I'm clumsy," said Kate. "Need to get out of here before I start knocking everyone's drinks over too." She turned abruptly and headed for the door. For a moment Claire sat, staring at nothing. Then she rose to her feet and headed after her.

CHAPTER FIFTEEN

Kate was sitting at her desk when Claire got back, staring grimly at her computer screen. Claire tried to catch her eye as she passed, but Kate ignored her. Probably just as well, Claire thought. We both need to put a little distance between what just happened and how we deal with it. She spent the rest of the afternoon holed up in her office, reviewing and editing the notes Mark had done for the asphyxiation post-mortem. She thought about examining the case file for the Alice murder but felt too anxious to look at it. Instead, she rang home. She did this every day now. Her aunt had agreed to stay with them for a couple of weeks to take care of Toby. He was still going to nursery every day, with her aunt managing the drop offs and pick-ups. The phone call was to make sure they had both got back safely.

Her aunt was slow to pick up and Claire could feel the panic already rising in her chest by the time she did answer. She had told her aunt everything that had happened, including her belief that Toby was also now a target. For some reason, which she struggled to explain even to herself, she had not told Sean. Was it because he might accuse her of paranoia, a manifestation of her illness rather than a real threat? She was unsure; their relationship had been difficult for a long time now and she was no longer certain she even wanted him in her life.

"Hello, Claire – I almost missed your call. Toby was insisting I help him with his Lego castle. I'm afraid at the moment it looks more like a shed than a castle, but he seems happy enough."

"Sorry, just wanted to make sure you'd both got back safely from nursery."

"Yes, all good. Look, you don't need to ring me every day like this – I can just send you a text once we get home."

"Yes, sorry, you're right… but what if someone got hold of your phone, pretended to be you?"

"Oh, Claire, you must stop worrying like this – you'll drive yourself mad."

"I know, I know, I just can't—"

"Look, it's fine, just go on ringing me. If it makes you feel better then just carry on. If you're in a meeting or otherwise tied up, I'll text you. Then you can ring me once you're free again."

"You're a saint, Brenda, I'd be lost without you. I should be home by seven – I'll do some stir-fry for us both."

"Don't worry – save it for the weekend. I'm doing us a pasta dish – you know, the one with goats' cheese and pesto."

"That's great – I love that recipe. Is Sean going to be eating with us?"

"I'm not sure, he seems to be getting back later and later these days. More often than not, he's also already eaten – look, if he's home, fine, he can eat with us, otherwise, he'll have to sort himself out."

"No problem. See you later, then."

*

Driving home, Claire thought again about the conversation with Kate in the pub. She didn't consider herself bisexual but she thought everyone's sexuality was fluid to an extent, both sexes capable of being captivated by a beautiful woman or man. It was impossible not to be drawn to them. But to go further? She pushed it to the back of her mind. It was not as though she didn't have enough going on in her life. Which brought her to Rachel. She knew, she was sure of it. She would need to speak to Alan again.

Brenda was in the kitchen when she got home. She didn't hear Claire enter the house and when Claire found her, she was bouncing around the kitchen, a spatula held in one hand and a jar of green pesto in the other as she listened to the Supremes' "You Can't Hurry Love". The sight was so comic Claire burst out laughing. Shamefaced, Brenda lowered her arms.

"Don't stop for me," said Claire. "You're obviously enjoying yourself."

"Yes, well, just a tiny bit embarrassing," said Brenda.

"No, don't be daft. If I was listening to that I'd find it impossible not to dance round the kitchen too. I love Motown.

Takes me back to my childhood, singing along with a hairbrush in front of the wardrobe mirror."

"I used to get my mates round," said Brenda, "so we could practice our dance moves for the school disco. Completely wasted on the boys, of course: they just stood around the edges with their arms folded trying to pretend they weren't interested."

"Until the slow dance at the end," laughed Claire. "As soon as "House of the Rising Sun" came on, they were practically sprinting across the floor trying to grab you before their mates got there."

"Long time ago now," said Brenda. "Well, for me, anyway."

Claire looked at her. Brenda suddenly looked older, shrunken somehow, her untidy mop of grey hair spilling down into her eyes. It was impossible to look at her, though, and not be immediately reminded of her own mother. Brenda and her mother had been twins, practically inseparable as children. Then that awful Friday evening when Claire's mother had killed herself, found hanging from a roof beam in the garage when her father got home from work. After that he had become withdrawn, a silent presence in the house. Grief had erected a tent in his heart, and he never recovered. Claire had been three years old when her mother died, the same age as Toby. The feeling of abandonment she felt then had never left her. After that, Brenda had tried to spend as much time with her as she could manage, taking her out for treats like the circus and pantomimes, going shopping with her for ballet pumps and school uniforms, and consoling her when she got dumped by her first boyfriend. Brenda's own marriage broke down when she found she couldn't have children. Painful endometriosis, followed by a hysterectomy. Claire became her daughter.

Toby came rushing into the kitchen, arms outstretched as he hurled himself into Claire's arms. "Mummy," he cried.

Claire swept him up into her arms. "Gosh, you're getting heavy."

"Auntie's doing paste."

"She is indeed making paste and I'm sure it will be delicious, a special treat for us both."

"I don't like paste, it's horrible."

"But darling you've never had it before; you'll absolutely love it."

"I want beans, beans and chicken. I like chicken."

"Well, look, if you don't like it, I'll make you beans and chicken nuggets afterwards. Just try a bit of the paste first and see if you like it."

"Can we do aeroplanes?"

"You and your aeroplanes," laughed Brenda. "Of course we can do aeroplanes." She waggled her eyebrows at Claire.

"Join me in a glass of wine?" said Claire lightly. "I've had a really rough day and I need something to calm me down."

Brenda frowned. She was all too aware that Claire's drinking was getting out of control. "Are you sure?" she said cautiously. "I hesitate to say this, but I think you've been overindulging lately. Might be an idea to give your liver a break."

"What's a sliver?" asked Toby.

"No, not 'sliver' – liver. It's something we all have in our tummies," smiled Claire.

"Does it hurt?"

"No; it's very important, though, and helps us to stay well."

"Am I well?"

"Yes, you are, my darling, you are the wellest child in the whole wide world." She hoisted him higher and kissed him tenderly on the forehead.

"I'm wellest, Auntie," Toby giggled.

"You are the wellest," said Brenda, smiling. There was a loud beeping sound from the timer on the oven. "I think our food's ready. Can you give me a hand serving, Claire?"

"Yep, no problem."

"I'll pour us all some water, shall I?" There was a challenge in Brenda's gaze as she said this.

Claire sighed. "Water's fine. I'll set the table." She carefully put Toby down on the floor again, went into the dining room and started to lay out the cutlery and placemats for their meal. Her aunt usually retired to bed early, around nine, and she consoled herself with the thought that she could have some wine then. The bottle could be hidden afterwards. Her thoughts drifted back to Kate. As though my life isn't complicated enough already. She stared out at the garden. Light flooded upwards from the LEDs buried in the decking, brilliant white spotlights illuminating the trees and shrubs. Claire suddenly felt very vulnerable; could someone be out there watching?

She hurriedly switched off the kitchen lights and stood there for a while, waiting for her vision to adjust, the garden slowly swimming into focus. There appeared to be a shadow off to the side of the summerhouse. She tried peering more closely; it seemed to move and then disappeared.

CHAPTER SIXTEEN

She lay awake, staring into the darkness. It was just after six. Sean lay snoring gently beside her. Alan. She needed to speak to him; if Rachel was at the bottom of all this then if she got rid of Alan then that should get rid of her as well. The threats should stop. If they didn't, then it would prove at least that she hadn't sent that horrible invitation, that someone else must be at the back of it. Whichever way she looked at it, ending the affair with Alan would simplify things. Toby was her priority now; she needed to do all that she could to keep him safe. Alan would already be at work, she knew; his firm was notorious for its long-hours culture and the partners set the tone.

Throwing on a dressing gown, she crept downstairs. Easing her bare feet into a pair of old shoes she kept near the back door she gently opened it, straining to be as quiet as possible, and, stepping out, walked to the far end of the garden. The artificial turf spat water up onto her feet; in places rainwater had simply pooled on the surface. Bloody stuff. It hadn't been laid correctly, with poor drainage. Sean had promised to sort it out, but having got their money, the contractors seemed to be in no hurry to come back. Claire found Alan's direct dial number for his office. He picked up immediately.

"Hi, Alan, can you talk, or should I phone back?"

"No, no, it's fine. My first meeting's not until 8.30 so now's fine. How are you? Our last conversation didn't—"

"Not so good actually. Look, Alan, I've been thinking; we need to end it."

"Sorry, end it? End what?"

"Our relationship, Alan," said Claire impatiently, "if we can dignify it with that word."

"Claire, why? Why would you do that? You know I—"

"You don't love me, Alan, so let's not pretend you do. We're both grown-ups. It was nice while it lasted, we had some fun, but now we need to call a halt."

"I still don't—"

"Toby. Toby's my priority now. Despite what you say, Rachel knows about us. I don't know whether she's responsible for this hoax, but I can't chance it either."

"I already told you, I'm sure she doesn't—"

"She knows, Alan, believe me, she knows. How else do you explain those phone calls?"

There was a silence at the other end. "Sorry, you're right. She must know. And you're right about us, too. I really don't want to lose you, Claire, but all of this is too much of a risk. I love Rachel – I know she can be difficult, but at bottom I still love her, and I don't want to lose that either."

"Good. It's settled then."

"Yes, it's settled." A pause. "Can we still at least be friends?"

Claire gave a hollow laugh. "Yes, of course, we can – in the time-honoured phrase – still be 'friends'. Oh, and Alan? Get rid of that phone."

CHAPTER SEVENTEEN

"I want a divorce."

Claire stared at him in shock. It was a Sunday morning. Brenda had taken Toby to the park; she had wanted to join them, but when Brenda was in the hallway getting ready with Toby, Sean had pulled Claire to one side, said there was something important he needed to talk to her about. Now they sat in the kitchen. Sean asked her if she wanted a coffee, but Claire waved him away, saying she'd already had too much. As he carefully poured the pungent beans into the coffee maker, he dropped his bombshell. He said it casually, his back turned to her as he reached for a mug from one of the cabinets. He placed the mug into the machine, a toy which had cost the thick end of £600.

"What? What did you say?"

He turned to face her, still holding the mug. "I want a divorce. I've had enough; I can't cope with your moods anymore." The coffee machine made a hissing sound, an audience at a pantomime booing the villain.

"And I suppose I can cope with yours? You've been foul to

me for months. At least I have the excuse that I have a disease – you're just nasty."

Sean turned back to the machine. The coffee was ready. He lifted the mug out and brought it to his lips, savouring the taste. He was gazing quite calmly at her, as though she were a mild domestic problem which needed to be dealt with; milk past its sell-by date, cat litter which needed throwing out.

"You complete bastard," said Claire. A thought struck her. "Are you having another affair? Is that why you're doing this?'

Sean looked coldly at her. "I know you're fucking Alan. Rachel told me weeks ago."

Claire was stunned. So, Rachel did know. "Really? Well, if I am 'fucking' Alan as you so delicately put it, that's hardly a surprise given you've been shagging anything with a pulse ever since we got married."

He seemed amused by this. "I'm actually quite choosy," he smirked. "Well, apart from the mistake I made in marrying you."

"You fucking evil bastard." Trembling with rage, she flew across the kitchen. He was still holding the mug of coffee and her first blow smashed it against him, tipping the contents down his T-shirt and navy-blue chinos. He raised his arms to defend himself, but she knocked them aside and began pounding his chest with her fists. For a moment he was too startled to do anything, then he grabbed her arms and gave her a hard shove. She fell, her hip banging hard against the tiled floor, and she screamed in pain.

He stared at her, breathing hard. Then he turned and left the kitchen, slamming the door behind him. As she attempted to stand, a sharp pain knifed up through her. She groaned and sank back down again onto her knees. She could hear him moving around upstairs, the floorboards creaking with his weight. Gripping the edge of the marble worktop, she slowly hauled herself to her feet. She felt nauseous, a sour acid bursting upwards through her throat. She vomited again, and then again, her stomach going into a series of painful spasms until, at last, there was nothing left to bring up. The foul smell of her own vomit made her gag again. It not only covered the floor but had splashed up onto her shoes and leggings. She heard the front door open and then bang shut, and she burst into tears.

CHAPTER EIGHTEEN

It was bitterly cold outside, the sky an iron grey. As she approached Judith's Field it started to snow, a heavy drifting snow which blanketed the ground in minutes. She cursed her choice of footwear; thin trainers, already soaked inside. Brenda and Toby were standing in the play area, Toby giggling as he bent to pick up handfuls of the snow, flinging them into the air where they burst into powdery clouds.

She waved to them, and they both waved a greeting back to her. Looking at her chalk-white face, Brenda knew immediately something awful had happened.

"Claire, are you okay?"

"Sean," she whispered, her voice hoarse and strained. Toby looked up at her anxiously.

"Mummy, why are you crying?"

Claire attempted a smile. "I'm not crying, darling, just got some of the snow in my eyes. Brenda, can we go back to your house? I don't want to go home at the moment."

"Yes, of course. My house is closer anyway and if we leave it much longer, we'll be up to our waist in this snow. Come on, Toby, back to Auntie's."

"I want to stay here; I want to make a snowman."

"We can make one in the garden when we get back," laughed Brenda.

Claire caught his hand, Brenda took the other one, and they swung Toby between them, Claire grimacing in pain, at the same time trying to hide it from her son. "Up, up and *away*," they sang, as they lifted him high, pretending to launch him in the air. He squealed with delight.

The snow grew heavier, erasing their footprints, covering them in a white shroud.

CHAPTER NINETEEN

A lthough it now had a tiled roof, Brenda's house had been built in the seventeenth century. A wooden plaque, carved with the date 1610, stood above the front door. Thick oak beams provided the skeleton of the building, arranged in a lattice framework on the exterior and threaded through the walls and ceilings of the interior. The external walls had been rendered and painted a creamy burnt umber. One end of the roof was bowed and leaned forward over the street as though to better hear the conversations of passers-by. The house was listed, and Brenda had facetiously described it in a poem as listed, listing and listening. Claire had responded that, perhaps, the listening could more be accurately described as eaves dropping. I agree, said Brenda, but that would ruin both the alliteration and assonance, although, it was a pretty decent pun.

Claire loved old houses, but Sean decidedly didn't, so they had moved into a new house in Brampton, and while Claire searched the dozens of packing boxes scattered around the house for a bottle opener, Sean started to draw up plans to extend the drive and patio areas and investigate whether the grass at the back of the house could be replaced with Astroturf. Still without a bottle opener, sweating in the noonday heat, Claire pointed out that all he would achieve by putting down Astroturf would be to replace the lawnmower with a broom. At least that was eco-friendly, he said, and then delivered the coup de grâce by saying that Astroturf was not only better for the environment but would substantially increase the value of their house.

Claire conceded with an ill grace and returned to her now even more desperate search for a bottle opener. The Astroturf was duly laid the following week by some moonlighting carpet fitters. Now, in high summer, their garden glowed a rich and unearthly green amidst the parched brown lawns of their neighbours.

Every other inch of their garden had been tamed with hard paving and composite decking. Plants were grudgingly confined to a few scattered pots, although even here Sean had insisted on planting herbs which, he said, at least had a culinary value. Claire had rolled her eyebrows at this because his idea of a herb was tomato ketchup.

The house itself was pleasant enough and stood in a close overlooking a small pond. Even better, this was overhung by an enormous oak tree which, as the subject of a protection order, the builders hadn't been allowed to touch. The house was also close to a garden centre and golf course, the latter flanked by a waste recycling site. A mountain of brown earth marked the boundary with the course, an occasional yellow digger patrolling the top. On a hot summer's day, the windows of residents' houses would be flung open in a vain attempt to cool the interiors. An hour later they would be closed again to block out the pungent smells emanating from the plant. The Environment Agency said they were monitoring the situation. Presumably from a safe distance, thought Claire.

Brenda's house faced onto a wide road lined with mature plane trees; the streets on Claire's estate were lined with cars. The narrow roads forced the cars to encroach onto the pavements, children adding their own obstacle course with scattered bikes and toys. Recycling and waste bins completed the barricades. The paths blocked off, young mums travelled in convoys down the roads to the local school, struggling with prams and pushchairs, their other kids trailing behind.

*

Once safely ensconced in the living room of Brenda's house, Claire told her everything that had happened; the funeral invitation, the temporary marker on the freshly dug grave in the cemetery, and the final awful row with Sean that morning. As she talked, she struggled to keep the tears from her eyes, carefully wiping them every few seconds with a tissue to try and stop her mascara running. She chose, though, not to tell her aunt about her own affair with a married man, and she didn't tell her about the possible threat to Toby's life. Even thinking about this was terrifying; to tell her aunt would not only worry her but make the threat even more real, and at that moment, she was desperately hoping that her potential attacker was only interested in killing her, that the threat to Toby was simply another mechanism to ratchet up her level of fear. She had, however, told her aunt to watch Toby like a hawk and never to lose sight of him. She pretended her bipolar disorder was making her even more anxious than normal at the moment and she needed to know that Toby was safe.

"He could stay with me for a while if you feel that would help?" said Brenda.

Claire hesitated, her hands twisting nervously in her lap. She remembered she had forgotten to take her medication that morning, although, that was hardly surprising given everything that had happened.

"I know this is a lot to ask, but could we both stay here for a while? I'm frightened going back to the house. Sean was so nasty last time—"

Brenda put her hand on Claire's. "Of course you can – I would love to have you both here, you know I would."

"Are you sure?"

"Don't be daft – of course I'm sure. I spent all those years putting up you with as a child, I'm sure I can manage a couple of days now, particularly if you do all the cooking and housework. That reminds me, the garage needs a good clear-out as well."

Claire laughed. "I think I'll leave you to do the cooking, you know I'm a rubbish cook."

"That's true; I remember one of your boyfriends telling me

that you were going to boil an egg in the microwave before he managed to stop you."

"True, unfortunately. It hadn't occurred to me it might explode. I then suggested that, if that didn't work, could we try microwaving some bacon instead? He was equally unimpressed, said bacon cooked in a microwave can be carcinogenic."

"Did he say why?" enquired Brenda.

"He did tell me, but I'd fallen asleep by the time he'd got to the end of it. Lovely bloke but, boy, was he dull. Not exactly one of life's risk-takers. I think he was an actuary. Or was it an accountant? Whatever it was, he was dull, anyway. Personally, I was well up for seeing what happens when a microwaved egg explodes. Especially since it was his microwave."

They both laughed. Claire glanced outside. It was still snowing heavily.

"God," said Claire, "it feels like it's been snowing forever. I wouldn't mind, but I need to go back to the house to pick up clothes and stuff. I've also still got to collect my car from Judith's Field."

"True, I'd forgotten you'd left it there so Toby could enjoy the snow walking back. Look, let me drive. I can drive us both back to your place and then we can sort out what you need."

"Are you sure you don't mind? I can easily do it on my own."

"No, no problem at all. Anyway, I don't like the idea of you going over there on your own. He might have come back."

"Oh, God, no, the last thing I want is to see him at the

moment. Just the thought of it makes me physically sick. What about Toby, though? We can't leave him here on his own."

"We'll take him with us; we'll only be there half an hour, I'm sure he can cope with that."

"Are you sure you don't mind doing this?" A thought suddenly occurred to her and her face paled. "What if he comes back while we're there?"

"It's possible, I suppose," said Brenda. "Look, here's what we'll do; we'll drive over and, if his car's in the drive, we can just turn round and come back again."

"Yes, that would work. What if he turns up when we're there, though?"

"We'll just have to take that chance. At least I'll be there, and if he starts being nasty then I'll show him what nasty really looks like."

Claire laughed. "I bet you would. Okay, you're on – let's go for it."

*

When they pulled up, the house was in darkness. Claire breathed a sigh of relief; his car wasn't there. It was now late evening. The snow had turned to a cold, sleeting rain. Toby had fallen asleep on the journey back.

"Brenda, it might be best if you stay in the car with Toby," she whispered. "If he wakes up then bring him in, but I'll go in and start collecting stuff. It shouldn't take long. We don't need that much."

When she entered the main bedroom, she noticed that she had left the window ajar; the blind, caught by the wind outside, made a soft tapping noise against the frame. As she went to close it, she heard a car pull up at the lights outside. Despite the snow, the driver had wound down one of the windows; he was playing an old Motown song. *What becomes of the brokenhearted?* She was immediately transported back.

*

"You're late."

"Sorry, needed to get a presentation finished for a meeting tomorrow. I'm completely knackered." She had heard the key turn in the lock and had come into the hallway to confront him as he entered. Sean had been looking down as he spoke, but now he stared at her, as though seeing her for the first time, a look of astonishment on his face. Claire stared back, defiant, and lifted the glass she had been holding to her lips.

"You're not drinking are you – that's not—"

"What if it is?"

"Claire, you know you can't drink; the baby—"

Then he realised; his mobile phone was on the hall side table. He had forgotten to take it with him that morning but had reassured himself that it didn't matter. He had been careful to change the PIN several months ago.

"So, who is she?"

"Sorry, who is *who*? I don't understand what you're talking about."

"The slut you've been shagging – who is she?"

"Look, I don't know what the hell you're talking about. You're five months' pregnant and I come home and find you drinking. You know how dangerous that is; are you manic again – is that what this is?"

"You bastard, you complete shit!" She suddenly lunged for the phone and hurled it at him, striking him on the shoulder. He winced in pain. "Tell me who it is and *stop* fucking lying to me!"

"I don't know what you're—"

"I've seen the texts, Sean; I've seen the disgusting stuff she's been sending to you. I'm pregnant with your child, Sean, your child, and you're shagging someone else. You bastard!" She hurled her drink at him. Wine splattered his jacket and trousers, the glass shattering on the oak-timbered floor. Then she punched him hard on the side of his jaw. His head jerked back with the force of the blow, and he crouched, facing away from her, one arm raised protectively above his head.

"You bitch... you fucking bitch. I should—"

"You should what, Sean? Hit me back? Have me sectioned again?"

"You're mad, completely fucking mental. You've ruined this jacket."

He rose slowly to his feet. "Are you going to hit me again or can I trust you to be sensible, to act like a grown-up?"

Claire laughed bitterly. "If there's one thing you're not, Sean, it's a grown-up. So, don't you dare try and claim that I'm not one.' She suddenly felt exhausted. Her hand ached where she had punched him. With the rush of adrenalin, she had felt nothing initially, but now there was a dull throbbing ache. She hoped to God that she hadn't broken anything.

"I'm going to bed. You can sleep in the spare room. Tomorrow, I want you to leave; I don't want you in the house."

"Claire," he said softly.

"Don't. I don't care anymore; I need to sleep."

*

Sean had moved out the following morning. He hadn't been that bright. He had changed his PIN but Claire had easily guessed the new one: the date they had got married. Ironic, really.

In the weeks that followed, Claire continued to drink, consumed with self-pity. Each night she told herself that this would be the last time, that tomorrow she would stop, and each night she would repeat the same promise to herself even as she reached for one of the chilled bottles of wine which were now a permanent fixture in the fridge. Sean made several attempts to contact her, all of which she rebuffed. Then, one night, she saw a shadow through the glass of the front door. There was a rattle of a key in the lock and there he was, ashen, with a pleading look in his eyes. She suddenly found herself in his arms and they both stood for a while, hugging each other, both in tears.

Of course, she had taken him back; she still loved him,

despite the hurt and grief he had caused her. Then there was the baby, the tiny creature growing inside of her; if she destroyed her marriage then she would be a single parent, struggling to bring up a child on her own. She didn't feel she had the strength to do this; it was too much. She was too vulnerable, too frightened to walk out on her marriage. So, she stayed. And stopped drinking. What she couldn't stop was the guilt, the agonising fear that their child would not be born whole, that he would be damaged. She read as much as she could about the effects of foetal alcohol syndrome; she was looking for reassurance, of course, a grain of comfort in the stark presentation of the facts. There was none; a child with foetal alcohol syndrome could suffer from irreversible brain damage. At the very least, they might suffer from a low birth weight, learning disabilities, poor co-ordination and delays in speech and language development. Then the most horrifying statistic of all: the average life expectancy of a child with FAS was thirty-four years. Thirty-four years; the age she was now. She was so frightened; her first pregnancy had ended in a stillbirth. Now it looked as though she had made sure her second pregnancy would end in disaster as well.

As it was, Toby was perfectly healthy when he was born. His birth weight was normal. She anxiously watched for the signs of FAS during that first year; there were none. She had dodged a bullet.

*

The sound of the front door crashing open startled her. A man's voice.

"Claire!"

Forcing herself to stay calm, she walked out to the top of the stairs and gazed down. "What do you want, Sean?" she said coolly.

"Where's Toby?"

"He's in the car with Brenda outside."

"You're not staying here, then," he said, gesturing to a suitcase which lay in the hallway; Claire had left it open, and it was already half filled with clothes.

"No, I'm staying with Brenda for a couple of days – I thought—"

He looked away. "You can stay here; I've found somewhere else anyway. I won't be moving back."

She felt a surge of relief, immediately followed by resentment. Why shouldn't she stay in the house? It was her home. He was the one who had decided to destroy their marriage. Of course she was staying. She was too tired to be angry anymore, though, she just wanted him gone. He looked at her, his gaze softening.

"I'm sorry, Claire, I really am, I just can't cope—"

Tears pricked her eyes and she angrily wiped them away with the back of her hand.

"Don't, don't start."

"Look, I just need to pick up some more stuff and then I'll go. I won't be long, honestly."

"Fine, just do it," she said wearily. "Please be quick – Toby's asleep: I don't want him seeing you, he'll be too upset."

"He might be awake and see me when I leave, though, and short of putting a bag over my head—"

"Look, I'm going outside, and we'll drive around the corner. We'll wait fifteen minutes and then come back. Is that enough time?"

"Yeah, should be, should be more than enough."

"Good, hurry up then."

She turned away but he called her back.

"Claire?"

"Yes, what now?" she said impatiently.

"'I've got a solicitor. You might want to get one too."

"Right. Good to know where we stand. So, not an amicable divorce, then?"

"I see no reason why it shouldn't be."

"Really? Well, we'll just have to see, won't we?

CHAPTER TWENTY

2011

"In your post-mortem report you state that there was a basal fracture to the deceased's skull. For the benefit of the jury members, can you tell us first what a basal fracture is?"

Claire stared at the barrister; he reminded her of Shere Khan in Disney's *Jungle Book*, bald with a thrusting jaw and a look which was both supercilious and cunning. She was often called as an expert witness at a trial, but she frequently felt inadequate to the task, a situation where her fear of being unmasked as an imposter was at its most acute. She had been careful to avoid looking either at the accused or the jury. Dust swirled in the shafts of light from one of the windows and for a moment she gazed, transfixed.

"Mrs Evans, I asked you to explain what a basal fracture is. Or does that particular nugget of knowledge now elude you?"

Claire stared at him. How dare he? "A basal fracture is – as it sounds – a fracture to the base of the skull. There was clear evidence of this on the CT scan. In addition, during the autopsy there was periorbital ecchymosis; in layman's terms, bruising around the eyes. There were also crescent-shaped bruises behind the ears; these are a classic symptom of a basal fracture. It's known at the Battle sign and was first identified by an English surgeon, Doctor William Henry Battle, in the late 1800s."

Stung, she had said too much, at the risk of now appearing condescending and arrogant herself. Khan gave a sardonic smile. "Well remembered, Mrs Evans. Now, the prosecution alleges my client strangled Sarah Davis, and the basal fracture is evidence of a violent death rather than accidental asphyxiation. There is also evidence showing the presence of the victim's blood, hair and tissue on the door handle. The prosecution's conclusion is that my client deliberately struck the victim's head – by shoving her backwards, I presume – against the door handle as part of his attempt to kill her. Is it not the case, though, that she could have struck her head accidentally against the door handle?"

"It's possible, but unlikely; the fracture to her skull would require considerable force. I cannot see that such a fracture would have been sustained accidentally."

"But it is possible, is it not?"

"No, I don't agree that such an injury might have occurred accidentally. I also visited the victim's flat and examined the bedroom door; from the measurements I carried out of the elevation of the body against the door she must have been lifted up and back to strike the door handle. I very much doubt this could have happened during an accidental asphyxiation."

"If the victim had been kneeling rather than sitting wouldn't this have raised her to such a degree that no lifting would have been required?"

"It's possible, yes, but the crime scene photographs show the victim as slumped forward and sitting on the floor. She was not kneeling at the time of death."

"No, but the injury could have been sustained at an earlier point, perhaps prior to the asphyxiation itself? They were, after all, having what has been described as rough sex?"

Claire gave an audible sigh. "If she had sustained such an injury at an earlier point – that is, prior to the act of asphyxiation – I very much doubt she would have been either willing or capable of continuing. In any case, I would have expected her boyfriend to also want to call an immediate halt at that point. He would have needed to have sought urgent medical help for her."

The oily tiger looked deflated; his main point of attack had been blunted. He pressed on, though, desperate to introduce an element of doubt in the jury's minds. "But it's also possible, isn't it, that the injury could have occurred during the asphyxiation itself? That she could perhaps in a moment of sexual abandon or excitement have raised herself up and accidentally struck the door handle?"

"It's possible but I don't see that as likely."

"But it's still possible? You can't rule it out, can you?"

"No, no, I can't."

Tiger Face was triumphant, victory rescued from the jaws of defeat.

"No further questions, Your Honour."

*

It had been a gruelling cross examination and Claire was anxious that she hadn't done enough to convince the jury. She risked a glance at the defendant as she left the witness box. He looked to be in his late twenties, podgy with a pasty complexion, already receding badly at the temples, his hair combed forward in a fringe in a vain attempt to hide this. He looked nondescript and it was difficult to imagine him as someone capable of murder. What caught her attention, though, was the look of hatred directed at her from a man sitting towards the back of the court room. She looked away and, head bent, made her way out.

*

"So, how did it go?" asked Claire.

"Well, we got a conviction. Majority verdict. Life sentence with a recommendation from the judge that he serve a minimum term of 15 years. The minimum term might get overturned by the Home Secretary, of course, but I very much doubt it," said Hamlin.

"That's a relief. I thought I'd ruined it with my testimony."

"No, far from it – it was your testimony which was largely responsible for getting him convicted. I owe you a drink."

"I might well take you up on that. By the way, there was a bloke giving me the evil eye when I left. Unnerved me a bit."

"What did he look like?"

"Fairly chunky. Looked like he spent a lot of time lifting weights. Shoulder-length blond hair, both arms heavily tattooed. I'm not very good at guessing ages, but he looked around thirtyish."

"That's the guy's brother, Craig. Nasty bit of work. Got done for GBH a few years back. Bottled some poor girl in a pub."

"God, why am I not feeling reassured?"

"You should be alright – no reason why he should target you. More likely to come after me, I reckon. Either that or his barrister." He laughed. "He did do a fairly shit job defending him."

"Do you know anything more about him?"

"Well, both brothers came up through the care system. Usual story, mother a drunk, father a druggie. Social services got involved. They used to run a garage together; Craig still does, matter of fact."

"You seem to know a lot about them."

"I like to keep tabs on the villains in my patch. Craig did a spell in Wandsworth, and I confidently expect him to find another prison berth at some point."

"Okay, well, thanks for letting me know."

"No trouble," said Hamlin. "Have you spoken to Madison about the Alice trial? It's just that the 8th November's only twelve days away now."

"No, I've been meaning to ring her. I'll make it my next call."

"Are you nervous about it?"

"A little – it's a big case. Too much in the public glare for me."

"I wouldn't worry. Madison's going to have to do the heavy lifting."

"What, you mean I'm just the understudy?"

"I didn't mean that. I just meant she'll be the one in the spotlight, not you."

"I certainly hope so; I'm quite comfortable staying off stage."

"You'll be fine."

Claire rang Madison that afternoon. She'd read through the case notes, including the post-mortem report on Alice and the original autopsy report on the first child, Amanda. She thought a microbiological report had been requested for Alice, but there was nothing in the file. She decided she would ask Madison about this when she spoke to her. She was feeling low again, a familiar vague feeling of dread having again enveloped her.

"Hello, Joan?"

"Ah, Claire. I was just about to ring you. How are you?"

"I'm fine. Overworked as usual, but just about managing to cope. How are you?"

"Alright. My mum's not been very well so I'm a little worried about her. She's been losing weight and complaining of headaches."

"That does sound worrying; has she had tests?"

"She's got an MRI on Monday."

"How old is your mum?"

"Eighty-seven – now, I know people will say she's already had a good innings, but it doesn't work like that, does it? Inside that old woman of eighty-seven is someone who still thinks she's in her teens, and she's not ready to go. And I'm not ready either. Dad passed away ten years ago, and I still miss him."

"No, I know what you mean. My dad's now in a care home, unfortunately. He's got dementia. My aunt looked after him for a while, but he got too much for her in the end. I love him to bits, but he doesn't always recognise me when I go into to see him. He has lucid moments, but even those are becoming few and far between now."

"Dementia's a terrible disease," said Madison. She paused. "Right, now we've managed to depress ourselves, shall we talk about the trial? I'll obviously be the main witness, but your testimony is equally important, so we need to make sure we're singing from the same hymn sheet. Do you think we need to get together to go over everything?"

"I think it would be useful. When are you free?"

"Next Tuesday would be good," said Madison. "Does first thing at 8am work?"

"Yes, that should work. I've got to drop Toby off at nursery, but I can get my aunt to do that. Shall I come to you, or do you want to come here?"

"Would you mind coming here? I've got a meeting at 10 AM

which I can't really afford to miss. We'll have two hours, which should be enough I'd have thought. What do you think?"

"Two hours should be plenty. Great, I'll see you then."

When she rang off, she suddenly remembered she'd forgotten to ask about the microbiological report. No matter, she could ask Joan when she saw her the following week. She got up from her desk and stared out of the window. A dense fog hung in the air, oozing up from the ground, sinking down from the grey sky. It felt as though a wet suffocating blanket had been thrown over everything. The fog mirrored her depression.

Her mind drifted back. Three years ago, she had been sectioned with psychosis. It wasn't voluntary. It was shortly after the stillbirth of her first child, a period when her depression had spiralled out of control. She started hearing voices, hallucinating. In truth, she thought she was going mad. But then, for a while she was mad, wasn't she? Why else did Sean have her committed? Fulbourn Hospital diagnosed her as bipolar. She didn't know whether this had been triggered by the stress of the stillbirth and her subsequent depression, or whether it was something she had suffered from most of her adult life without realising. She could recall periods when she had felt euphoric, the centre of attention, almost wildly charismatic, and she also remembered times when she had endured lacerating bouts of depression. So, there was something there, wasn't there, something hidden in the depths, watching her, biding its time?

She had suffered a mixed episode, apparently, one in which her depression and mania had co-mingled, creating an explosive mix, combining a terrible sleeplessness and agitation with a vertiginous depression. Fulbourn itself was an odd place. The Mulberry Ward in which she stayed was part of a modern complex; the rest of the hospital sprawled in a spidery mess of buildings over the landscape, the gatehouse an almost Disneyesque gingerbread fantasy with a pointed hat roof to its side and narrow rectangular windows that seemed deliberately designed to hide its interior. The main building looked like a poor man's idea of a stately home: narrow columns of alternating red and yellow bricks rising forlornly into the sky at its margins, the same narrow windows, a stone rooftop balcony. She found out it had originally been the pauper lunatic asylum. Lunatic: an interesting word, conjuring up a gibbering, gurning creature, scarcely human.

She had recovered. They had put her on lamotrigine to stabilise her moods, control her depression. Three weeks after she had been admitted she was discharged back into the care of her husband. Two months later she felt well enough to return to work. No-one there knew, of course; they had simply been told she had suffered a very bad case of postnatal depression. Which she had, in a way. But not in the way they imagined.

CHAPTER TWENTY-ONE

Twenty-One Days Left

Walking up the street where she lived that evening she noticed a car parked almost opposite her house on the other side of the road. The headlights were on. Blinded by the lights, she could just make out the silhouette of a figure in the driver's seat. Was it the same car? It had been impossible to tell last time what colour or make it was; in the dark all colours morphed into a dull grey. She peered more closely. She was sure it was a woman. Claire crossed the road towards the car but even as she neared it, she could hear the engine starting up. It lurched forward and quickly disappeared.

The glare from the headlights had stopped her identifying the number plate, but she was certain the person driving was Rachel. She stood for a moment, deep in thought. Had Alan told her their affair had ended? No, of course not. If he told her, then he was admitting to the affair in the first place. The coward would much rather pretend Rachel didn't know, and hope it would all go away. What the hell was she going to do about it, though? If Rachel thought the affair was still ongoing then she would continue to threaten Claire. Assuming it was her behind the hoax. Claire had hoped that by ending the relationship she could at least eliminate her as a suspect, but her plan had failed. There was only one thing for it; she would have to confront Rachel. Tell her about both the affair and the hoax and see how she reacted. It would probably damage Alan's marriage, but that was his lookout. He should have come clean. Her life was being threatened and possibly Toby's as well, so what did he expect?

Just as she approached her front door, Jessica opened it from the other side. "Sorry," she laughed. "Saw your shadow outside. I've just got Toby off to sleep. How was your day?"

Claire gave a tired smile. "The usual grind. I thought Brenda was picking Toby up from nursery today?"

"She was going to, but she asked me to do it; apparently a friend rang asking if she wanted to go for a drink this evening."

Claire was annoyed but tried to hide it. She didn't mind Brenda having time to herself, but she would have liked her to have at least rung her to let her know.

"Are you okay? You look a little pissed off, if I'm honest," said Jessica.

"No, no, I'm fine. What would I do without you both? You're lifesavers."

"Never mind all that. You'd do the same for me."

"Fancy a drink? I can knock us up something to eat as well if you're hungry."

"Sounds great; I'm starving."

Once they had settled themselves in the kitchen, Claire having first poured them both a glass of wine, she decided that this would be a good opportunity to tell Jessica of her suspicions about Rachel. "Jess... I thought you should know – I've broken it off with Alan."

"Oh, Claire – I thought you really liked him, and God knows you need someone now that Sean's walked out on you."

Claire felt irritated. What made Jessica think that she needed a man in her life to complete her? In truth, for the first time in years, she felt a wonderful sense of freedom; she could breathe again. She could shape her own life rather than trying to fit it around a husband or lover. "I'm fine, Jess. In fact, I'm better than fine. If it wasn't for these horrible threats—" She stopped, tears filling her eyes.

Jessica covered Claire's hand with her own and gave it a reassuring squeeze. "I can't imagine what you're going through. Brenda told me... about the other grave..."

Claire stared at her. "So, you know, then?"

Jessica nodded. She leaned forward and hugged her friend to her. Claire was suddenly in floods of tears, trembling in her embrace, her body wracked by sobs. They stayed like that for a while and then Claire slowly disengaged, hauling herself to her feet. "I need to sleep, Jess, I'm just so exhausted."

"You get yourself off to bed – I'll clear the plates and sort out the dishwasher."

Claire looked at the half-empty bottle of white wine on the

table. "I'm tempted to take this up with me, you know."

Jessica lifted it by the neck and handed it to her. "Take it if you want – I certainly wouldn't blame you. If I was going through what you're going through I think I'd be on the hard stuff by now and probably finishing off a bottle a day."

Claire grimaced. "I shouldn't really, I'm drinking too much." She hesitated for a moment and then returned the bottle to the table.

"I could stay if you like."

"You haven't got any stuff, though. I can rustle up a spare toothbrush but what about clothes?"

"It's only one night, I'm sure I'll manage," Jessica smiled. "We're about the same size; I just need a spare pair of knickers. Unless, of course, you've got any expensive designer outfits I might borrow?"

"Well, there is the off-the-shoulder Stella McCartney dress I could let you have; perfect for the weekly shop in Lidl's," smiled Claire.

"Tracky bottoms and a T-shirt is more my style, really. Never rated Stella McCartney."

"Are you sure staying over isn't a problem?"

"Course I am. You get yourself off to bed, and I'll stay up for a while and binge on *The West Wing*. I might also help myself to what's left of that wine, given you've come over all abstemious."

"Thanks, Jess – you're a star."

*

Of course, she didn't sleep. Her bedroom sat directly above the living room and even though Jessica had been careful to keep the sound of the television as low as possible, she could still hear it. Worse, she had already binge-watched all the episodes twice herself, so as she lay there, and even though she was unable to hear everything that was being said clearly, she couldn't stop herself completing the lines of dialogue in her head. Fortunately, Jessica watched just the one episode. Claire heard her creeping up the stairs before she retired to the guest bedroom and then, finally, the house was quiet again.

Still, she couldn't sleep. Rachel. She needed to find out if she was her tormentor. She must be. Why else was she making those frightening phone calls? Confront her; it was the only way. And it needed to happen soon.

CHAPTER TWENTY-TWO

laire steeled herself. It was 8.30 AM. Around her, and through the car's sealed window, she could hear the muffled cries and footsteps of the school run. One or two of the mothers glanced briefly at her as they passed. Claire could see what they were thinking by the angle of their heads, the look of puzzlement, antennae ever alert, probing for risks, for whatever there was out there that might possibly threaten the safety of their children. Was she waiting for someone? Making a phone call? Did she look upset? Or was it something more sinister? She looked harmless enough, but was she? Claire ignored them. She took out a small compact from her bag, and carefully reapplied her lipstick, tamping down with a tissue between her lips to finish. The puffiness around her eyes she hid with concealer. Ready for battle, she stepped briskly out of the car.

Alan's house was at the end of a long, gravelled drive which swept upwards from the road. Stopping in front of a forbidding set of ornate iron gates, Claire had to get out of the car to access the intercom. It was immediately answered by Rachel. "Hello, Claire."

Claire stepped back in shock.

"Sorry, didn't mean to startle you. You're on CCTV, I can see you at the gate."

Claire laughed nervously. She looked up; a camera was mounted directly above her on one of the concrete gate supports and, turning to the left, she could see a second one on the other pillar. She realised that this was only the second time she had visited the house, the first being the fateful dinner party which had led to Alan and her becoming lovers.

"No, it's fine. I should have realised."

Rachel's next sentence, though, was chillingly cold. "Why are you here?"

"I need to talk to you."

"About what?'

So, she was determined to make her suffer.

"I think you know why I'm here."

There was a brief silence, and then, the soft click of the release mechanism as the gates slid open.

The last time Claire had been here it had been dark and she had failed to get a real sense of the scale of the house. Now she could see it was huge, brick-built, the brickwork itself stitched together with dark, heavy oak beams beneath a clay-tiled roof. Although it was obviously a modern build, it was a faithful recreation of a Tudor manor house. It was one of those rare winter days with a blue cloudless sky and a hard bright sun. There was a smell of woodsmoke and rotting leaves. A smouldering pyre of torn branches sat by a distant fence. There was the damp cough of sheep from a field above the house.

Rachel was waiting at the top of the stone steps in front of the door, her arms folded across her chest. Claire started across the gravel, her head bent.

"Wait! Don't come any closer; I'm not inviting you in, you know."

Claire looked up at her. Rachel looked thinner than the last time she had seen her, thinner and paler, and somehow less present, a painting bleached by the sun. Her face was unadorned, free of makeup, and she was dressed quite simply, a lime-coloured dress matched with thick black tights. There was a brief silence, the air between them congealed and heavy. Then: "I know about you; I know what you've done."

Claire's face flushed with shame. "I'm sorry… it was a mistake… it should never have—"

"No, it shouldn't. It shouldn't have happened. But you couldn't leave him alone, could you, couldn't keep your filthy hands off him? You filthy fucking slut."

Claire stared in alarm. Rachel looked deranged, consumed by hatred; her whole body shook with it. Then, remembering Toby, anger flared in her too.

"It was you, wasn't it? It was you sent me that bloody card! And it was you that dug that grave. How dare you try and frighten me, and how dare you threaten the life of my son?"

"What card? What fucking grave? What the fuck are you talking about you, crazy bitch?"

Claire looked at her and in that moment she knew. Rachel's

face was ugly with rage, tears and snot marking her cheeks, but she also looked genuinely astonished. Claire's anger leached out of her. She felt ashamed, beaten.

"I shouldn't have come. I'm sorry." She turned back towards the car, then turned, staring back at her opponent. "It's over. I finished it. I'm sorry, I really am."

Rachel slumped against the doorframe. She was no longer looking at Claire, staring unseeing into the distance. "You're not the first, you know. Not by a long chalk."

"I – I didn't know... I'm sorry."

Rachel fell silent. As she drove away, Claire glanced back at her in the rearview mirror. She was still there, still staring into the distance, as though turned to stone.

CHAPTER TWENTY-THREE

"Claire, when I took you on, I said that I wouldn't sugarcoat anything. I said divorce can be a rough business and my job is to fight for your interests, but I wouldn't pretend things were good, or would turn out well when there was a very good chance that they wouldn't. Do you remember?"

"Yes, of course, I remember and, of course, I wouldn't want you to sugarcoat things, but now you're beginning to worry me—"

"I'm sorry, Claire, that's not my intention but…"

"But what?"

Her solicitor, Helen, looked anxiously at her. When she had first met her, Claire had warmed to her immediately. She was attractive, with shoulder-length dark hair, feisty and formidably bright, but also personable and funny.

She wasn't smiling now, though.

"Sean's solicitor has been in touch. They're applying for a residence order."

"Meaning what, exactly?"

"A residence order determines who a child will live with. It also determines who has day-to-day responsibility for a child's care and for making any routine decisions with respect to their welfare. Sean wants to be Toby's primary carer."

"I'm sorry, I still don't understand. Toby is living with me. Why would—?"

"Sean's arguing that your bipolar disorder and lifestyle mean you're not competent to look after Toby."

"What? He can't do that – I'm his mother, surely the court—?"

"The fact that you're his mother does weigh very heavily in your favour, but this is serious. I've known of other cases where a mother's mental illness has resulted in her children being taken away from her. It can happen. He says you were sectioned with a psychotic episode shortly after a miscarriage. Is this true?"

"Yes, but it was for only a very short period, three weeks at most. I had a stillbirth; it was just an awful period in my life. But I'm fine now. Yes, I'm bipolar but it's controlled through medication. I'm fine."

"He's disputing that; he says you still have episodes."

"I do still have mood swings," said Claire slowly, "but that's not the same as psychosis. I'm fine, I'm stable."

Helen sighed. "Is there anyone responsible for your care at the moment? A psychiatrist? A GP who could vouch for you?"

"I have sessions now and then with one of the psychiatrists at the Newtown Centre in Huntingdon. Not that regular, maybe every two or three months?"

"Right. We're going to have to ask them for a report on your mental health that we can submit to the court. You may also need an evaluation by an outside psychiatrist, who hasn't worked with you before, to provide an expert report to establish Toby is safe in your care."

Claire was feeling both increasingly anxious and angry. How dare he do this? She was the one who did the lion's share of looking after Toby. She was the one juggling childcare arrangements, arranging for Brenda to look after him, and Jessica on the occasions Brenda couldn't do this. What the fuck did he do? And wasn't she looking after Toby now, whilst Sean was off shagging his new squeeze? Assuming he was shacked up with someone else, and she would bet her life on it that he was. All that crap about not being able to cope with her moods anymore. Complete bollocks: he was shagging someone; she was sure of it.

She stood up and walked to a window. The first time she had met Helen it had been at her home in a small village close to Hitchin. This time Helen had asked to meet her in London at her firm's offices in Bloomsbury, an impressive four-storey Edwardian house in a crescent of similar houses overlooking a small, gated park. She watched a harassed-looking mother kneel down in front of a child, an impish-looking girl with untidy blonde curls. The woman spat onto a paper tissue and vigorously wiped the girl's mouth, which had been smeared with what looked like chocolate.

Despite her own internal agitation, Claire smiled. She shut

her eyes and leaned her forehead against the cool glass.

"Claire, are you alright? Can I get you some more tea? Coffee? I can have a fresh pot brought up?"

Claire turned and looked at her. For a moment, she felt faint, the world starting to blur and spin. She shut her eyes again. The feeling passed.

"I'm fine," she said. "Just... *shocked*, you know. I never thought—"

"I know this is difficult," said Helen, "but we will get through this, I promise. I'm sure we can persuade the court that Toby should be in your care." She hesitated. Then: "Have social services had any involvement with Toby?"

"What? No, no, of course not. Why do you say that? Why would I have anything to do with social services?"

"Sorry, I didn't mean to... look, when this goes before the court Cafcass will get involved—"

"Cafcass?"

"Sorry, it's a bit of a mouthful – Cafcass is the Children and Family Court Advisory and Support Service. They advise the court on any safeguarding concerns and recommend what they think the court should do in the child's best interests. They may well turn it over to social services to investigate and report to the court, depending on what Sean tells them, especially if they've been involved before. I just wanted to know whether—"

"Yeah, I get it – whether I'm the sort of crap mother social services spend their lives monitoring. Or failing to monitor given they usually fuck it up. Sorry, I'm getting worked up, I know. It's just I'm a good mum, you know, no, I'm a *brilliant* fucking mum and I love my… I love my *son*."

Tears filled her eyes.

"I know you are, Claire, I know you are. Do you want a—"

"Got my own, thanks," Claire grimaced, reaching into her handbag for a crumpled tissue. "I expect you get a lot of this."

"The men are the worst," smiled Helen.

Claire laughed despite herself. "So, what's next?"

"Well, first, there'll need to be a Conciliation Appointment. I don't yet have a date for that but it's fairly informal. No wigs and gowns. So, there'll be the judge, Sean, and his solicitor and counsel, and then us plus our legal team. The purpose of the Conciliation Appointment is to see whether you and your ex-partner are prepared to try mediation first. If that looks possible the next step will then be for you both to sit down with someone from Cafcass and, hopefully, agree a way forward. If the mediation fails, then it will go to court, with each side preparing and submitting statements. Cafcass will also prepare a statement.

"So, let's hope, first of all, that Sean sees sense, agrees to mediation, and allows Toby to continue to live with you. If it does go to court, though, they'll obviously try and present evidence around your mental health; I imagine there'll be a statement on this from your ex and we'll need to present our own evidence. I suggest we start with a letter from your psychiatrist. Will you be able to get that?"

"Yes, I think so, but can't all of this wait until we know the outcome of the Conciliation?"

"We could wait, but at the same time I don't want us to be scrambling around at the last moment if the Conciliation goes against us and Sean wants his day in court. It's better to prepare the ground now. Do you think you can also sort out getting a report from an independent psychiatrist?"

"God knows. I don't even know who… I'll talk to my own psychiatrist and see if he can recommend anyone."

"I'm sorry to ask this, Claire, but how is your bipolar at the moment? Would you consider it to be well managed? Do you still have mood swings?"

Claire looked at her. How honest should she be? The truth was that her medication had taken the edge off her lows, but she was still experiencing mania, and in those manic episodes she would sometimes stay awake for two or three days at a stretch, becoming progressively more and more exhausted. Was she a good mother in those periods? She closed her eyes.

"I'm more stable," she said slowly, looking down at the floor, "but I do still have mood swings."

"And how bad are they? Do they affect your ability to look after Toby?"

She sighed. "If I'm honest, a bit. The lows are fine; the medication I'm on means I just have a workaday sadness like everyone else rather than a suicidal, can't-get-out-of-bed depression. I still have manic episodes, though. It depends how you look at it; when I'm high I just have lots more energy.

In a way, I'm just more me when I'm high."

"So, you don't feel it has any impact on Toby's care?"

"No, no, of course not."

Of course not, apart from the terrible insomnia, apart from falling asleep in the car when I'm driving to nursery to pick him up, apart from that time I almost tipped hot tea over him when I was cradling him, my eyes closing even as I raised the cup to my lips. Of course not.

"And your psychiatrist will back you up?'

"Yes, I'm sure he will. Yes, of course."

Of course not, of course he won't; he scarcely knows me. And at our last session I told him I was still having problems. I told him I was barely coping, that the manic phases were wearing me down, making me progressively more and more exhausted. He'd asked if I want to change my medication. We could look at lithium. No, no, I was fine.

But I wasn't fine, was I?

CHAPTER TWENTY-FOUR

2011

"Claire?"

"Hi, Joan, how are you? You sound upset. Are you alright?"

"It's Mum – she's got a brain tumour; they're taking her in for a biopsy tomorrow morning. I'm sorry, I can't do our meeting, I've got—"

"Oh, Joan, I'm so sorry. That's awful. Don't worry about the meeting – is there anything I can do?"

"No, no, it's fine. I'm really sorry to let you down like this."

"Honestly, Joan, it's not a problem. The important thing is your mum. I'm sure we'll get a chance to catch up before the trial starts next week."

"I'll give you a ring later in the week and see if we can sort out another time."

"Yes, that would be great; you just concentrate on your mum. You'll let me know how she is as well, won't you?"

"Yes, as soon as I hear anything. Thanks, Claire, I really appreciate this."

"It's not a problem, honestly."

*

But it was a problem. Claire didn't hear again from Madison; her PA contacted her later in the week to tell her that Madison's mum had been diagnosed with a glioblastoma, a particularly aggressive from of brain cancer. It had been decided it was too dangerous to operate so she was being treated with radiotherapy, but the prognosis was poor. Claire had to rely on updates from Hamlin on how the trial was progressing. He told her Madison had appeared as an expert witness and had put in a good performance, albeit she had looked both tired and, at times, distracted.

Now it was her turn. This was the first time she had seen the defendant. She was a small, shrunken woman and Claire guessed she must be in her mid to late sixties. It was impossible to imagine her as someone who had consciously and deliberately chosen to murder both her own child and her son's. Claire felt a stab of pity for her; this felt wrong. In both looks and manner she reminded her inescapably of Brenda, and then of her own mother. If she had lived, she too would now be in her mid-sixties.

For most of her life she had fought a deep-seated hatred of her mother; she had hated her for abandoning her, for being weak, for what she had done to her father. At three years old, she had scarcely begun to know her, and the few memories she had were just fragments, images which disappeared even as she stared at them: her mother lovingly braiding her hair into a ponytail and fastening a large pink bow for a birthday party; her laughter when Claire dropped a spoon into a mixing bowl, showering them both in flour.

The prosecution barrister skilfully led her through the evidence contained in the autopsy, reminding the jury at various points of the conclusions which had been reached by Joan as the paediatric pathologist and asking Claire to reaffirm them. An energetic, muscular man in his forties, he exuded an effortless mix of both charisma and wit; Claire could see that some of the younger female jurors were almost spellbound by him, and she could not help inwardly smiling.

She felt far more anxious, though, as the counsel for the defence rose to face her. This was a woman; similarly middle-aged, attractive, dark wisps of hair clearly visible beneath her wig.

"Can we first deal with the supposed murder of Amanda, Mrs Turner's own child? I think we can both agree that this charge should be dismissed, don't you think? The coroner's verdict at the time was that this was an unexplained death. No evidence was found during the autopsy to indicate otherwise and obviously, given the length of time which has elapsed and the physical impossibility of reexamining Amanda's body, none can be produced now either. Do you agree?"

Claire's mouth felt like ash. She did agree but she could hardly say that. How did Joan deal with this? She should have checked with Hamlin. "Although it's no longer possible to examine the body, there is other evidence of abuse we can look at. Amanda did suffer a life-threatening event when she was just five weeks old; she was taken to hospital, her body was limp and there was evidence of oxygen deprivation—"

"Yes, yes, but we both know from the literature that such events are not uncommon in infancy. If we decided that every admission such as this was a clear indicator of murder, then we'd have to lock up tens of thousands of parents; the courts would scarcely have time to deal with anything else."

"Yes, but—"

The barrister pointed at Turner, who was looking on anxiously from the dock. "Let me ask you this: do you believe there is sufficient forensic evidence to justify this poor woman being charged with the murder of her own child, Amanda?"

Claire hesitated. Her hands were clammy with sweat. She looked across to where Hamlin sat. He was staring back, trying to appear impassive. "On its own, no," she said weakly, "but—"

"On its own, no. So, in other words, if we consider Amanda's case in isolation – and I'm asking you to do precisely that – then there is insufficient forensic evidence to justify this charge. Do you agree? Yes or no?"

"Yes."

"Yes. Thank you. Let us turn now to the forensic evidence which has been presented to this court to support the charge of murder with respect to Alice. There is a classic triad of symptoms used to support a diagnosis of shaken baby syndrome, all of which are present in the forensic report produced by you and Doctor Madison: retinal haemorrhaging, a subdural haemorrhage and hypoxaemic encephalopathy. To put these in simpler terms we can all understand, we have a bleed to the retinas of the eyes, an internal bleed to the brain and a lack of oxygen to the brain. Let's take the retinal bleed first. Is it not true that retinal bleeding is quite common in newborns? Particularly where there has a been a rapid vaginal delivery?"

One of the male jurors gave an involuntary snort of laughter at this, the judge giving him a warning glance.

"Yes, that's true, but retinal bleeding of this kind usually fades or disappears quite quickly, certainly within four to six weeks at most. Alice died at ten weeks old, so our determination was that the bleeding occurred very close to her death."

"That's your determination, but from a statistical point of view it's much more likely that the retinal bleed occurred during Alice's birth and not, as you've concluded, as a result of smothering. Or are you saying the statistics are wrong?"

"No, I'm simply saying that our conclusion was that—"

"But you can't be certain, can you? Certain beyond a reasonable doubt, which after all is the standard being applied here. So, a simple question: are you certain beyond a reasonable doubt that the bleeding occurred as a result of smothering?"

"No, I…"

"Thank you."

"The prosecution's case is that Alice was murdered as a result of violent shaking, which would have caused haemorrhages to the brain and a deprivation of oxygen leading quickly to her death. Was there any evidence of trauma to the spine or the neck?"

"No physical injuries to either the spine or neck were observed during the post-mortem, but this does not mean shaking didn't take place. We do have the haemorrhages to the brain, which is a telltale for possible shaking."

"But wouldn't you normally expect to find evidence of injury to the neck muscles and spinal cord with shaking? The physical shaking of a baby is quite a violent act, is it not?"

"It can be," said Claire cautiously, "but it's possible for a baby to undergo shaking in a way which can cause damage to the brain without visible trauma being inflicted elsewhere on the body."

The barrister paused. "The bleeding to the blood vessels of the brain – your report stated that this must have been caused by physical trauma. Is that the case?"

"Yes."

"But is it also not true that such bleeding could have been caused by disease, or possibly a bacterial infection. Is that not another possibility?"

"It's possible, yes, but we found no evidence of disease, or any trace of infection, during the post-mortem."

"But you would agree that there are other reasons you might see haemorrhaging of the blood vessels in the brain other than as a result of a physical injury?"

"Yes."

The barrister turned triumphantly towards the jury. "So, to sum up, none of the classic symptoms associated with shaken baby syndrome are present. There's no evidence of damage to Alice's neck muscles or spinal cord. The only evidence we have is bleeding to the brain, which can be the result of infection or disease, and the retinal haemorrhages, which are fairly common in any case and can be caused during a child's birth." She looked up at the judge. "No further questions, Your Honour."

*

"Well, that was a disaster."

"Not necessarily, Claire. I wouldn't beat yourself up about it," said Hamlin. "The prosecution has called a number of expert witnesses and Joan herself did extremely well."

"So, it's just me that let the side down then?"

Hamlin sighed. "Look, just between us, I don't think you really believe this woman is guilty, do you?"

Claire glanced around her. They had grabbed some coffees from the vending machine in a hallway and seated themselves on a bench outside the main courtroom. Minutes earlier, there had been a swarm of lawyers, relatives and witnesses from one of the other courtrooms, but for the moment it was quiet. Two men stood talking to each other at the other end of the hallway, but it was unlikely they could hear what Claire and Hamlin were saying.

She gave a long sigh. "No, I don't. I just felt sorry for her, if I'm honest."

"So, you wouldn't mind if she got off?"

"No, I wouldn't. I'm sorry – I know how much time you—"

"Don't worry, Claire. It's difficult to take pleasure in the conviction of a woman in her sixties and even I can see this is a complex case. Who knows where the truth really lies? I much prefer nicking straightforward villains. That way I can sleep easy at night – with cases like this there's always that doubt."

"Joan seems so certain about it all, whereas I struggle to be certain about anything."

"Yeah, I know. If it's any consolation, though, I'm in your camp."

*

It was later that evening that Claire remembered the microbiological report. How important was it? If there had been an infection of the kind claimed by Counsel, the report would have picked it up, but Joan had made no mention of anything. So, there can't have been. Claire felt uneasy, though; she needed to see that report.

CHAPTER TWENTY-FIVE

2012

"So, you said you managed to find something interesting with the reverse search."

Claire looked expectantly at Kate, who was busy typing on her phone. They were sitting opposite each other at a small table in the same pub where Kate had made her breathless declaration of love a fortnight earlier. Kate had wanted to tell Claire earlier that morning what she had found, but Claire had said to wait until they were on their own and had an opportunity to discuss it properly.

"I most certainly did," said Kate, her eyes shining with excitement. "The search took me back to a Facebook page; it's Jessica's."

Claire blinked. "What? Jessica's? You mean…?"

"Yeah, it's your friend's page. Look, I'll show you." She lifted her phone.

Claire stared in disbelief. It was a group shot of her with Jessica and two other women; they were all smiling, Jessica holding a glass of red wine, her arm draped around one of the other women's shoulders. In the background she could just make out a banner: Exeter University 2000 Alumni. Of course, the reunion. That's where it came from. But then…"

"But she can't have… she wouldn't…"

"I was shocked too," said Kate quickly. "But although it looks suspicious, you have to really know what her privacy settings are. She may have allowed access to the world and its mother, and if she's done that, then anybody could have gone on her site and lifted the image."

"True," said Claire.

"It's also possible that photograph was shared on social media sites by other people at that reunion."

Claire twisted her hands anxiously in her lap. "It can't be Jess. It just can't. Oh God, what a mess – she's one of my closest friends."

"Are you okay?" said Kate anxiously.

Claire grimaced. "Not really. Finding out your best friend might be at the bottom of a horrible hoax like this is hardly the best start to a day. Look, email me the link and I'll show it to Pete, see what he thinks."

She was quiet for a moment.

"Kate, about last time…"

Kate flushed. "Look, Claire, it was a mistake – I've already forgotten about it. Please let's not talk about it. It's just too embarrassing. We're friends, we like each other, I completely misread the situation, so let's just move on."

Claire stared at her. "I'm sorry, I'm just not—"

"Please, Claire, I'm fine honestly."

"Okay… I understand. Another drink?"

"Yes, why not?"

CHAPTER TWENTY-SIX

It was only after that she had settled Toby down to sleep that evening that Claire allowed herself to reflect on the afternoon's events. She poured herself a glass of wine and brought both the glass and the bottle into the living room. The room was dominated by a cream sofa which formed a large L-shape. Orange scatter cushions lay across it and Claire pulled one against her back as she sat down. The only light in the room was from a blue Tiffany lamp perched on a small glass table next to the television.

Infinitely tired, she rested her head against the sofa and closed her eyes. Jessica. It was impossible to believe she was responsible for the hoax. No, Kate's explanation was surely correct: Jessica's settings allowed everyone to view her posts and it was almost certainly in that way that her tormentor had gained access to the photo. Either that or they had taken the photo from another site where it had been shared. So, that was the answer to that problem. What was she to do about Sean? She couldn't let him get away with stealing Toby from her; she had to confront him. Anger boiled up inside her and she unconsciously curled both of her hands into fists.

Tomorrow evening. I'll have it out with him then.

*

She was drunk. She shouldn't have driven. Yet here she was, parked opposite Sean's house, a terraced cottage, pebble-dashed, the cream surface studded with cracks around the narrow windows, more cracks snaking up from the top of the faded timber front door. She sat there for a moment, summoning up the courage to confront him. As she stared, a car suddenly pulled up and swung into the driveway to join one already there, Sean's blue BMW. It was dark but the body shape seemed familiar. A woman stepped out and moved quickly to the doorstep. As the door opened, light flooding outside, Claire gave an involuntary gasp. Jessica. A figure just inside the door leant forward and embraced her, a lover's hug, long and lingering. Claire shrank down in her seat, anxious not be to be seen.

She felt a surge of anger. Waiting until the door closed and the street was in darkness again, she emerged from the car and strode purposefully across the street. There were no lights on at the front of the house and she guessed Sean and Jessica must therefore be occupying one of the rooms at the rear. Probably one of the bedrooms, she thought sourly. Unbidden, an image rose up of them having sex, rutting animals, slippery with sweat, pawing at each other. She was filled with disgust and hatred.

Her first thought on leaving the car had been to confront

them, but as she neared the house, she changed her mind. Jessica's car was a battered red Peugeot. She thought of keying it down its flank but that was too obvious. She needed something a little more subtle. Kneeling, she removed the plastic cap from the front tyre on the car's passenger side and depressed the tyre valve using her car key. The air hissed angrily. Not too much, she thought, just enough to cause a problem. She replaced the cap and rose to her feet, falling back against the car for support as a wave of nausea swept over her. She shut her eyes, waiting for it to pass.

It was once she was back home again that she started to regret what she had done. But by then it was too late.

CHAPTER TWENTY-SEVEN

Ten Days Left

"Kate – I've done something terrible…"

"What? Are you okay? What's happened?"

"I don't really want to say on the phone, it's too awful. Look, could we meet up so we can talk? Would you mind? I'm happy to come to you if it's easier. Toby's asleep and I can get Brenda to pop over whilst I'm out."

"To be honest, I've already had a drink so that might be better, if you don't mind. Are you sure, though? Perhaps we could go for a drink after work tomorrow?"

"No, no, I really need to see you now. I need someone to bring me down off the ceiling, frankly; I'm afraid I don't really know where you live. Can you give me your address?"

"It's out in the Fens, near March. It's a shame this isn't all happening next week, I'm moving to the new house on Friday. Then I would only be ten minutes from you, if that. The address is – have you got a pen? – 23 Lady Bower Lane PE29 3NU."

"Lady Bower? Is that why you chose it?"

Kate giggled. "It might have played a part. It is a nice place though, just a bit too small now for all my bits and pieces."

"I'll be there in half an hour."

*

When she arrived, Claire drew Kate into a long desperate hug and to her own surprise, burst into noisy sobs. "I'm such a fuckup, Kate. My whole life is fucked up and now this…"

"Everyone's fucked up, Claire, it's just that some of us are better at hiding it than others. What's happened then? What's so terrible?"

"Sean. The bastard's been fucking Jessica. I found out last night." She stopped, lifting her head from Kate's shoulder so she could look directly at her. "I've done something awful, Kate."

"Why? What have you done?"

"I tampered with the air pressure in her tyres."

"Well, that doesn't sound that horrendous; did you do all the tyres? Were they completely flat?"

"No, I was more cunning than that – oh God – I just took some of the air out of one of the tyres."

"How much air?"

"Not that much; I didn't want her to notice. But it's still enough to cause a tyre blowout and that could—"

"Oh, Claire, you're over-worrying. Most of us drive round with under-inflated tyres all the time. I once drove round for a fortnight with the low-pressure gauge winking at me, and I'm still here to tell the tale. What car was it?"

"A Peugeot, red, quite old."

Kate laughed. "Thank you for the 'red' – that's important. Well, if it's red we don't have a problem. Everyone knows red cars self-inflate their tyres on a daily basis."

Despite herself, Claire laughed too. "So, you think I'm over-angsting?"

"Just a tiny wee bit, yes. It also sounds as though the bitch deserved it. I'd have done a lot more than take a little bit of air out of one of her tyres; I'd have taken a tyre iron to her. Look, it's too late for you to drive back now, why don't you stay the night?"

Claire hesitated. She had to admit she was very tired. It had starting raining again, and driving the Fen roads in the dark and the rain wasn't remotely appealing. "Well, I must admit, I am tired. Are you sure, though? Are you sure I wouldn't be imposing too much?"

"Sure, I'm sure; the only condition is you give me a hand changing the bedlinen. Had a friend stay over two weeks ago and I never got round to changing the sheets."

"It still seems a lot of trouble – are you sure you don't mind?"

"Don't be daft."

"But I don't have anything with me – no makeup or toiletries, not even a change of clothes."

Kate grimaced. "I can't lend you a toothbrush and you can even borrow my makeup. Not sure about the clothes, although I'm sure I've got something that'll fit. So, is it a deal?"

"Deal. I'll need to ring Brenda though, because she'll have to stay over with Toby. I'll also have to leave early because I'll need to get back in time to take him to nursery. I could ask Brenda, but she already does too much as it is."

"What time will you need to leave?"

"Probably around seven."

"Sounds good. If that's the case, and given I'll still be in bed, can you bring me up a cup of tea in the morning? Oh, and perhaps a slice of toast."

"You cheeky mare – as a guest you should be bringing me tea."

Kate grinned. "Not that sort of hotel, I'm afraid."

*

The drive back in the morning reminded her how much she hated the Fens; she remembered the first time she had seen them, when her parents had driven her and her younger brother to the seaside resort of Hunstanton. The landscape had felt alien, otherworldly; a vast expanse of flatness, punctuated by irrigation ditches, the odd tree appearing almost as an afterthought. Although the land sat below sea level, such was the unending vista that it felt as though you were standing on a mountain gazing down on a plain far below. How else was it possible to see so far in all directions? It felt almost as though, rather than gazing out at the landscape, it was looking back at you, not only looking back, but peering into your very soul. And finding you wanting.

It was still dark, the low sun peeping over the horizon as though reluctant to make an entrance. Mists rose off the fields, hovering in the air, curling around trees, sinking down into the ground. Every now and then she would catch a glimpse of the drainage ditch adjoining the road, glints of silver from the water, straw-coloured bullrushes spattered with cobwebs. She had slept badly, having finally got to bed just before 2 AM. She felt exhausted, scarcely able to keep her eyes open.

There was a loud bang. The car juddered, skidding across the road.

CHAPTER TWENTY-EIGHT

Her heart hammering in her chest, Claire braked hard, steering the car as close as she could manage to the edge of the drainage ditch. She had to be careful because the ditch was steeply banked, and it would have been easy to miscalculate and plunge the car down into the river below. Heavy cloud cover obscured a gibbous moon, but there was sufficient light to pick out the sinister gleam of the river below.

She switched her hazard lights on and, checking to make sure no other vehicles were coming up behind her, eased open the door and glanced back. There was a strong smell of decay, of rotting vegetation. Roughly ten yards away there was a dark mound of what seemed to be matted fur and blood. Presumably the animal she had hit.

She got out of the car and walked slowly across. A fox. Worse, it was still alive; she could see the laboured rise and fall of its chest. It was too badly injured to survive, and she couldn't just leave it like that either. She would have to kill it. But how? She glanced quickly at both sides of the road. The riverside was bordered with rough grass and reeds. On the other side stretched freshly ploughed fields. Neither would provide a weapon. Then she remembered; there was a jack in the car.

The jack was an awkward rhomboid shape and, at first, she was uncertain how best to deploy it. In the end, she simply held the jack by one of its arms and rammed it hard down on to the fox's head. There was a high-pitched yelp and then silence. Still kneeling, she shut her eyes. When she opened them again, she could see dark staining on her jacket. She gingerly dabbed at it with a finger. Blood and soft tissue. Not very bright of her really, should have found a way of killing it without ruining her jacket; she was, after all, supposed to be an authority on blood spatters. Including how to avoid them.

CHAPTER TWENTY-NINE

The day had started badly. Now it got even worse. Hamlin rang.

"Hi, Claire. I've got some horrible news, I'm afraid. Janice Turner – she's topped herself. Found hung this morning in her cell."

"Oh my God – that's terrible. That poor woman."

"Yeah, it's not great, is it? Now, normally at this point I'd be wishing you a Happy New Year, but that hardly seems appropriate, does it? Apparently, from what I could glean, the poor woman was being badly bullied by some of the other prisoners. She was close to starving; she'd collect her food and then someone would take it away from her. That or tip it on the floor, or just spit in it. She also got badly beaten up on one occasion – two broken ribs, badly bruised face and a fractured jaw; ended up with a week's stay in the prison hospital. Too frightened to say who'd done it, of course. The prison governor was trying to get her moved."

"But why? Why would some of the other women do that? Surely, she didn't deserve—"

"She murdered two kids. That put her beyond the pale.

Bullying her was their way of showing that they were better than her, of making them feel better about themselves."

"Yes, I suppose so. Still, it's so sad."

"Life's sad – it's just that most of us cope by pretending it isn't. Of course, the son's appeal is now dead too, if you'll excuse the pun."

"Oh God, I'd forgotten about the appeal. Do you know what the grounds were? Sorry, professional curiosity, obviously doesn't matter now."

"Yet to see what they had, to be honest, but I've been told they were going to argue that the second child, Alice, may have died from a massive bacterial infection, that it was a natural death."

A feeling of cold dread settled in the pit of her stomach. The microbiological report. If high levels of infection had been present this would have been picked up there. Yet Joan had told her there was nothing to worry about. She needed to see it. This wasn't good. Not good at all. This poor woman's death could be her fault. She could try and blame Joan but that still didn't excuse her own behaviour; she should have made sure she saw that report.

"How's Joan, by the way, Claire? I hear she's on compassionate leave?"

"Yes, her mum died just before Christmas. Cancer, a very aggressive brain tumour. Do you know, from the point of diagnosis to her death was only five weeks? Awful, isn't it?"

"Poor Joan."

"Joan's a tough soul but also a lonely one, unfortunately; she lived with her mum and I'm not sure she's got anyone else."

"I always found her a bit of a queer stick, I'm afraid."

"She's a prickly soul but I still like her."

"You like everyone, Claire. You'd probably have been best mates with Jack the Ripper."

"Well, that's a backhanded compliment if ever I heard one."

"Sorry, it's the only sort I know."

"Well, at least you know your limitations."

"Always know your limitations, Claire. Always."

*

She rang Madison as soon as she got off the phone with Hamlin. As she anticipated, Madison was in a low mood and seemed entirely disinterested in the case. Even the news of Turner's death failed to penetrate her apathy. She spoke about her anguish during the remaining weeks of her mother's life and how empty the house now seemed without her. Her mother had been Irish, and her last wish was that her ashes should be taken back to her hometown of Bray. Madison was planning on travelling the following week. The ashes could be carried in her hand luggage, apparently, but she would need both a death and a cremation certificate. Claire was only half listening, waiting patiently for Madison to finish.

"Joan, I need to see a copy of the microbiological report for Alice. Can you arrange for a copy to be emailed to me?"

"Yes, I can do that. Why do you need it, though? There

won't be an appeal now. Don't you have a copy already?"

Claire struggled to hide her exasperation. "Joan, I've never seen it."

"No?" Madison sounded surprised. "Well, no matter, there's nothing in it. Why do you want it?"

Claire hesitated. She didn't want to worry Madison unduly, especially since the appeal wouldn't be proceeding. Still, she needed to know. "They're claiming the report showed evidence of a bacterial infection and that this was the real cause of death."

"Not from my reading of the report; there was a bacterial infection but that had no connection with her death. Sounds a little desperate to me," Madison sighed. "Give Roger a ring at the lab; he can email one to you. Do you know it took three weeks for the crematorium to produce the certificate? It was absolutely appalling; I'd booked a flight on the premise that it would only take a couple of days and I had to cancel the flight and rebook. I've got a good mind to send them the bill for the additional costs—"

"Sorry, Joan, I've got a meeting which is just about to start. We must catch up properly together. Look, I'll ring you at the weekend and perhaps we can get together for a meal or something—"

"What? Oh, yes, of course, that would be nice. I'm flying out Tuesday and I'll be gone for four days, but when I get—"

"Great – I'll ring you Sunday. Look after yourself, Joan, I know you've had a horrendous time of it."

"Yes… yes, and you. Take care."

Having rung the lab, Claire received the report within the hour. She printed it out but was careful not to look at it; she wanted to study at it at home that evening. If it was as distressing as she suspected it might be, she needed to be armed with a glass of wine before she started reading. The phone call with Madison had calmed her nerves a little, though; if there had been a serious bacterial infection Madison would surely have identified this. She said there had been an infection but nothing that rang any alarm bells.

If she had felt a little calmer that afternoon this quickly disappeared when she finally read the report.

CHAPTER THIRTY

The bacterium, *Staphylococcus aureus*, was present in huge quantities throughout Alice's tiny body, infecting every one of her organs. There was no doubt, no doubt at all, that this was the real cause of death. How could Madison have ignored this? Claire felt a sick churning in her stomach; this was beyond awful. But the defence would have seen the report too – why hadn't they raised this at trial? It was inconceivable. It was true the defending barrister had mentioned a bacterial infection as a possible cause of death, but why hadn't she delivered a coup de grâce by presenting the report as evidence? It didn't make sense. Hamlin. She needed to speak to him.

"Hi, Claire – twice in two days. I'm honoured. To what do I owe the pleasure?"

"I've read the report; Alice died from a massive bacterial infection. It wasn't SBS, Pete. We should have picked this up. It should never have gone to trial."

"What? You're absolutely certain about this? But if that's the case, then why wasn't it picked up earlier? Why didn't you or Madison—?"

"I never saw the report, Pete. I kept asking for a copy; Madison never gave it to me."

"But what about Madison? She must have seen it, surely?"

"She's said she did, but she also told me there wasn't anything in the report to worry about."

"Did she now?" said Hamlin quietly. "Well, this is a worrying development, to say the least, particularly given Turner's suicide. Are you absolutely sure Alice died from a bacterial infection? There's no room for doubt on this?"

"None whatsoever."

"And what does Madison think? She must be devastated."

"No, that's the problem; she doesn't think the report matters. She's maintaining it's still SBS."

"Is she now?" said Hamlin grimly. "Is she indeed?"

Claire hesitated. "Pete? I take it the report was given to the defence as part of the pretrial disclosures?"

"Yes, I presume so; it must have been."

"It's just odd, really. If they had received that report, it would surely have formed a major plank of their defence and yet…"

"Well, they threw all sorts of mud against the wall, hoping some of it would stick. They did mention the possibility of a bacterial infection too, come to think of it, in your cross-examination."

"Yes, that's true," said Claire, "but only in passing. If they had seen the report, I would have expected them to not only give the jury copies but to have read from it at length in the courtroom and yet none of that happened. Can you doublecheck they did receive a copy of the report?"

"Yes, of course, I'll make some phone calls now. I'll ring you back as soon as I find out."

*

Hamlin rang back that afternoon. "Sorry it took so long. I couldn't get hold of the defending barrister – she's up in Leeds somewhere on some DUI manslaughter caper. I did manage to speak to her clerk, though; that report was never given to the defence. They never saw it."

"But why the hell not? What happened?"

"I don't know, Claire, I really don't. It would have been Madison's job to make sure that report was included in the bundle going across, but somehow, it's been left out."

"But what does this mean?"

"Nothing good, I can tell you that. There's going to be one hell of a media storm once this leaks. I think it's hold on to your tin hat time. I'm just pleased I'm retiring."

"You'll be alright, it's Madison and me that will bear the brunt of it. We could both lose our right to practise over this, get struck off the register. Then I assume we may face a civil suit as well from Turner's son. This couldn't get any worse. This is awful. And do you know what the worst of it is? Madison doesn't even seem to really care – assuming she even realises how serious this all is. Oh, for fuck's sake, Pete.

I need a drink, several drinks. Are you free this evening?"

"Can't I'm afraid. Theatre trip. I'm not that keen, but Liz arranged it months ago."

"What are you seeing?"

"Do you know, I'm not even sure. No, hang on, I think she said it was *Macbeth*. Yes, that's it, bloody Shakespeare."

"Pete, I love that play. Everyone goes for *Hamlet,* but I'm a *Macbeth* groupie."

"*Hamlet* – isn't that the cigar ad? I can't stand Shakespeare; why couldn't he write in English?"

"God, you really are a lost cause. Seriously, you'll enjoy it – it's a copper's wet dream."

"Why's that then?"

"It's basically a thriller with a twist at the end, and murder at the heart of it. It also, like your good self, has a fairly bleak view of human nature."

"Perhaps I will enjoy it then." He was silent for a moment. "So, now you don't have me as a partner in crime for this evening, what are you planning to do?"

"A quiet night in with my aunt and Toby, I'm afraid."

*

But the night was to prove far from quiet. Claire had just put Toby down to bed when her mobile rang. She had left it downstairs charging in the kitchen and Brenda brought it to her just as Claire reached the bottom of the stairs. "It's Pete," she mouthed.

"Claire? Madison's had a serious fall; she's in UCH in London."

"What? How? What's happened? Is she okay?"

"I'm not quite sure; I just had a phone call from the Met – they're still trying to talk to anyone who might have seen what happened. She fell down one of the escalators at King's Cross. It was probably an accident, although, there's also speculation she might have been pushed. They should know more once they've had a look at the CCTV footage."

"Oh my God – that's awful. Has anyone spoken to the hospital? Found out how she is?"

"Claire..." he said softly, "it must be serious. She's in an induced coma. There's a serious bleed and swelling to the brain."

Claire felt her hand fly to her mouth. Tears ran unchecked down her face. She felt physically sick, slumping slowly to the floor in the hallway, her back pressed against the wall. She shut her eyes. The door to the living room was half open and through it she could hear the strains of the *EastEnders* theme tune as the programme ended. They always ended on some manipulative note of high drama, the cynical bastards. Keeping you hooked for the next life-sapping episode. God, she hated it. Give her *Coronation Street* any day. At least that had some humour. Brenda was an addict, though. Never missed an episode.

And now it feels like I'm trapped in an episode of *EastEnders* myself. At a moment worthy of that horrible music.

"Claire? Claire? Are you still there? Are you okay?"

"Yes, sorry, still here. It's just the shock really…"

"It's awful, I know. Look, I've got to go, but if I hear anything more—"

"Thanks, Pete. Yes, let me know."

"You sound—"

"No, I'm fine, honestly. Look, I've got to go. Ring me if you hear anything."

She hurriedly ended the call. Poor Joan: I only hope to God she survives. And she's got no-one: the only person who cared about her is dead, a jar of ashes tucked into her hand luggage. Perhaps, I should try and… but she's in a coma, how would that help? She took a deep breath. No, best wait for Pete to ring again; if she's well enough to be brought out of the coma then that would be the time to see her. But now…

But now what?

CHAPTER THIRTY-ONE

Eight Days Left

Claire's solicitor rang her just as she was about to leave the house. "Oh, Claire, I'm so glad I caught you. The court hearing's been cancelled. Sean's been granted a postponement."

"Why?"

"A friend's been involved in some sort of accident, apparently; her car went into a river."

Claire's heart stopped. "God, that's awful; who was it rang you? Was it Sean?"

"No, his solicitor."

"Do they know what happened?"

"He said it was a tyre blowout, but he didn't know much more than that, really. The woman's been taken to hospital."

"Did he say how she was? Is she alright?"

"He didn't know, I'm afraid. I'll ring him later today and see if he's got any more news. Obviously, I'll ring you if I do hear anything. I also need to try and agree a new court date with him. A delay might work in our favour anyway, because it should give you a chance to try and get an independent psychiatrist's report."

"Yes, I suppose so – I'll do my best."

"It's important, Claire."

"Yes, I know. Don't worry, I'll sort it."

*

She eased herself into her car, a grey Ford Fiesta, now six years old.

It was Jessica; she knew it was her, and she was responsible for nearly killing her. Correction: if Jessica died, she *would* have killed her. Murdered her.

She needed to find out. She was too anxious to wait for anything her solicitor might learn. But how? She could hardly ring Sean. Elaine: Jessica's younger sister, she would know. Her hands shook as she searched for her number.

"Elaine?"

"Claire. I was just about to ring you." Her voice was dull, lifeless. Strained. "It's Jess. She's had an accident—"

"Oh my God. I tried ringing her this morning, but it just kept going to voicemail. What happened? Is she alright?"

"Her car ran into a dyke. Burst tyre apparently. We think she's alright but we should know more tomorrow, hopefully. She's in Addenbrookes. She's got a lot of facial bruising and there's a nasty gash just above one eye. They've had to stitch that up. They were also worried about possible internal injuries, so they've done an MRI, but we've yet to get the results. At least she's alive though. She could have died. Mum's in bits. She wanted to stay overnight but I've persuaded her to go home. Said I'd stay."

"Oh, Elaine, that's awful. I'm so sorry. Where did it happen?"

"It was up near Chatteris. The Forty Foot Drain?"

"God, that's a notorious black spot. There been a number of accidents there. And fatalities."

"Exactly. Jess was so lucky. She could easily have drowned. The car pitched into the river and sank almost straightaway. She tried breaking out through the driver's side window, but it was impossible. In the end, she got out by kicking out the windscreen and then scrambling out that way. She literally only had seconds left."

"I'm so relieved she's okay. God, I can't believe it." Claire laughed nervously. "I'm shaking from head to foot here."

"Well, I know you two are close."

"Look, I've got to go. Can I ring you again tomorrow to see how she is?"

"Yes, of course."

"Would I get in the way if I came in to see her tomorrow?"

"Well, we're hoping to speak to the consultant in the morning and we're still not sure of the extent—"

"No, no, of course," said Claire, hurriedly interjecting, "I understand. Would it be alright if I rang you tomorrow afternoon for an update?"

"It might be better if I rang you. Look, I'll ring as soon as I know more."

"Thanks, Elaine. I'm so sorry, I feel like I'm being a nuisance when—"

"No, don't be daft, Claire, you're one of her oldest friends. I'll ring you as soon as we learn anything. Then, hopefully, it should be okay for you to visit as well."

"Thanks, Elaine, you're a star."

Claire rang off.

What have I done? What in God's name have I done?

CHAPTER THIRTY-TWO

The following day was a Tuesday, but Elaine didn't ring with an update and nor did she ring the day after. Claire became increasingly anxious, and it was late afternoon on Friday when she finally called.

"Hi, Claire, sorry I haven't been in touch. It's all been a bit grim, to be honest, and we've been frantic with worry."

"Why? What's happened? Is—"

"Jess had a ruptured spleen. She almost died. They had to take her down for emergency surgery Monday night."

"Oh my God. Is she alright now?"

"She is, but it was a close-run thing. She's been in intensive care for the last two days and it was only this morning that they decided she was well enough to move onto one of the general wards."

"Poor Jess. Can I come and see her?"

"Yes, it should be fine to see her now. I'm sure she'd love to see you."

"Right. Well, I'll try and pop in tomorrow afternoon, if that's okay. Are you sure she's well enough to see people now?"

"She's fine, honestly."

"Great. Well, I'll see her tomorrow, then. Which ward is she on, by the way?"

"F6."

"Okay, great. Thanks, Elaine."

She ended the call, her heart beating furiously. Elaine hadn't told her, but she knew they would have had to remove her spleen. The spleen was an important organ, but it was possible to live without one, other organs in the body, including the liver, adapting to take over many of its functions. The point was, she had almost died and if she had, it would have been Claire's fault. How was she supposed to sit beside the bed of a woman who not only had been having an affair with her husband, but who she had also almost killed?

CHAPTER THIRTY-THREE

The meeting had been arranged at the Newtown Centre in Huntingdon, a tired red-brick building on two floors. There was only limited parking at the Centre, so Claire parked in the ugly cedar-cladded Sainsbury's multistorey immediately opposite. Although she had grown to love living in Godmanchester, she was less enthusiastic about Huntingdon itself, a cancerous growth to the north of the town, expanding ever faster, uncoiling brash new housing developments which were tightening and crushing it.

The psychiatrist introduced herself as Siobhan. She was an attractive girl in her late twenties, with a shock of curly red hair and a dusting of freckles across her face. Claire liked her immediately. She told Claire she had been born in Ireland, but her parents had come across to England when she was seven, hence the absence of an Irish accent. "I fall into it quick enough, though, when I go back to see my cousins," she laughed. "Anyway, enough of me; I'm supposed to be interviewing you. How are you doing at the moment?"

"Not great, but then it's difficult to be too upbeat in the middle of a divorce where your husband is doing his best to take your son away from you."

"No, that must be very tough. Do you keep a mood diary at all?"

"Yes, I started keeping one when I was first diagnosed."

"And when was that?"

"Isn't it in my notes?" Claire said coolly.

"The notes say your first episode was almost five years ago. Is that right? Is it possible you'd had previous episodes, but they hadn't been identified as such at the time?"

"It's possible," said Claire cautiously, "but I don't really think so, if I'm honest."

"Your mother committed suicide, didn't she? When you were just three years old? That must have been a terribly traumatic time for you. And for your dad, of course."

"It was, yes."

"Do you want to say any more about what happened?"

"Not really, no."

Siobhan sighed. She had been resting Claire's case file on her lap while she studied it, but now, she snapped it shut and placed it on the desk behind her. "I'm trying to help you, Claire; if I'm to write this report I need to know as much as possible about you. I can't really make a full assessment without that."

Claire softened. She was right, of course. It was just all so depressing; why should she have to prove her mental competence to look after her own child? How did they think she'd been managing for the last three years? The whole process was just insulting, a joke.

"How would you say you are now? Are you having mood swings or is the medication keeping that under control? You're on lamotrigine, aren't you? 200mg, once a day. Is it working, do you think?"

"It's good at damping down the depression – although it doesn't completely get rid of it. Hasn't helped with the highs at all, though; I still have periods of mania where I just can't sleep."

"That's not too surprising; lamotrigine only has limited success with respect to mania. Has anyone suggested changing your medication? Trying lithium, for example?"

"My psychiatrist suggested it, but I'm concerned about the side effects."

"Lamotrigine has side effects too."

"Yes, but the long-term side effects of lithium seem much more worrying – possible kidney and thyroid damage."

"Most people don't suffer those side effects and we do carry out regular monitoring of your bloods to make sure the level of lithium in your bloodstream is safe."

"Even so… Anyway, I was told that if I did switch, I would have to take lithium for a minimum of two years. That's quite a commitment for a drug that might not even work."

"If you were having an adverse reaction to the drug then we would take you off immediately. Initially we would also start you off on a very low dose whilst carrying out weekly monitoring of your bloods. It would only be after we were comfortable that there were no issues and you were tolerating the lithium that we would then try and move you to a therapeutic dose."

"I'm still not convinced, I'm afraid."

"Would it help if I told you that I'm bipolar and that I take lithium?"

"What? I didn't think…"

"That someone with a mental illness could also be a mental health practitioner?"

"No, I – I'm just surprised." In truth, she was embarrassed. She blushed and looked at the ground, unable for a moment to look directly at Siobhan.

"Who better to help, really?"

Claire looked at her and they both burst out laughing. "The blind leading the blind…"

"Exactly. Some are more blind than others, of course."

"When did you have your first episode?" asked Claire, suddenly curious.

"When I was eighteen; during my first year at university. I was studying medicine. Then there was a bad breakup with a boyfriend and I was struggling with the workload, pulling all-nighters studying. I started hallucinating, hearing voices, seeing stuff. I'm Catholic, so you can imagine what sort of things: visions of the risen Christ, hosts of angels filling the sky, all sorts. Quite exciting, in a way. I became convinced I'd been put on this earth to find a cure for cancer, but unseen forces were trying to stop me. Well, unseen until I decided they'd taken shape in the form of one of my histology lecturers. Anyway, you know the rest: psychosis, hospitalisation, disgrace, ruin and, of course, intense embarrassment and shame once you've recovered. The usual bipolar gamut."

"But you obviously recovered enough to restart your medical studies?"

"Yes, I had to take a year out, but Southampton were kind enough to allow me to resume. I'm not sure that would have been true at other universities."

"I was at Cambridge and I'm not sure they would have let you back there."

"No, perhaps not. I was lucky. Once I qualified, I decided to specialise in psychiatry; felt I had to give something back and help others with a mental illness. The point is, Claire, I'm on your side; I want you to win custody of Toby. I think what your husband is doing is cruel, almost medieval. I've got a four-year-old, Maddy; I would be devastated if someone tried to take her away from me."

"I am devastated," Claire said slowly. "Toby is everything to me; he's my life. I couldn't imagine—"

"No, I understand. We just have to make sure we beat the bastards, then."

"And you think lithium might help?"

"Yes, I think it might; it would also be something tangible we can offer the court, evidence that with new medication you are now stable and sufficiently high-functioning to be able to take care of your son. I'll write a report to that effect and your own psychiatrist will support that too."

Claire thought about it for a moment. If it meant she kept

Toby, it had to be worth doing. It might also finally cure her, or at the very least minimise her symptoms to the point where they were manageable. "And has it worked for you?"

"It's not a wonder cure, Claire, but it's a damn sight better than the alternative."

"And what are your mood swings like now?"

"I still get depressed sometimes, but then don't we all? I also have occasions where I might be described as a little too cheerful and energetic, but I quite like that anyway. Those are the only times I get anything done. The point is, it's managed to dampen it down to a point when I can live a normal life. And isn't that what you want too, Claire?"

"Yes, yes, it is. I just want to be normal." And to her surprise, and unable to stop herself, she burst into tears.

CHAPTER THIRTY-FOUR

I t had been raining steadily all morning; rain the weather forecast app on Claire's phone had failed to predict, which was why she was now sitting in the waiting area outside Helen's office with ruined hair and soaked tights.

"You obviously got caught," smiled a sympathetic Helen as she emerged from her office.

"It wasn't supposed to rain," Claire grimaced. "I wouldn't mind, but I washed my hair this morning as well."

"Can I get you a drink to warm up? Tea? Coffee? Brandy?"

Claire smiled. "Now if you were asking Brenda, my aunt, she'd want both – tea with a drop of brandy. Or is it brandy with a drop of tea? I can never remember. Depends on the time of day, I think. Tea would be great, if that's okay. Excuse me wittering on. Always do when I'm nervous."

"Milk? Sugar?"

"Just milk is fine. Not too strong, though."

"I'm the same. I have a friend who likes her tea so strong she just leaves the teabag in."

"Not Irish, by any chance?"

"Yes, how did you know?"

"Just a wild guess," said Claire. "It's either that or Yorkshire."

Once they were settled, Helen pulled out a file from the two-drawer filing cabinet she kept behind her desk. She quickly flicked through its contents before extracting and opening a thin buff folder.

"I've read this report from the independent psychiatrist. I see they've started you on new medication. How are you finding it?"

Claire raised an eyebrow. "It's too early to tell; I've only just started taking it. First, I had to have blood tests to measure my renal and thyroid function. Then they start you on a very low dose, take more blood tests for lithium toxicity and, assuming everything's okay, finally give you what's described as a therapeutic dose. By which time, of course, you've lost the will to live."

"Well, we've still got a bit of time. The Conciliation Appointment's on the 28th, which is over three weeks away. Will the meds be working by then?"

"Apparently. The psychiatrist told me that you normally start to see benefits within two to three weeks."

"Great, so the 28th should be fine; not that I'd be able to move it even if I wanted to. It might also be an idea to schedule another appointment with your regular psychiatrist closer to the date and ask him to produce a note on how well you're managing with the new meds."

"Assuming that's true, of course."

"Sorry, assuming what's true?"

"That I am managing, and they are having a benefit."

"Do you think they might not work, then?"

"I honestly don't know," Claire sighed. "Oh, let's assume they will. They certainly need to; being bipolar is wearing me out. I swear it's shortening my life."

"Your new psychiatrist seems to think they'll help."

"She's bipolar herself, by the way," said Claire.

"Oh," said Helen, surprised. "Does it matter? Is she on lithium too?"

"Yes, she is on lithium and, no, it doesn't matter that she's bipolar. Makes her more relatable, to be honest."

Helen was pensive for a moment. "On second thoughts, I think what we'll do is to ask your regular psychiatrist to give us a report and then ask the independent – Siobhan Walsh, isn't it? – to give us a revised report covering the change of medication and her belief that you're now stable. Would she be willing to do that?"

"Yes, I think so. Just don't ask her to turn up in person. I've seen ten-year-olds that look older than her."

Helen gave a snort of laughter. "Okay, I'll bear it in mind."

CHAPTER THIRTY-FIVE

Claire felt increasingly nervous as she made the long walk through the hospital corridors, worried that Sean would also be there when she finally reached Jessica's room.

It was with relief, therefore, that as she opened the door, she could see no-one else was present. She would have Jessica to herself. Which was just as well, given the complex wash of emotions she was currently feeling. Jessica was lying on her back, her eyes closed. She didn't appear to have heard the door opening and seemed to be asleep. Claire stood for a moment watching her. People were always at their most vulnerable in hospital, their bodies weakened by illness, unshaven or stripped of makeup, their hair tangled and uncombed. In hospital you were closer to the bone, the skin stretched more tightly against the skull.

It was as Claire was making an inventory of the detritus around the bed – the mandatory half eaten box of chocolates, the ruby-coloured grapes in a bowl on the bedside cabinet, the unwanted banana already partially blackened – that Jessica suddenly opened her eyes.

"Claire. It's so nice to see you. Sorry, I was asleep. How long have you been here?"

"I've only just arrived. How are you? I've been so worried about you."

"Well, I've been better," Jessica smiled, "but I could have died, which would have been a whole lot worse."

"Elaine told me about the accident; it must have been so frightening."

"It was absolutely terrifying. I very nearly did die, the car was almost completely underwater. I just couldn't get the windows open. In the end I kicked out the windscreen with my feet and got out that way. My lungs were bursting; I must have swallowed half the bloody dyke by the time I got out."

"So, what happened then?"

"It was a really steep bank, and it took me forever to crawl up it; I think it was just adrenaline that got me through. At the top I just collapsed. A car stopped – an off-duty policeman, ironically – and they called an ambulance, and the rest is history."

Claire was uncertain how to react, or what to say, her brain paralysed by conflicting thoughts and emotions. Laying a hand gently over one of Jessica's, her eyes filled with tears. She didn't trust herself to speak. It was Jessica who broke the silence, pulling her hand away.

"Claire, I need to tell you something. Please don't hate me, because I couldn't bear it. You're one of my oldest and closest friends and I don't..." She trailed off and was crying herself now.

Claire stared in alarm. She knew where this was going and all it would succeed in doing would be to increase her own sense of guilt, perhaps even impel her to confess what she herself had done.

"Jess, it's fine. Whatever it is it can wait. You've had a horrible time – you just need to—"

Jessica cut across her. "No, it has to be now." She had been looking down but now stared directly into Claire's eyes. "I've had an affair… with Sean."

Claire shut her eyes. God, no, I really don't need this. She opened them to find Jessica still staring at her with a horrible intensity.

"I'm so sorry Claire, I'm so ashamed. I…"

"When did it start?" said Claire coldly.

"I… a year ago. I'd had a really bad day at work… you were in London at a conference. You'd asked me to babysit… Sean…"

"You were looking after *Toby* when you—"

"I'm sorry, I'm so sorry. I know I betrayed you, betrayed our friendship—"

"And did you fuck him that night?"

"What?"

"Did you fuck him while you were supposed to be looking after my son?"

"Claire, please…"

"You know he wants to take Toby away from me; are you helping him with that?"

She looked shocked. "No, I didn't know that. Why would he—?"

"Because he thinks I'm mad, that's why, that I'm not fit to look after my own child. You did know, didn't you? You must have known."

"No, no, I swear. Claire, I've broken it off with him – I told him last night. I've just felt so ashamed and guilty, it was all a mistake, it should never have happened."

Claire was silent. She had her own shame to deal with, her own guilt.

"I was feeling vulnerable when it happened," Jessica went on. "You know I'd just been dumped by Matt; I suppose I felt flattered. But I've had a lot of time to think lying here and I've realised that our friendship's far more important to me than... please, Claire..."

Claire looked away. For a moment she struggled with her anger. Then, as suddenly as it had flared up, it disappeared. She felt exhausted. Surreptitiously, she glanced at her watch, then glanced back at Jessica.

"It's alright... I understand, it's okay, Jess, it really is."

"I'm so sorry."

Claire gave a wan smile. "God, it's a good job we're in a private room rather than out on the general ward, we're both a complete mess."

"Are we okay? Sorry, I don't mean are you alright with this because, of course, you aren't... I mean you can't be but... do you think you can forgive me?"

"Yes, I forgive you. God knows I can't pretend I haven't fucked up in the past as well." She smiled ruefully. "At some point I think we all fuck up – it's just a question of when."

CHAPTER THIRTY-SIX

laire felt dismayed as she walked up to the local branch of Cafcass. In front of her stood a scruffy 1930s semi. There were two blue recycling bins to one side, one of them tipped sideways on the ground, bits of cardboard, food wrappers and plastic cartons spilling out onto the gravel drive. She hated mess and for a moment she thought about pulling the bin upright and retrieving the escaped waste. No, chances were she would get food stains or something worse on her dress or jacket. Wiser to leave it alone.

She had spent a long time that morning deciding what to wear. Initially she had thought of wearing a suit. That would project an air of competence and no-nonsense professionalism and she had two "court" suits which would have been ideal. Then she realised the mediation meeting was about persuading Sean to accept that Toby should live with her; for that she needed something more feminine. In the end she went for a dress and jacket. Instinctively, she had reached for a dress that Sean had often complimented her on before reluctantly putting it back on the rail. She wasn't trying to please him; he was now the enemy. Her final choice was the dress she had worn at Toby's christening; a subtle reminder of the journey she had made in giving birth to and nursing her child.

The doorbell was answered by a tall man with a mane of sandy-coloured hair, a broad flat nose and an unkempt beard. The Cowardly Lion from *The Wizard of Oz* made flesh. Although she guessed he must only be in his early thirties, he already had the beginnings of a pot belly and, dressed in black chinos and a crumpled white shirt, his appearance mirrored the shabby untidiness of the interior. He introduced himself – Claire expected Zeke or Clarence but apparently his name was Graham Holt – and then ushered her into a small room towards the back of the house. Sean was already there. He was sporting a newly shaven head, which Claire found unflattering and which also gave him a vaguely military aggressive air. She wanted to comment on it and tell him it was a mistake but bit her tongue; it wasn't her place anymore to give him advice on how to dress or look.

"Tea or coffee, anyone?" said Holt brightly.

Neither Claire nor Sean wanted anything, so Holt made some tea for himself and there was an awkward silence while they waited for him, Claire trying a brief smile which Sean affected not to see, staring straight ahead.

"So," Holt said, opening a buff folder, "my role today is to see if the two of you can reach an agreement on the custody arrangements for Toby." He studied the case notes in front of him for a moment. "Sean, my understanding is that you're seeking a residence order which will allow Toby to live with you."

Sean shifted a little in his chair, still refusing to look at Claire and directing his full attention towards the Cafcass Officer. "Yes, that's correct."

Holt looked at Claire. "And you're contesting this?"

"Yes."

"Right. So, our task today is to see if we can reach some form of compromise, i.e., an arrangement with which you're both comfortable. And above all, of course, we need to make sure that whatever we agree is in Toby's best interests. Now, for me, that would normally mean that both parents take an active role in parenting with perhaps shared residence. Sean, perhaps we can start with you telling us why you want Toby to live with you rather than staying with his mother?"

"Claire suffers from bipolar disorder. She's been hospitalised in the past with psychosis and is unstable; I think Toby's safety and welfare would be at risk if he were to stay with her and she was his primary carer."

"And how would you respond to that, Claire?"

"Yes, I have bipolar disorder, but it's fully controlled by medication. Toby is now three years old and I'm the one who's been caring for him for his entire life, with Sean only an occasional presence, and Toby is living with me now. There's no way the judge will award a residence order in Sean's favour, and he knows it." She glared at Sean, but he quickly looked away, his hands clasped in front of him and trembling slightly as he tried to control his anger.

"You're out of control, Claire. Toby's not safe with you."

"That's rubbish and you know it. You also have a full-time job – who would be looking after him whilst you're at work?"

"My mother's offered to look after him; she'll move in with us."

Claire gave a derisive laugh. "That's rich; that woman couldn't even find the time to come to his christening. I can count on one hand the number of times she's offered to look after him. You're an only child, Sean, and there's a very good reason for that; the woman hates children. You were just an excuse for her to give up work."

"You fucking bitch—"

"Sean, can we not—" said Holt.

"I'm sorry, I didn't mean to—"

"Look," said Holt. "The bottom line is this: either we can find some common ground today and agree on a solution you're both content with, or it goes back to court and the judge decides for you both. The problem with that, of course, is that I can guarantee both of you are going to be unhappy with the outcome. The best you can hope for is that one of you will be slightly less unhappy than the other one. Either way, it will be miserable. Do you want to take that chance?"

Claire sat silent, waiting for Sean to speak. It was his fault they were here; he was the one who needed to compromise. He sat staring down at the table, looking at neither of them. Holt swept a hand back through his hair and glanced briefly at the door as though eyeing up his escape route. There was a sheen of sweat on his face. For a professional mediator he didn't appear to be someone who relished conflict.

"I'd rather take that chance than leave Toby with her."

Her. He wasn't even using her name now.

"Are you certain about this? Even if the court grants a residence order in your favour, Claire will still need to be involved in Toby's life; he'll need both of you and it's his needs that are important. It's that you need to focus on."

"I *am* focused on that. Believe you me, that's *all* I'm focused on," said Sean.

Claire glanced at him and, for the first time in the meeting, he stared back at her. It was a look of pure hatred.

CHAPTER THIRTY-SEVEN

"Claire?"

"Oh, hi, Pete – how are you?"

"I'm okay, but I'm afraid I've got some bad news – Joan Madison's died. Someone I used to work with just rang me – thought I'd like to know."

"God, that's terrible, that poor woman. I thought she was in an induced—"

"She was. The family took the decision last night to turn off the ventilator. An MRI showed irreversible brain damage, apparently. To be honest, I think the MRI was done shortly after she'd gone into the coma, but it's taken a while for them to reconcile themselves, I suppose."

"God, I don't know what to say. Do you know when the funeral is? I think I'd like to go."

"I'll see what I can find out for you."

"Did you ever find anything on the CCTV footage, by the way? Was it an accident?"

"It was inconclusive, unfortunately. The station was busy, a lot of people milling around. Lots of pushing and shoving, people running down the escalators, usual nonsense. There were half a dozen people who stopped to help, including a nurse, and the Transport Police were on the scene pretty quickly as well, but we never did get to the bottom of it. Sorry, I've just realised there's a very bad joke in there somewhere."

"And what do you think?"

"Think of what?"

"Do you think it was an accident?"

"I honestly don't know. Probably an accident is my best guess. Anyway, I'm retired now so it's no longer my problem. Are you okay? Have you heard any more on that threat?"

"No, I haven't. I try not to think about it really, because I've got enough problems as it is. It was probably just a nasty hoax; I hope so, anyway."

"So, what else are you struggling with?" asked Hamlin.

"Oh, nothing much – I'm getting a divorce and Sean wants Toby to live with him. Apart from that—"

"I'm sorry to hear that. Was the divorce your idea?"

"Oddly, no, although I should have divorced him years ago."

"And he wants custody? I thought the courts always favoured the mother."

"You'd think, wouldn't you, but apparently not. It doesn't help that I'm bipolar, because he's using that as a stick to hit me with."

"Surely the court wouldn't give him custody based on that?"

"They might – my solicitor told me she had a client with bipolar a number of years ago and that's exactly what happened."

"Well, if you need someone to speak on your behalf, I'd be happy to step up."

"It's fine, Pete, Brenda will be there, and I've also asked an independent psychiatrist to attend on my behalf; she's bipolar as well, believe it or not, so I'm hoping her testimony will nail it for me – after all, despite being bipolar she's still holding down a responsible job and is allowed to go out and about without being pounced on by men in white coats. Sorry, my sarcasm got the better of me; I'll have to rein that in at the hearing."

"Sounds as though you've got it covered. Still, if there is anything I can do—"

"Don't worry, Pete, it'll be fine, I'm sure."

Claire ended the call. It wasn't true that she had stopped thinking about the hoax. On a purely rational level she was now convinced it was just a prank, but there was still a part of her which was worried, which was anxiously counting down the days to the 13th June.

Four days away.

CHAPTER THIRTY-EIGHT

Four Days Left

Kate's new house was in a quiet cul-de-sac. It was part of a neat terrace, brick-fronted and slate-roofed with grey shutters framing the windows. There was no response to the doorbell, but there was a gate to the side and, walking through, she saw Kate standing near the bottom of the garden. She was wearing stout purple gardening gloves, which made a colourful and striking contrast with the rest of her attire, a loose yellow blouse and faded blue jeans. Claire watched for a moment as she bent over a rose bush, snipping off branches and dropping them into a wicker trug.

"I never took you for a gardener," said Claire.

Despite the cold, there was a sheen of sweat on Kate's face. Her eyes glowed and she looked alive in a way she never did in the office. "Why?" she said. "Because only crusty seventy-year-olds are supposed to like it?"

"I just thought you might find it a bit dull, like fishing or doing embroidery."

Kate smiled. "I actually love it, it's like meditation, it just takes you out of yourself. Plus, it's a lot cheaper than drugs."

"I've never really found the time," said Claire. "Too many balls in the air – I can see its attractions, though."

Kate stared off into the distance and when she next spoke it was as though she was talking to herself, had forgotten Claire was there. "I find it quite spiritual. Birth and decay, death and renewal… you know, like watching a rose bloom, stunningly beautiful and then a brown mush within days. It sort of reminds you of your place in things."

"What, as brown mush?" Claire pushed a strand of loose hair back from her face. "You never cease to amaze me, Kate. How did you get to be such an old soul?"

"I never told you about my childhood, did I? Well, my dad's idea of entertainment was to beat the shit out of my mum. At the start it was on the rare occasions when he'd had too much to drink, then it was when he was sober as well. I was a four-year-old, hanging off my dad's leg trying to stop him killing her and then wiping the snot and blood off her face after he'd pissed off up to bed. I was four, but I already felt like a hundred years old."

"Did he ever hit you?"

Kate didn't answer. She knelt and picked up the trug. "Let me get rid of this and then I can show you round. It needs a lot of work, I'm afraid, so you'll have to make allowances. The agent described it as a 'project'."

"Meaning it's a disaster?" smiled Claire.

"I understand the classic definition is a house which will

require, at the very least, a complete demolition and rebuild – or as the agent put it, a house which needs a little updating but provides a wonderful opportunity to put your own stamp on it."

"Ah, a complete money pit then. "

"*Exactement, ma chère amie.*"

*

They shared a scrambled-together dinner of quiche and salad, with hunks of a freshly baked sourdough Kate had made. Claire asked if there was any wine and after a little scrummaging Kate offered up two bottles, a French Merlot and a half-finished bottle of Italian Gavi.

"Which you would prefer? There isn't as much of the Gavi as I'm afraid I had a glass of that in the garden earlier."

"Would you mind very much if I had the Gavi as well?" said Claire. "I have a real problem with red wine. For some reason it all seems to taste of Ribena. Are you sure you don't mind, though? If you prefer the Gavi then I'm happy to settle for water; I probably shouldn't drink anyway because I'll have to drive home later."

"No, you have the white; I think I've already had enough. And don't worry about the driving; the food will soak up the alcohol and you're more than welcome to stay, anyway."

It took a while to take Kate through everything that had happened since they had last been together. Some of it Claire had already shared over the phone: the car accident and Jessica's confession that she had been having an affair with

Sean. The revelation that Madison had died was new, though, and Kate was shocked.

"God, Claire, that's awful. Do you think it's linked to the hoax, or is it just a horrible coincidence?"

"I don't know – I hope to God it isn't linked because that would mean—"

"You need to go back to the police. They have to take it seriously now; they'll have to do something."

"Do what, though? Even if they do take it seriously and start to investigate, where would they even start? And if that bloody grave marker is right, there are only four days left."

"But they could at least arrange some additional protection for you."

"Yes, possibly, I suppose. But Toby would need protection as well – the second grave, remember?"

"Well, you need to talk to them. We're not talking about round-the-clock month-long stuff, you just need them to protect you on 13th June."

"I don't think whoever sent this is quite that fastidious. If he – or it could be a woman, I have no fucking idea – if he doesn't get me or Toby on the 13th, then what's to say he won't have a go the following day? If I thought it was that easy, I would just stay under the bedcovers on the 13th and get Pete to stand guard outside."

"Well, I think you should do that anyway," said Kate. She was quiet for a moment. "You don't think Sean's mixed up in this, do you?"

Claire looked shocked. "What? No, that's ridiculous, Sean would never get involved in anything like this. I might not feel too fondly about him at the moment, but we were married for nine years and for most of that time, I was in love with him. Still do love him, in some ways; he's just being such a bastard about Toby." Sighing, Claire looked at her watch. "Just gone nine. I need to get back home, unfortunately."

"Couldn't you stay? Brenda can look after Toby."

"No, I'd love to, but I can't." She stood up and stretched, suppressing a yawn.

"You will ring the police, won't you?"

She gave a tired smile. "Of course I will – first thing in the morning, I promise. I'll also talk to Pete – see what he can do to lean on them. Tomorrow will be three days, Kate; I've only got three days left to find out who this bastard is and stop them."

CHAPTER THIRTY-NINE

Three Days Left

T he first surprise was that there were three magistrates rather than the one Claire had been expecting. There were two women who Claire quickly judged to be in their late forties, both dressed almost identically in dark jackets and skirts. They could virtually be twins, she thought. Perhaps they'll speak in unison, like a sort of Greek chorus. She suppressed a smile.

The male judge was different, wearing the sort of tweed jacket beloved of pipe-smoking sports teachers and with receding grey hair of a gossamer lightness reminiscent of candy-floss. He was much older too: early sixties? Older still?

Claire looked at Helen, raising an eyebrow.

"There's usually one judge, but this sometimes happens," Helen whispered. "Two women might help, though." Claire wasn't so sure.

Helen had had the foresight to buy them all coffees from a coffee shop immediately opposite the court, explaining the vending-machine coffee in the building itself worked better as an emetic than a beverage. Taking a sip, Claire studied her surroundings. It looked like someone had taken a normal courtroom and then done their best to make it less forbidding. There was a lot of wood panelling in a subdued honey colour, with the judges seated at a level only slightly higher than their own. A series of desks had been arranged in a loose square in the middle of the room. Claire, Helen and Siobhan occupied the front of the square with Sean and his solicitor taking one of the sides, together with a man Claire didn't recognise. Sean had nodded briefly to Claire as they entered, but was now studiously ignoring her.

"Who's that sat at the end of the row with Sean?" whispered Claire.

"I was introduced this morning," Helen whispered back. "That's his barrister, apparently."

"*What?* He's appointed a *barrister*?"

"It happens a lot, actually, providing a claimant can afford it, of course."

"In my experience, barristers don't come cheap."

"Don't worry; I've come across him before – he's not that good. Still expensive, though."

"I hope you're right."

The judges introduced themselves and then asked everyone to explain who they were and their role in the proceedings. Everyone had been given the same bundle of papers to refer to during the hearing and the three judges consulted these frequently whilst evidence was given by each side. Sean's barrister spoke first, presenting an alarmingly formidable case as to why a residence order should be granted in Sean's favour. He also made great play of the psychotic episode which had led to Claire's hospitalisation and their fear that her current mental instability could, in the professional view of their psychiatrist, easily lead to another such episode, with profound consequences for the physical safety and mental welfare of Toby.

It was a compelling presentation and if Claire had been a neutral observer she might have believed it herself. As it was, she sat rigid with anger, pressing the nails of one hand into the palm of the other with an intensity fierce enough to draw blood. Helen noticed and gently placed a hand on her forearm. "Relax," she whispered. Claire gave a brief nod and unclasped her hands.

Shortly after that a recess was ordered, and it was announced that Claire's team would be invited to put their side of the case in the afternoon session.

"So, what do you want to do?" asked Helen. "We can either pop out and get a quick bite in a pub or grab a sandwich from one of the vending machines here and set up in one of the interview rooms."

"I don't mind," said Claire. "I'm too nervous to eat anyway, but you two have something."

"Siobhan?"

"The vending-machine sandwiches here are pretty dire; usually by the time you get there they've been cleaned out anyway and the only thing left are stale packets of crisps or a cheese and onion bap."

"Right, that settles it," said Helen. "I'll find us a pub. The Old Bridge Hotel is only about five minutes' walk from here and the food's pretty good, so I suggest we adjourn there. How's that suit?"

"Fine by me," said Claire.

Siobhan smiled. "Gets my vote."

*

"I'm nervous," said Claire. The rain had stopped and, looking across and through the window, she could see the sun had embroidered the river with shimmering bands of gold. She had ordered a smoked salmon sandwich on sourdough but had barely eaten, pushing the salmon around her plate with a fork while she talked. "Their barrister did a pretty good demolition job on me."

"Claire, you're making us all look like gannets; you've scarcely touched that," said Helen.

"Sorry, I'm just not hungry – my stomach's in knots. I shouldn't have ordered it."

"No, it's fine, I get it, honestly, I do. I know how important this is to you and also how terrifying. But, please, don't worry, we'll get what we need out of this."

"So, you mean Sean won't get custody?"

"I can't see them granting a residence order, no."

"But how can you be sure? You can't, can you? Not really."

A look was exchanged between Claire's solicitor and Siobhan. "Look," said Siobhan, "I'll settle up here and then perhaps the three of us could go for a short walk along the river before we have to go back."

"No, no, don't worry about that," said Helen, "I'll sort the bill. You and Claire go for a walk together, and I'll see you both back at the court. I need to nip back early anyway to give me a chance to review the papers for this afternoon."

*

As they stood waiting to cross the road, Siobhan said, "Did you know that when the Romans built this bridge they started from both banks at the same time?"

"No," said Claire. "Why?"

"Well, it explains the slight kink in the middle; they don't line up properly."

Claire stared at the bridge. "Really?"

"So, they weren't too bad at building, but they were lousy mathematicians."

"God," laughed Claire. "Imagine what a mess they'd have made of Tower Bridge."

They were now beside the river; the opposite bank gave onto a broad meadow spotted with clusters of cows. On their side of the shore, Claire watched a grey bearded man in his fifties carefully inflating a blue paddleboard with a hand pump.

"I had a client once," said Siobhan, "whose daughter was killed in a horrific car crash. She was supposed to have been on a night out with friends. Now, I know what you're thinking – one of them must have got horribly drunk but still insisted on driving. But it wasn't like that at all. It was a high-speed police chase, the police pursuing some kids who were joyriding. The police car took a corner too fast, lost control and smashed into his daughter's car. She wasn't even driving, just a passenger, but the police car took out her side of the vehicle."

"God, that's so awful. Her poor parents."

"Yes, her poor parents. That's not really the point of the story, though; the point is that after this my client – let's call him Ian – well, Ian was very quickly diagnosed with clinical depression. And one of the features of his depression was the OCD which he'd always suffered from became much worse."

"In what way?"

"Well, to give you one example, he found he was unable to go to bed at night until dozens of small rituals had been performed. All of the plugs in every washbasin in the house had to be inspected to ensure they hadn't been accidentally left in the plugholes. They also had to be carefully positioned on the ledge of each basin in such a way that they couldn't accidentally slip down into it during the night and block the plughole. All the taps had to be given a twist to ensure they had been properly turned off and then the gas jets on the hob had to be checked to ensure they were off – anyway, you get the picture."

"That poor man – that must have been so exhausting for him."

"And the real question is, why was he doing it? Why did he feel compelled to act like that? Well, I asked him, and do you know what he said?"

"No, tell me."

"He said he felt compelled to do these things because if he missed even one of them, then something terrible would happen. So, it was an attempt to exercise some of form of control, even though rationally he knew this was nonsense."

She stopped and turned to face Claire. "And we all do it. Every day, we try and control what's around us, pretend to ourselves that if we do it well enough, then nothing can go wrong. But deep down we also all know how deluded we are. When you first told me about the funeral invitation, you know what I thought? What I actually thought?"

Claire frowned. "No, I don't. Sorry."

Siobhan turned away to gaze over the river. Two young lads glided silently past them in a kayak. A grey heron stood on the far bank, perfectly still, its head lifted as though to listen.

"I thought what a perfect metaphor that is: an invitation to your own death. Because when we're born, that's what happens, we all receive an invitation to our own death. As soon as we are born, we start to die. And I suppose the challenge for all of us is what we do with that information. How should we lead our lives, knowing we are going to die? Sorry, Claire, I've just been banging on and I'm not even sure if anything I've said is really helping you."

"No, it has helped, honestly; it's been fascinating."

PATRICK MACDONALD

"Well, what I meant to say before getting sidetracked with the meaning of life was that what my poor client was doing was catastrophising; everywhere he looked he foresaw possible disasters, unimaginable horrors just waiting to happen. And that's what you're doing now, Claire. You've convinced yourself that Sean is going to win, that you're about to lose Toby. But you can't live your life like that. You have to break it down into manageable chunks, to tackle what's in front of you rather than conjuring up imaginary horrors or dragons down the road which you feel you must fight now. It's too exhausting and it will literally drive you mad."

"So, what should I do? I don't think you understand; I am frightened. Terrified—"

Siobhan held her by the shoulders. "I do understand, Claire, I really do. Here's what I want you to do. When we're back in that courtroom I want you to have this image in your head: picture yourself returning home tonight, entering your house and sweeping Toby up in your arms, knowing that you've won your case and that Toby can stay living with you. And if any of the testimony gets difficult and seems to be going against you, close your eyes, take slow breaths, and conjure up that image. Do you think you can do that?"

Claire gave a sad smile. "I'll try... but what... what if he wins?"

"Then fuck it – we both go and get steaming drunk."

CHAPTER FORTY

The judges said they were anxious to learn more about Claire's bipolar condition, so Helen called on Siobhan as her witness. She briefly ran through Siobhan's qualifications, drew attention to the report she had produced and then invited the judges to ask questions. It was the male judge, Hopkins, who spoke first, and Claire couldn't help but notice that as he spoke his nose twitched from side to side. It was a little bizarre and made it difficult to concentrate on what he was saying. Was it a physical tic of some kind, like Tourette's, or was it just some peculiarity of his physiognomy? He looked like a nervous rabbit worried the juicy carrot which had just been offered to him was about to be snatched away. Still, his questions seemed sensible enough.

"Your report concludes that Mrs Evans' condition is well controlled by medication and you wouldn't therefore expect a repeat of the psychotic condition for which she was hospitalised four years ago. Is it also your belief, therefore, that she is now capable of raising her son and that Toby would not be at risk if he remained living with her?"

"Yes sir. When Claire – Mrs Evans – had the original

psychotic event she hadn't at that stage been prescribed any medication. It was as a result of her breakdown that she was given a mood stabiliser. She was able to function perfectly well with that medication and went on to not only hold down a very demanding and stressful job as a forensic pathologist, but to have and raise a child, Toby."

Sharp-nosed and with piercing blue eyes, one of the female judges, who had introduced herself as Mayhew, jumped in.

"But I see from your report you've changed her medication. Why did you do that if you're saying she was stable on her previous meds?"

Siobhan hesitated. "Claire was on lamotrigine, which is primarily an anticonvulsant used in the treatment of epilepsy. It has also, though, been found to have a therapeutic benefit for bipolar disorder—"

"But why change it, then?" interrupted Mayhew.

"Lamotrigine is better at treating the lows, or the depressive episodes, in bipolar disease, but perhaps less successful in dealing with mania—"

The third judge, Mackenzie, a grey-haired woman Claire judged to be in her early sixties, now intervened.

"So, I assume you feel lithium is successful at controlling both aspects of the illness, the mania and the depressive episodes; is that correct?"

"Yes, that's exactly right."

"But from what I've read, it has several potentially toxic side effects, doesn't it?" Mackenzie continued. "It can damage your kidneys, your thyroid – these are potentially very serious side effects, aren't they?"

"All drugs have side effects, and you have to weigh the benefits of any particular drug against the possible harm done by such side effects. With careful monitoring of the lithium levels in a patient's blood, it's very unlikely severe side effects will be experienced."

"And would you say Mrs Evans' mood swings are more stable as a result of this drug?" asked Mayhew.

"Yes, I would."

"So, you don't consider Toby would be at risk in any way if he remains with her?" she continued.

"No, certainly not. Toby is a very well-adjusted little boy who plainly adores his mother. And his mother adores him. It would do huge psychological damage to both of them if they were separated."

"Whilst preparing for this hearing," said Hopkins, "I read a very interesting statistic – apparently between twenty-five and sixty per cent of individuals with bipolar disorder will attempt suicide at least once in their lives. This seems hugely worrying to me; would you care to comment on that?"

"Only a very small proportion of those, though, actually go on to commit suicide; I believe the figure's around four per cent."

"Ah, yes," said Hopkins, with a note of triumph in his voice, "but I also looked up the overall suicide rate and that, according to the Samaritans, in 2019 was eight per 100,000.

So, I've done a bit of maths and that works out as a suicide rate of one in twenty-five if you're bipolar and one in 12,500 for the rest of the population. Pretty stark, don't you think?"

"There is no record of Claire ever attempting suicide. From a psychological point of view, I consider her to be an extremely stable individual and no more likely to be at risk of suicide than you or me."

"Mrs Evans has a full-time job and I imagine it must also be a very demanding one," said Mackenzie. "What are the current arrangements for Toby's care whilst she's at work?"

"I think I can answer that," said Helen. "Toby goes to nursery during the day and Claire's aunt collects him in the evening, taking care of him until Claire comes home."

"And does this aunt live with Mrs Evans?"

"She lives locally, but will often stay over at Claire's if Claire has to work late, for example, or attend a work function such as a conference or dinner."

"And does Mrs Evans drop Toby off at the nursery or does the aunt do this?"

"Brenda – sorry, her aunt – usually drops Toby off, but on occasion Claire also does this."

"Thank you. Claire, I'm so sorry, I know you must be finding all of this extremely stressful. Is there anything you want to add or wish to say?"

Claire's mouth felt dry, and she forced herself to take a sip of water from the plastic beaker in front of her before she spoke, her hand trembling slightly as she lifted it to her lips.

"I – I only want to say that I love Toby with all my heart and I know he loves me, and if I'm separated from him, I know he will be devastated. I will be devastated. It will destroy both of us. I believe young children need structure and routine, they need the familiar, and if you take that from them that can only be damaging. He has friends at nursery, and he has a very loving and close relationship with his aunt; all of that will be destroyed if he has to move to Scotland."

"But won't it be equally damaging for him to be separated from his father?" said Hopkins.

Claire felt a surge of anger and Helen, seeing this, quickly intervened. "It's Toby's father's choice to move to Scotland. Claire wants both parents to be involved in Toby's care; by seeking a residence order, Sean is seeking to remove his mother from his care. By moving to Scotland, he's also making it extremely difficult for Claire to even have access or visit her son."

Mackenzie leaned across to whisper something to her two colleagues. Hopkins gave a brief nod and began pushing papers into a binder. "I think we've heard enough to try and reach a decision on this," he said. "I suggest, therefore, that we break for an hour and then my colleagues and I will give our decision when we return." He glanced at this watch. "It's just gone three o'clock, so if everyone's happy with this, we'll meet back here at four. If we need longer, we'll get a message to you and, with that in mind, perhaps the lead solicitors for each of the sides can leave a contact number we can reach you on."

Helen looked at Claire. "Happy?"

"Yes," said Claire. "Fine."

Sean also nodded his assent to his solicitor.

"Everyone happy?" said Hopkins. "Splendid; we'll meet back here at four, then."

Once they were outside the building, Claire turned to Helen. "So, what do you think?"

"I'm not sure, Claire. I would expect them to deny Sean's application for a residence order but as a battle-hardened lawyer I've sometimes seen the courts make the most appalling decisions. We'll just have to see. What do you think, Siobhan?"

"I think I need a caffeine fix. Probably a sugar one as well, if I'm honest."

"I think I need something a lot stronger than caffeine," said Claire, "but that may have to wait until this evening. Coffee's fine."

Helen smiled. "Great – I spotted somewhere on the High Street which looked fairly decent, so let's head for that."

As they started to walk away, something made Claire look back. There on the steps of the court building stood Sean, his solicitor and barrister, all engaged in conversation with Hopkins. Nothing wrong with that, perhaps, but they were all laughing as though they were enjoying a particularly good joke. Was she the joke?

CHAPTER FORTY-ONE

Helen had also noticed the three men standing together.

"I'm not happy with that," she said.

"No," replied Claire. "I'm not either. Should I be worried?"

"As a judge, Hopkins shouldn't be talking outside proceedings to either party. Put it this way, if the decision goes against you then I'll be making a formal complaint."

"Have you come up against him before?"

"Yes, several times. He's a bit of a maverick, our Hopkins. Still, having said that, I've always found him to be fair, so let's wait and see."

*

It was a little after five when they returned to the court building. Claire had forced herself to drink a latte, but it had made her nausea worse. When the court had rung Helen to explain more time would be needed to reach a decision, she had felt almost physically sick. Now, she sat anxiously scanning the judges' faces as they filed into the room. Nose Twitcher spoke first.

"I apologise first for all of this taking a little longer than I anticipated. We have now reached a decision, though, and my colleague, Patricia Mayhew, will take you through this."

Claire stared at Mayhew, anxiously trying to read the result from her expression. Mayhew coughed and took a sip of water from a plastic cup in front of her and Claire noticed her hand shook a little as she raised it to her lips. Was that nerves, she wondered, or a simple hand tremor of the sort many people develop in late middle age? As Mayhew placed the cup back down on the table Claire watched her glance briefly at Sean and then at her. Was there the hint of a smile there?

"Having heard all of the evidence presented by both parties," she began, "we have decided to reject the residence order application filed by Toby's father. It is the decision of this court that Toby should continue to reside with his mother, Claire Evans. Toby's father will be granted visitation rights and the details of this should be agreed between the two parties. I'm sorry we kept you all waiting for our decision."

Claire felt a wave of relief sweep through her; exhausted, she stood up and almost immediately felt as though she was about to faint. Helen stood as well and swept her into her arms, unaware of how close Claire had been to falling. "Congratulations," she said.

Siobhan stood smiling a little awkwardly to the side. Claire could see she wanted to join in the hug but was uncertain as to whether it was appropriate, so she extended her arm and drew her in. Claire was crying and both Helen and Siobhan were soon in tears as well.

CHAPTER FORTY-TWO

Two Days Left

"Claire, I'm at the nursery – did you arrange for Toby to be picked up?"

There was an urgency and panic in Brenda's voice which immediately sent Claire's heart rate soaring.

"What? What do you mean? You're picking him up. Where are you?"

"I'm at the nursery now. He's not here, Claire, they're telling me someone collected him half an hour ago."

"That can't be right. Are you sure? He *must* be there – is he outside, in the toilet? Check again."

"No, he's gone. Someone picked him up."

"But I told them the only people allowed to collect him are you, me and Jessica – who picked him up? Was it a man? Was it Sean? Can they describe them?"

"I don't know. It was a bloke, apparently, and it could have been Sean, but he's only ever been here once or twice before and hardly any of the staff know what he looks like anyway. I hope to God it was him. Has he been in touch?

Did he tell you he was picking Toby up?"

"No, I haven't heard from him since the court hearing. What the *fuck* are they doing? I told the manager, Elaine, not to allow anyone else to collect him other than us three *and* to let me know if anyone else did try that. Is Elaine there? Put her on so I can speak to her."

Elaine had obviously been standing beside Brenda and listening to the call because she immediately came on the phone, sounding both panicky and scared. "Claire, I'm so sorry, it was one of the juniors here, she's only been with us a week and—"

Claire cut her off. "I don't care about that – what the *hell* are you playing at? I told you never to allow anyone apart from me, Brenda and Jessica to pick Toby up. How the hell did this happen?"

"I – I had a dentist's appointment, I had to go out for an hour. Toby was picked up when—"

"Don't you talk to your staff? Have you never heard of inductions? I swear if any harm comes to my son I'll have you closed down."

"I'd *told* her, all the staff knew—"

"Well, they clearly didn't know, did they? I want to speak to the person who allowed this to happen. Put them on now."

"Yes, of course. She's very upset, so—"

"*I'm* very upset. Let me speak to her."

There was a muffled, fumbling sound as the phone was

handed across. A brief silence, then a young girl's voice. Nervous. Frightened. "Hello…"

Claire could immediately picture her, face blotchy and red from crying. Her normal instinct would have been to comfort or console. Not now. "I'm sorry, Elaine hasn't told me your name."

"Sam… sorry, Samantha."

Claire took a deep breath, forced herself to speak normally. "Sam, what can you remember about the man who picked Toby up? What did he look like? What was he wearing?"

There was an agonising silence; Sam was clearly in shock, her brain's normal thought processes frozen with fear. "I – I don't know," she stammered. "He just looked normal, you know, average. I'm so sorry, I didn't know, nobody told me, he seemed so nice, I—"

Claire was struggling to keep the anger out of her voice. "What's *normal*, Sam? What did he *look* like?"

"He was… tall, slim, I think. Black hair?"

Like Sean.

"Do you remember what he was wearing?"

"Jeans… a T-shirt… navy blue?"

Claire grimaced. Sam was employing an upward inflexion in her speech so many youngsters seemed to favour. In any other situation, she might have found this endearing. Now, it was completely maddening.

"What sort of T-shirt? Did it have any logos on it or—?"

"I can't remember… I don't think so."

"Do you remember what his shoes looked like?"

"I… I didn't really look; I was trying to put Toby's coat on, so… I… I think they might have been trainers?"

Sean always wore trainers.

"Are you *sure* they were trainers?"

"No, I think they were but…" There was an anguished sobbing.

Claire took a deep breath. "Alright, Sam, that's fine. Thank you. Can you pass me back to Elaine, please?"

"Elaine? I'm going to call my ex-husband to see if it was him that picked Toby up. I'll then call you straight back. Please don't let any of your staff leave until you've heard from me again. If this wasn't my ex, then my next call will be to the police and I'm certain they'll want to talk to you and your staff. Can you pass the phone back to my aunt, please?"

There was a muffled fumbling as the phone was given back to Brenda.

"Brenda, did you hear what I just said?"

"Yes, I'll stay here as well."

"Thanks, I'll call you back."

She rang off and brought up Sean's number. It went to voicemail. "Sean, Toby's missing. Can you ring me back urgently?" She followed this up with a text for good measure. Was he deliberately avoiding her call? Because he had picked up Toby up and was even now driving north with him? Either way, she couldn't wait any longer; she had to phone the police.

Recognising the urgency in her tone the call handler

immediately patched her through to CID. A woman picked up the call, listening intently as Claire explained what had happened.

"Do you have your ex-husband's address in Edinburgh? If you think he might be travelling up with Toby, I can get someone from Lothian to go round and check later tonight."

Claire scrolled through her phone for Sean's new address. "Do you want his mobile number as well?"

"Yes, please, and any other contact numbers you might have for him. Do you have a work number, for example?"

"Yes, yes, I do." She hurriedly gave the details.

"Right. Give me the nursery address and I'll come over now. Look, it's quite late, 5.30 – will there still be any staff there?"

"Yes, there will – I asked them to stay. I told them I was ringing you and you would probably want to speak to them."

"That's great. Can you meet me there? I'll also need a recent photo for Toby, a head shot, full profile – ideally a couple of photos. Can you organise that?"

"Yes, of course, I'm sure there are some suitable ones on my phone."

"Right, text them through and I'll see you at the nursery."

Claire ended the call. She suddenly had a thought; Sean's mum lived in Edinburgh. Perhaps she might know where Sean was. She only had a landline number for her but, hopefully, she was at home. The phone seemed to ring a long time and she had almost given up when it was suddenly answered.

"Hello?" An anxious, timid voice.

"Oh, hi, it's Claire. How are you?"

"Oh, hello, Claire, haven't heard from you in—"

Claire cut her off. "Is Sean there?"

"Sean? Yes, he is. Did you want to speak to him?"

Claire's stomach lurched. If Sean was there, then he couldn't have picked up Toby from nursery. It would have taken more than six hours to drive to Edinburgh. Someone else must have collected him.

"Please, it's urgent. Can you put him on?"

"Urgent? Why? What's happened?"

"Let me speak to Sean – he can explain afterwards."

"Alright, I'll just get him." She heard her calling her son, her voice now even more anxious and alarmed. Sean must have picked up on this because he also now sounded anxious. Anxious and a little wary.

"Hi, Claire. What's up?"

"It's Toby – he's missing. Someone – a stranger – collected him from nursery this afternoon."

"What? Well, how the *fuck* did that happen?"

"Don't *shout* at me, I'm stressed enough as it is. I'd told them the only people allowed to collect Toby is me, Brenda, or Jessica. They *knew* that. Some bloody youngster they hadn't trained up properly allowed this. Anyway, forget that; the point is he's missing, and it looks as though he's been kidnapped." Her voice broke on the word *kidnapped*, as she finally confronted her worst fears. She started to sob.

Sean softened. "Don't worry, Claire, we'll find him. Have you spoken to the police?"

"Yes, I've just rung them. I'm seeing someone from CID at the nursery now."

"Alright, that's good. I'm coming down."

"You don't need—"

"He's my *son*, I'm not—"

"No, no, you're right. You'll need somewhere to stay; you don't know how long you'll need to be down here. Do you want to stay with me?"

"No, don't worry, I'll find somewhere."

"No, you can stay with me. Honestly, it's not a problem."

"Well, if you're sure? You don't mind?"

"No, of course I don't."

"Alright, I will. Thanks."

"Look, I have to go; I need to get across to the nursery, but I'll obviously ring you if I hear anything."

She rang off. She was struggling to stay calm, her heart racing, her whole body trembling. One thought consumed her.

If Sean hadn't picked Toby up, who had?

CHAPTER FORTY-THREE

It was gone midnight when Sean finally turned up, looking haggard after his long drive, worry etched across his face. Why had she invited him to stay with her? She had told him he could stay on the spur of the moment; it was only afterwards she asked herself why. The truth was he was as invested in Toby's welfare as she was, the only other person on earth who would really understand and share the terror she was feeling at potentially losing him.

When she opened the door, they both fell into a long wordless hug. Claire was immediately in tears again, her body shaking. Sean gripped her tighter. Slowly, she regained control of herself, eventually calming down enough to trust herself to speak.

"I'm so frightened."

"I know. What did the police say?"

She looked up at him. His eyes were bloodshot, she noticed, but then if she bothered to look in a mirror it was unlikely hers were any better. "The nursery's got CCTV just near the entrance. The police are analysing that now and have promised to give me an update in the morning."

"Does it cover the car park?"

"There's another camera overlooking the car park so, yes; with luck they can link the footage showing whoever picked him up with the car he used."

"Let's hope to God they can do that. I know it's late, but I need a drink."

"I've done you some food, I thought you might be hungry."

"You didn't have to—"

"Don't get too excited; it's only some roast chicken and some salad."

"That sounds great, I'm actually ravenous. I didn't get time to eat, just jumped in the car and came down. Didn't even bother to pack."

"Don't worry, I can lend you a toothbrush," smiled Claire. "Some of your old clothes are also still in the wardrobe; I thought about taking them to a charity shop but haven't got round to it yet." What she didn't tell him was that she had been reluctant to get rid of them, that sometimes she would take out one of his old jumpers and press it to her face, inhaling the complex mixture of smells which reminded her of him; of sweat and after shave, of damp and cut grass. Did she miss him? How could you not miss someone you had spent years making a life with? She still both loved and hated him, but to hold on to hate too strongly risked poisoning the well of their memories together, of destroying the happier times they had shared: their wedding day, Toby's birth, their first Christmas as a family, Toby delighting in playing more with the cardboard boxes and a wooden spoon than the presents they'd so carefully chosen. Writing off their past would be like erasing part of herself.

They sat up talking most of the night. Claire was convinced Toby's abduction was linked to the hoax funeral invitation, but she hadn't told Sean about the second smaller grave. She looked at him; he looked tired and beaten. How would he take this?

"Sean, I need to tell you something, but before I do, please don't be angry with me."

"Why? Why would I be angry with you?"

"There was another grave, a smaller one. It appeared a couple of days after the first one."

He looked confused. "But so what? What has this got to do with—"

"It was a child's grave."

Realisation dawned. "Christ, Claire – why didn't you tell me? How could you hide this from me? Do the police know?"

"I've told the police. I've told them everything about the hoax and now, finally, they're taking it seriously, when it's too *fucking* late."

Sean's eyes blazed with anger. They had been sitting at opposite ends of the L-shaped cream sofa in the living room but now he stood up, looming over her. "Why didn't you tell me?"

Claire looked back at him defiantly. "Because I didn't want to frighten or worry you."

"You should have told me. If you'd told me then maybe—" He stopped.

"Then maybe *what*? Maybe it wouldn't have happened – is that what you were going to say?"

He was quieter now, more anguished. "I don't know, yes, maybe, just maybe, I don't know, *but* you should have told me."

Claire was sobbing. She was so tired. It had been a mistake inviting him to stay with her. She knew that now. He sat down again, this time drawing her towards him and wrapping his arm around her. "If you cry any more tears, I'll have to get a mop," he said gently.

"I'm so tired and frightened. If anything happens to him…"

"He'll be alright, we have to believe that."

"I can't go to bed… I can't rest until I know…"

"I know. Look, let's just go for a walk. Do you think you can manage that?"

*

Sunrise found them pacing slowly around the lake in Hinchingbrooke Park and, despite her despair, Claire marvelled at how beautiful it was; deep crimson framing the jet black of the trees, merging into the softest of pinks and then the deep blue of the sky. It was strange how in life such stunning beauty often coexisted with the deeply ugly or horrific. When she was depressed, everything seemed a threat and it was impossible to find solace in anything; it seemed as though what appeared to be normal or safe was the thinnest of veils laid over life's surface which could be ripped away in an instant to reveal the horror underneath, the skull beneath the flesh. Strangers would stroll innocently past her in the street and out of the corner of her eye she would suddenly see them spasm and jerk into grotesque menacing gargoyles before suddenly morphing back. She would watch crows settle in vast throngs in the branches of trees as though massing for an attack, and the delighted screams of children in a local playground would slice the air like knives.

And at the moment she was beyond depression. It was as though her entire skin had been stripped from her body, every nerve ending lying exposed and jangling with pain. They walked in silence as the sky slowly brightened, the sun glinting off the surface of the lake. Not so long ago, she thought bleakly, we'd have been walking hand in hand. And Toby would have been walking in front of us, running off and then checking back, excited, mischievous, asking for ice cream and Haribo in the same breath.

It was as they moved away from the lake, walking up towards the park's café, that her phone rang. "Hello?"

"Claire? It's DI Chambers; we met last night?"

"Hi. Thanks for calling. Is there any news? Have you—"

"We've got a possible lead. We've got an address in Grantham that we're checking out now. The local police have got it under surveillance and we've got a team about to drive up."

Claire stood still, hardly daring to breathe. Sean was close to her, straining to listen to the other side of the conversation. "How did—"

"CCTV footage from a local garage. I can't go into the detail, though, because we're literally about to leave. I just wanted to give you a heads-up."

"No, thank you. Please ring me as soon as you—"

The line had gone dead. Tears filled her eyes. "Did you hear—?"

"Yes," said Sean, and he pulled her towards him. For a long time, they stood hugging each other.

CHAPTER FORTY-FOUR

Twenty-Four Hours Left

It was mid-morning when Chambers rang again. "Claire? We've just left the suspect's address. He's not there. We've spoken to neighbours and, apparently, it's been a few days since he was last seen."

When Claire spoke, her voice was barely a whisper. Sean was standing beside her. Neither had slept. "So, what now?"

"We're trying to track down any family members he might have. I want to also tell you his name in case it's familiar in any way to you. I'm sorry, I should have told you last night, but once we had an address that became the priority."

"No, of course, I can see that."

"His name is Adam Turner; does that mean anything to you?"

Claire felt the hairs on the back of her neck stand up. "Sorry, did you say Adam *Turner*?"

"Yes – do you know him? Does that—"

"I've never met him, but I might have seen him in court; I

think he may be the son of a woman I gave evidence against in a trial."

"Really? Where are you now? Are you at home?"

"Yes."

"Great – look, stay where you are, we'll come to you. We should reach you in under an hour. I need to know everything you've got about this trial and this woman—"

"She committed suicide," said Claire. "In prison, just after Christmas – January. But there's more I need to tell you as well—"

"Right – we'll go over everything once we're there."

*

Chambers arrived with a colleague who she introduced to Claire and Sean as DS Peterson, a tall, gaunt man with greying hair. Claire guessed he was in his early fifties. Chambers, by contrast, was petite and youthful, pretty, her short brown hair expensively cut. They both looked hollow-eyed and exhausted, though, and Claire invited them through to the kitchen, where she busied herself making everyone tea with a strong black coffee for Chambers. They then all sat there whilst she took them through everything that had happened; the trial, Turner's conviction and suicide, Madison's fall and subsequent death, and how she now believed all of these events were linked to the funeral invitation and Toby's kidnapping.

"When you found the second smaller grave why didn't you go back to the police?" said Peterson.

"Because you didn't take it seriously the first time!" said Claire.

"I would have taken it seriously," said Chambers grimly. "I would have taken it seriously when you tried to report the first grave. It was a threat to kill, plain and simple."

"Well, when I did try, I was given the brushoff," said Claire. "I had to rely on an ex-DS to try and help me."

"Who was that?" asked Chambers.

"Pete Hamlin."

"Oh, I know Pete," said Peterson. "Lovely bloke, bloody good at his job too."

"I didn't know him, I'm afraid, I moved up from the Met two months ago," said Chambers. She looked worried and was quiet for a moment. "Remind me, what was the date of your supposed death again, I mean, on that marker?"

"Tomorrow – 13th June," said Claire.

"Right, you're going to need round-the-clock protection until we catch this bloke."

Claire was startled. "Sorry? What does that mean?"

"We'll have someone stay here with you. The alternative is we take you to a safe house – that might be the better option, frankly."

"No, I'm not leaving my home."

"Is protection really necessary?" said Sean. "I'm going to be here anyway; I can look after—"

"Yes, it is," said Chambers firmly, looking irritated. "We've got a suspicious death with Madison and now your son's been kidnapped. If Claire won't accept a safe house, then we'll have to have someone stationed here. I think I need to speak to Hamlin; it was his trial and I want to see what he remembers about the son. Claire, we took some photographs from Turner's flat – can you have a look at these and confirm this is the man you saw during that trial?" She passed two photographs across to her; one was a photo of Turner with his arm around a woman Claire guessed was his wife. Both were smiling and casually dressed, the man in a white polo shirt and khaki shorts, his sunglasses casually hooked into the neck of the shirt, the woman wearing a loose blue summer dress. His hair was longer and he looked younger than the man she had seen at trial. As she looked at the second photograph, a jolt of electricity ran through her. Turner was cradling a baby, a huge smile on his face: Alice, in what must have been just weeks or even days before she died.

"Yes, that's the man," she said. "You need to use the baby photograph; it's more recent and it's closer to how he now looks." She hesitated. "The baby in that photo; I'm pretty sure it's Alice, the baby alleged to have been killed by his mother."

"Alleged?" said Chambers sharply.

"Sorry, murdered... I don't know, I don't know anymore... she may have been wrongfully..."

"Why do you say that?" said Chambers, her eyes narrowing.

"There was a microbiological report; it should have been presented in evidence but... it showed a very high level of bacterial infection and that could have been the real cause of death."

"And Turner's son knew this?"

"It formed the basis of his appeal… but then, of course, with his mother's suicide—"

"Christ," said Chambers. "What a mess."

"No wonder—" said Peterson.

Chambers cut him off. "Right, we'll have these photos circulated. Claire, I've got to go, but Peterson will stay with you until the protection officer's arrived. I'll also need Hamlin's number, if that's okay. Give me your number now and I'll text you mine, which you'll need anyway. You can then text me his number."

They exchanged numbers and Chambers rose to leave. She turned to Peterson. "Can we have a word outside?" The two officers stood outside the front door; they had left it open but kept their voices low, so it was impossible to hear what they were saying. Claire gestured to Sean that they should move into the living room. Once there she turned to face him.

"I'm not staying here; I'm going to find him myself."

CHAPTER FORTY-FIVE

"Claire, that's madness. He's threatened to kill you; why would you deliberately put yourself in harm's way like that?"

"*Toby*," she hissed. "*His* life is in danger. I can't sit here while—"

They were standing quite close to each other. Claire could sense that Sean wanted to take her into his arms, but she quickly moved away.

"You can't, Claire – for a start, Peterson won't let you leave the house. Look, the police are dealing with this; you have to let them do their job."

"I can't… I can't. I need to do this; this is my fault; I need to find him. I couldn't live with myself if—" She crumpled to the ground and burst into tears. The pain of Toby's absence was unbearable, a knife twisted slowly round and round in her gut. Sean knelt beside her, cradling her with his arms.

"You need to rest, get some sleep. Once you've had some rest we can both try and look for him, but nothing we do now is going to help."

"I can't… I can't sleep. How can I? How can I?"

"Have you got any sleeping tablets?"

"No… wait… maybe… I don't know."

"I'll go up and look. Can I get you anything to drink? I could make you some hot chocolate?"

"No, no, I'm fine… perhaps some water."

"Okay, let me see if I can find the sleeping tablets first."

He stood up and left the room. Claire glanced at her watch. Nearly one o'clock. Toby had been missing almost a full day. She had no intention of taking a sleeping tablet, so she would have to fake it. She was suddenly aware of a shadow in the doorway and turned to look. It was Peterson.

"Sorry, I didn't mean to startle you."

"No, no, don't worry – you didn't," she replied.

She was still kneeling, and he looked embarrassed, as though he had somehow caught her doing something illicit or shameful. At that moment Sean reappeared. He was carrying a glass of water and his other hand was cupped, indicating he had succeeded in finding the medication. "Found it," he said. "You had a cache of them in your bedside table, enough to kill an elephant, actually."

Peterson gave a nervous cough. "What—" he began.

"Sleeping tablet," said Sean. "Claire needs to get some rest – she's out on her feet."

"Literally," smiled Claire, and she slowly stood up. She immediately felt dizzy, the room starting to spin. Peterson was the nearest and moved quickly to steady her.

"Sorry," she said. "Rush of blood."

"Are you okay?" he said.

"Tickety boo," she grimaced. "I think I will go up. Too tired to think straight anyway."

"Here," said Sean, handing her the water and the tablet. "Get that down you first and I'll help you upstairs."

"Roger that. Mr Peterson – sorry, I can't call you that. Do you have a first name?"

"Ivor."

"Ivor?" said Claire incredulously. "What, as in Ivor the Engine?"

"The very same," he said. "My parents were Welsh, you see."

"Ivor it is, then. I used to love that programme. Seems a very long time ago now, though, a very long time," she murmured sadly. "Oh, well, perhaps I'll wake up and it will all have been a nasty dream. A very nasty not-real-at-all dream."

CHAPTER FORTY-SIX

Once in her own bedroom Claire removed the tablet Sean had given her from her mouth, opened the window, and tipped it out. There was a reason she had accumulated so many sleeping pills and it certainly wasn't to euthanise an elephant. Hopkins' observation about suicide had been on the money. She stared out of the window. It was still quite light, and she could clearly see Peterson's police vehicle parked across the road, its distinctive blue and yellow livery in marked contrast to other vehicles around it, most of which were either grey or white. As she watched, a dark blue Ford Mondeo drew to a stop opposite. It hesitated for a moment and then moved forward, parallel parking a little further down the road. There was something familiar about it, but Claire's brain was too fogged with exhaustion to piece out why that might be. She sighed and drew the curtains.

Sean was right; she needed to sleep: not the dead coma, though, that a sleeping pill would produce, which might knock her out for five to six hours. No, she needed to find Toby and for that she could afford an hour's respite at best. Even that was too much, but she also knew that if she failed to get at least some sleep then she would of no use to anyone anyway. It would be like asking a sleepwalker to fly a fighter jet. Sean had elected to take one of the two guest bedrooms, with Claire sleeping in what had been the marital bedroom, the largest bedroom in the house, which also contained an ensuite. The house had five bedrooms in total and had had just three occupants; if they failed to find Toby that would shrink to just one. The rooms radiated out from a central corridor like the spokes of a wheel and to reach her own Claire could not avoid passing Toby's. The door was open. She glanced at it and then decided to enter.

The bed was neatly made up, exactly as she had left it the previous morning. His pink rabbit lay propped up against the pillow, its head turned towards the door, as though waiting for a visitor. With its pearl buttons for eyes, it looked vaguely sinister. She crossed the room and swept it off the bed so that it lay on the floor, face down. Lifting the pillow to her face, she inhaled deeply. A smell of shampoo and sweat, and the indefinable sweetness that was Toby. She started to cry, trying hard to muffle the sound of her sobbing.

She set an alarm on her phone to wake her in an hour, got undressed, and eased herself into his bed; it had been unseasonably hot, so she lay naked under just a sheet, the discarded *Star Wars* duvet heaped on the floor at the bottom of the bed. She stretched out her arms; he would often lie just so, his weight upon her arm as she pulled him closer, a book propped on her own chest. What had she read last to him? *The*

Twits? Something else? Then she remembered: It was *Love You Forever* by Robert Munsch. Where was it? She peered over at the small bookcase against the far wall. No, not there. Where, then? She had a sudden inspiration, reaching down the side of the bed pushed against the wall. Yes, there it was: she tugged it up and opened it. She had read the book to him many times and had seldom got to the end without crying. The first time it had happened Toby had been mystified. "Why are you crying, Mummy?"

"Because it's sad. Well, happy sad."

"What's happy sad?"

"It's when you're happy and sad at the same time."

He looked puzzled. "Haappy saad," he said, as though stretching out the syllables would somehow release their meaning. "*I know*," he said excitedly, "It's like when I'm eating ice cream. I'm happy when I'm eating it and sad when it's gone."

"Yes – brilliant. It's exactly like that. Anyway, that's enough for tonight. You need to go to sleep, young man."

"But I'm not tired and we haven't reached the end."

"Tomorrow, we can finish it tomorrow, I promise."

But we didn't finish it, did we?

A single tear rolled down her cheek. She shut her eyes. For a while she stared at the images which floated at the back of her eyes: a red spider's web of veins, a distant glow of pale green, the exit from a dark cave, which appeared for a moment and then vanished. She fell asleep. She had hoped to rest, but instead became entangled in a deeply unsettling dream. There was a vast ocean floor spooling away beneath and in front of her. An inky blackness enveloped her; she looked up, desperately searching for a shaft of light which might offer a possibility of escape. Then she saw him. Toby lay on the ground in front of her, eyes unseeing, fronds of seaweed settling around his face, sand drifting down around his still body. She started to scream, but the only sound was a muffled electronic beeping. It was growing louder, becoming more insistent.

Her eyes snapped open.

CHAPTER FORTY-SEVEN

13ᵗʰ June

Brenda opened her eyes, staring anxiously into the darkness. There had been a creaking sound, she was sure of it. The garden gate: someone had come through it. She strained to hear. The distant yowling of a cat, but otherwise nothing. Whoever it was must have paused, worried that the noise of the gate might have alerted someone.

Carefully, she eased herself out of bed and crept into the bedroom at the back of the house that faced onto the garden. She had left the curtains undrawn in this room, but by standing to one side of the window and gently lifting one of the curtains back, she felt she could peer out without being seen herself. Assuming there was anything there, of course. Her garden filled her with shame but the arthritis in her hands and the pain in her hip meant she no longer felt able to care for it. The roses she had cultivated over the years were smothered with brambles, and nettles had overrun the borders. Claire had kindly described it as cottagey, but Brenda suggested the word she should have used was rubbishy. She was resigned, though;

the garden's slow decline seemed to match her own and there was a sort of comfort in that.

She was stunned by the sight of the moon – it was a fierce blood red and looked huge, flooding the garden with light. A super moon: she had forgotten one had been predicted for tonight. She was completely captivated, when she suddenly noticed a movement below her out of the corner of her eye. She turned her head to try and focus more clearly on that area of the garden. Nothing. Had she imagined it? No, there it was again. There was a shadow near the bird feeder. An animal? A dog? A fox? The feeder stood at the far edge of the lawn, which itself was almost entirely in shadow from the house. If the wretched creature would only move further into the garden where it was lighter, then she might be able to…

Almost as though it had heard her, the shadow came closer. Brenda gave an involuntary gasp.

It was Toby.

He continued towards the house and as he came closer, she could hear his anguished sobbing. There was a garden pond in front of him, long neglected and virtually hidden beneath a tangle of weeds and brambles. Horrified by what was about to unfold, she screamed and banged the window with her fist. Startled, he looked up, but it was too late. He tripped and fell forward; there was a loud splash as he hit the water, then a frantic thrashing sound as he struggled to escape, his arms and legs flailing. Brenda raced from the bedroom, almost falling herself as she stumbled down the stairs. She always left the key to the back door in the top drawer of the oak dresser in the kitchen. It wasn't there. Swearing, she pulled the entire drawer out and emptied its contents on the kitchen table. Old invoices and circulars spilled to the floor as she frantically searched. Where the hell was it?

Her heart hammering in her chest, she gave up and ran instead to the front door. The key to this was always left in the lock to allow a rapid escape in the event of a fire. She threw it open and ran barefoot round the side of the house to the gate leading to the garden. The gate was ajar, and she pushed through, ignoring the sharp pains in her feet and shins from the damp lazy tangle of brambles and thistles which lay across the damp grass. Her heart stopped. Like a splayed starfish, Toby lay face down and motionless in the water, his blond hair a loose halo around his head.

She screamed.

CHAPTER FORTY-EIGHT

Kneeling, Brenda placed her hands around Toby's shoulders and lifted him clear of the water, her arms shaking with the unexpected weight. There was a sour smell of decay from the pond. She laid him face up on the grass and, wiping away strands of pondweed, frantically searched his face for signs of life. Nothing. His eyes were blank, his skin chalk white. She bent to listen for the sound of breathing. Nothing. She was too frightened to feel for a pulse and for a second sat back on her haunches, paralysed by fear.

Phone – I need my phone. How could I be so stupid as to come out here without it?

She ran back into her house, banging a toe hard against the wooden base of her bed and wincing with pain as she rounded it to retrieve her phone from the bedside table.

"Emergency, which service do you require? Fire, police or ambulance?" A man, his voice crisp, professional.

Brenda was already moving down the stairs, hurrying back to the garden. "Ambulance – it's my nephew—"

There was no response as the operator transferred the call. A new voice, female.

"Ambulance Service. How can I help?"

Brenda had already reached the garden and was staring at Toby's prone body as she spoke. "My nephew, he's not breathing – there was an accident, he fell into a pond. I—"

"Right. Give me your name and phone number in case I lose you and have to phone back. I also need your location."

"07700 886032, sorry, 038, 866038 – I can scarcely think. I—"

"You're doing fine. I just need your name and location."

"Brenda. 36 Hawthorn Avenue, Godmanchester."

"And the postcode, Brenda."

"PE29 6TW. Please hurry – I think he's—"

"I'm dispatching an ambulance now. Brenda, listen to me, this is important. How long was he in the water?"

She was struggling to breathe, her breaths coming in short panicky bursts. "Two, three minutes – I'm not sure. I had to—"

"Okay, try and calm down, Brenda. I need you to help your nephew – take some deep breaths, slow your breathing down. What's your nephew's name?"

"Toby."

"Toby, okay. And how old is he?"

"He's three, four in October."

"That's fine. Okay, have you tried CPR yet?"

"No, I don't know how… God, I'm so useless… I—"

"Okay, don't worry. I'm going to talk you through it. We're going to start with five breaths. Tilt Toby's chin up, open his mouth and cover it with your own, and breathe into it five times. You also need to pinch his nose when you do this. Can you do this for me?"

"Yes, yes… I'm going to have to put you on loudspeaker. Hold on. I'm just putting the phone down, God, my hands are shaking. There – can you still hear me?"

"Yes, I can still hear you. Five breaths – do it now."

Brenda bent over Toby's body. Despite the cool of the night, sweat dripped down into her eyes, blinding her, mingling with her own tears. Then, what seemed to her a miracle.

"His chest is rising – is that good?"

"Yes, that's good. Now we need some chest compressions. We need to do this thirty times: put the heel of one hand on his chest and press down – keep doing it for thirty compressions. Not too hard, his chest should be compressed by about a third."

"Where on his chest – I don't—"

"Pull his top up, Brenda. Put your hand between his nipples – that should be the right place." There was a pause. "Have you done that?"

"Yes."

"Right, thirty compressions, quickly now, and count them for me out loud so I can hear."

She began to count, furiously pumping his chest as she did so.

Nothing.

"He's still not breathing – I think he's—"

The dispatcher's voice again, an increasing urgency in her tone. "Two more breaths, Brenda – do that now and then another thirty compressions. The ambulance crew should be with you within the next five minutes. You're doing well – don't stop. Two more breaths. Come on, you can do this."

Brenda leant again over the small, inert body. *It's too late,* she thought.

It's too late.

CHAPTER FORTY-NINE

Claire lay staring at the bedroom ceiling. Was she mad? Was it better to just let the police do their job? What on earth did she think she could contribute? Then an image of Toby alone and in distress filled her mind and she knew she had to act. But how?

The police had failed to find Turner at his home address, but where else might he go? Did he have siblings or relatives where he might hide out? His mother. She was dead, but would he go there? She had to find her address.

Pete, I'll ask Pete; he'll be able to get her address through his contacts in the police force.

She glanced at the bedside clock. 4 AM. God, how long had she been asleep? Far too early to try ringing him. Plus, she would almost certainly be overheard. She needed to get out of the house. First, she needed her medication, though. She should have taken it last night, but had forgotten. She pulled the drawer of the bedside table open and peered inside: scrunched-up tissues, several small white boxes of sleeping tablets, a notepad with hard black covers, assorted pens and pencils, but no sign of the lithium pack. She started to sift through, searching for it. No, definitely not there. But she always kept it there. Where could it be? She didn't have the time now to look properly, but she knew that if she couldn't find the tablets it would take at least three to four days to get another prescription, by which time… No, can't think about that now. I need to move.

Hurriedly dressing, she quietly eased the bedroom door open. She could hear Sean's snoring from his own bedroom. I have to get out of here without alerting Peterson, she thought, but where is he? She peered down into the hallway; there was a light still on in the living room. Peterson was in there, she was certain. It seemed impossible that she could make it out of the house without alerting him, but she would have to try. She crept down the stairs; this was an art in itself. The floorboards always creaked on the left side on the bottom five steps, so she had to move over to the other side as she reached them.

She paused on the last step. The living room had two glass-panelled doors and light spilled out from these into the hallway. If Peterson had chosen to sit on the far sofa facing the doors, then he would have a clear view of Claire as she stepped into the hallway. Cautiously, she stepped down and peered into the room; if he was awake, she would simply say she couldn't sleep and had decided to get up. Peterson was sitting in an armchair with his back to the doors. Was he awake? His head was bent forward; he looked asleep. She had to risk it. Retrieving her car keys from one of the drawers in the kitchen, she slipped on some shoes and eased herself out of the front door, taking care to close it as softly as possible behind her.

It was both dark and cold and there was a heavy dew on the grass. Standing shivering on the drive, clad only in a thin summer dress, she realised she should have taken a coat. The dress was perfect for later on once the sun had made an appearance, but not so clever now. She paused, staring at her car in an agony of indecision. If she took it that would almost certainly alert both Peterson and her husband. Her mind made up, she began to walk briskly away from the house. She would walk to Hamlin's; it would take a good half-hour, but he wasn't going to be up yet anyway.

She had gone less than a hundred yards when her phone rang. "Claire. Thank God, I've reached you. It's Toby. There's been an accident; he almost drowned. I'm—"

Her whole body started to shake, and she felt as though she were about to faint. She slumped against a wall. "Brenda, is Toby alright? What accident? What's happened?"

Brenda sounded close to tears, her voice anxious and strained. "He fell into the pond in my garden – I'm at Addenbrookes. He's alright, I think. I spoke to one of the consultants and they think he'll be okay. I was so frightened—"

"You're not making any sense. How did he end up in your garden? I don't understand."

"I don't know, I don't know. He just appeared and then he fell into the pond. I did CPR – they had to talk me through it – and then the paramedics arrived. They were brilliant, Claire, if it wasn't for them… I thought he'd died, he wasn't breathing. I was so frightened; I've never been so frightened. I thought he'd died. They used a defibrillator on him and that brought him round."

"How long did he stop breathing?" Her professional training kicked in. She knew the cutoff for a toddler was five minutes; after that there was a high risk of brain damage.

"Three, four minutes? Maybe longer? I don't know, I was so scared, time seemed to stand still; I still feel as though I'm kneeling by the pond, everything feels so unreal."

Claire felt a surge of irritation. *Why don't you know? And never mind about the bloody pond.*

"But the consultant thought he was okay?" she asked in a tight voice.

"Yes, she thought so; she was really kind, gave me a hug, and I couldn't help crying. I think she was in tears herself."

"Is Toby awake? Have you spoken to him?"

"No, he's asleep – I haven't been able to speak to him yet."

"Which ward are you in?"

"C3, the children's ward."

"Okay, I'm coming now." She turned back to the house. Sod it; she was taking the car. If that alerted Sean and Peterson, then too bad. She ground the gears as she hastily put the car into first, the tyres squealing loudly as she pulled away. Sean: she should have told him. It would have to wait until she got to the hospital. She did a quick calculation. The journey should take roughly forty minutes, maybe less with so little traffic on the roads. He was going to be angry with her, but too bad. All that mattered now was Toby.

It was almost daybreak, and the sky was an angry red, the low sun blinding her as she made the final approach to the hospital. She should have aimed for the multi-storey car park on the site but instead drove directly to the main hospital building, taking one of the disabled spaces in front of it. She would probably be fined, but to hell with it.

CHAPTER FIFTY

The air in the ward felt hot with stale trapped air and there was the sour smell of disinfectant peculiar to all hospitals. Toby was on a general ward, but there was only one other child in the six-bay room, a young girl who was, perhaps, a year or two older than Toby, with dark curly hair and intense blue eyes. Despite the early hour, she was awake and stared at Claire with a frank curiosity as she passed.

Toby's bed was at the far end of the ward, next to an expanse of glass overlooking the entrance to the hospital. Ominous dark clouds were massing in the distance and the windows were already flecked with rain. She slowed as she neared his bed. Toby was lying on his back, eyes closed, his arms lying loosely by his sides. Brenda sat slumped in a chair beside him, her head bowed and seemingly asleep. Claire stood for a moment, uncertain as to what she should do. Then she bent forward over him, putting her ear close to his mouth; she could feel the touch of his breath on her ear, a wonderfully light caress. It was only then, as she exhaled with relief, that she realised she had been holding her breath from the moment she had entered the ward. She stared down at him, hungrily taking in the blond curls of his hair and the delicate curve of his nose. She flashed back to his birth and when she had first held him, cradling his head with her hand, both marvelling at and terrified by the delicacy of the soft fontanelle. When he had opened his eyes and gazed back at her it was as though he contained the wisdom of the ages and she felt an overwhelming surge of love such as she had never known before, not for Sean, her parents, or anyone else. It was primeval, astonishing and irresistible, as though the mystery of existence had suddenly been revealed to her, the veil torn away.

And that love had only grown.

Unable to help herself, she leaned across the bed again to stroke his face and, as she did so, Brenda suddenly woke with a start. "Claire – I—"

"How are you feeling?" said Claire. She put her finger to her lips to indicate she should keep her voice low to avoid disturbing Toby.

Her aunt rubbed the back of her neck. "Well, my neck feels as though someone's taken a hammer to it," she whispered.

"Can we go outside so we can talk?" said Claire.

"Yes, of course. Hold on." Brenda rose unsteadily to her feet, groaning softly as she did so. "I think my knees and back are both wrecked."

Claire looked at her, only noticing now that her aunt was dressed in a faded grey dressing gown. Mud and grass stains were caked around the base of her pyjamas. She started to say something, but stopped. Toby was the priority. Once they were in the corridor outside the ward she turned towards her aunt with a fierce whisper. "What *exactly* did the consultant say?"

"He said he thought he would be okay but they're going to carry out a CT scan in the morning – sorry, I suppose that's today now. I'm sorry Claire, it was all such a blur, he nearly died – I thought he was dead. I—" She burst into tears, hastily wiping them away with the heel of her hand. "I'm sorry, I was so scared."

Claire wrapped her arms around her. Brenda's whole body shook uncontrollably. For a moment they both stood, hugging each other, tears still spilling down Brenda's cheeks. "It's alright, you saved his life. If you hadn't been there—"

"I'm so tired," Brenda said. "I feel I could lie down and sleep forever. I can barely stand up."

Claire gently kissed the top of her aunt's head. She had never seemed so vulnerable, and Claire noticed for the first time that her grey hair was thinning at the crown, her pink scalp clearly visible underneath. "Has Toby been awake at all since the accident?" she asked. "I mean, has he been conscious?"

"What? Yes, when the paramedics revived him and then he was awake again for a while here."

"Did anyone carry out a physical exam on him?"

"Sorry, Claire, I'm not sure what—"

"Did anyone check his speech, track his eye movements, examine his motor co-ordination? I mean, could he lift his arms or shake someone's hand?"

"Yes, yes, they did – a doctor looked at him and then later

on, there was a consultant, a woman. She was great – I think they had to call her in. She looked exhausted, to be honest."

"And what did she say?'

"She said she thought he seemed alright. She said a CT scan should confirm that, though."

Claire drew a deep breath. "Did she ask you how long Toby had been unconscious for?"

"I told her four or five minutes – I wasn't sure, Claire. Everything happened so quickly, it was all a blur. It just seemed unreal, some horrible nightmare. It still seems unreal; I can't believe it's happened. I still don't understand why he suddenly appeared in the garden like that – why did that man suddenly let him go? And how did he know where I lived? I don't understand."

"I don't know. I can tell you what I have found out, though; it turns out he's the son of that woman who was convicted for murdering those two children."

"What? I'm sorry, I still don't understand."

Claire sighed. "His mother committed suicide whilst in prison – apparently he blames me; it was my evidence at the trial that helped convict her."

"God, that's awful, but surely, he can't blame you – there was so many others involved, the police, the courts. Why you?"

"There was a microbiological report that emerged after the trial – it showed the child she was looking after, Alice, died from a massive bacterial infection. It was a natural death – she should never have been convicted. I should have picked it up, so he's right to blame me."

As she said these last words, she burst into tears.

"But, Claire, even if this is true, it doesn't justify what he's done – Toby's just a child, he could have died."

"His mother's dead and so is his own child. It doesn't excuse what he's done, but it's understandable. Grief and hatred can drive people to all sorts of extremes."

"You should have told me – you shouldn't have had to deal with all this on your own. The divorce was bad enough, but this as well – I don't know how you coped with it, Claire."

Claire grimaced, tears still running down her cheeks which she made no effort to wipe away. "I didn't have much choice, did I? I didn't tell you because I didn't want to worry you. Anyway, what difference would it have made if I had done? What could you have done?"

"I don't know, probably nothing, but I still think you should have told me. I was looking after Toby – if he was in any danger at all, I needed to know."

Claire realised her aunt was right; in trying to protect her, she had placed Toby at risk. And she had still not told her about the smaller grave, the direct threat to Toby's life as well as to her own. "I'm so sorry, I've been so stupid. You're right. I should have told you." She hesitated. "There's something else I should have told you as well; I didn't say anything because I didn't want to frighten you—"

"What? What else is there?"

"I went back to the cemetery. I don't know why; I was hoping to find some sort of clue or something. I found another grave, a much smaller one…"

She looked into her aunt's eyes, hoping for a spark of understanding, reluctant to say anything more. Even to speak the words seemed to make the threat more real, to bring what had been hiding beneath the dark surface up into the light.

Her aunt hugged her tightly. "Oh Claire, you poor love. You must have been going out of your mind with worry."

It was as she stood in her aunt's embrace, staring into the darkness of the corridor over her shoulder, that she suddenly realised.

Today was the day she was supposed to die.

CHAPTER FIFTY-ONE

Her phone rang and she knew even before she answered that it was Sean. She had forgotten to phone him. "Sean," she whispered to Brenda, and walked a little distance away so she could concentrate on the call.

"Where the fuck are you? The police are in meltdown here. What the *fuck* are you doing?"

His words felt like a physical assault, but she forced herself to stay calm. "Don't shout at me; if you carry on shouting and swearing I'll end the call. Is that clear?"

"Just tell me where you are, Claire." He was no longer shouting but there was still a suppressed fury in his voice.

"I'm at the hospital – Addenbrookes. Toby's had an accident; he nearly drowned. We think he's alright, a consultant checked him out. They're doing a CT scan, though, so I should know more later this morning."

"You found Toby? But where? And how did he nearly drown? Where *was* he, for Christ's sake?"

"I don't know how this happened, but Brenda told me he just suddenly appeared in her garden last night. Then he stumbled somehow and fell into her pond. Brenda rescued him; she saved his life."

"Thank God Brenda got to him in time. Are you sure he's alright? Is he conscious – have you spoken to him?"

"No, he was asleep when I got here. Look, I'm sorry I didn't ring you. I left the house to try and find him and Brenda rang me even before I'd got in the car. After that, all I could think of was getting here. I was beside myself; I'm still shaking."

There was a silence and Claire could sense Sean struggling to get his anger under control. "Okay. I understand," he said slowly. "I'll drive to the hospital now. Peterson may want to come with me as well, but I'll talk to him. He's standing listening to all this, incidentally."

"Ah, right, well, give him my regards. I hope he's not too mad at me for rushing off like that."

"Well, put it this way, you're not his favourite person in the world at the moment. Anyway, that's your problem. Which ward is Toby in?"

"The children's ward – C3."

"Right, thanks."

*

Claire glanced down at the consultant's name badge. Sarah Raynor. She was small, with no discernible makeup, her brown hair pushed back behind her ears, dark rings beneath her eyes. Claire couldn't help wondering if she had returned home during the night for some much-needed sleep or had simply crashed in one of the side rooms reserved for hospital staff.

It was just after 9 AM; Sean had yet to arrive, no doubt with an irate and embarrassed Peterson in train. Toby was still asleep, Claire's increasing worry slowly turning her stomach to stone.

"So," said Raynor carefully, "we've got the scan results and I've also discussed them with colleagues. There's some evidence of swelling of the brain, which is consistent with oxygen deprivation." She waited a beat for this information to sink in, looking directly into Claire's eyes to ensure she understood. The heavy stone in Claire's stomach turned to ice.

"It's impossible to be certain about this and it may well be that Toby doesn't have any lasting ill effects, but you need to be aware that there may be issues—"

"What sort of issues?" said Brenda.

"It's impossible to say at this stage – there may be learning disabilities, memory problems, issues with motor co-ordination. Some of these deficits might only become apparent later on. On the other hand, Toby might make a full recovery – that's possible as well. We'll watch him very closely for the next few days and we might also need another CT scan."

Claire felt as though she herself were drowning, her throat closing, the air around her becoming dense and heavy. Raynor looked alarmed. "Are you alright? You look—"

She fainted. Brenda screamed. "Claire!"

She had fallen onto her side and Raynor swiftly knelt, turning her onto her back and loosening the belt of her dress.

She grabbed two pillows from the empty bed next to Toby's and placed them under Claire's feet. Moments later, Claire opened her eyes. She tried to lift her head but immediately felt dizzy and lowered it again.

"Careful," said Raynor. "You fainted. You're fine, just rest a little first before trying to get up. Try taking some deep breaths – slowly, not too quick."

"I'm sorry," Claire murmured, "you'll be giving me a bed next."

"You're fine," smiled Raynor. "Do you feel well enough to try getting up?"

"Yes, I think so." She lifted herself up onto her elbows, Brenda bending to help her. Slowly she got to her feet. She looked at Toby. He was still asleep. There was no colour in his cheeks. She started to cry.

CHAPTER FIFTY-TWO

S ean arrived shortly after the consultant had left the ward, Peterson trailing in his wake, the ward door almost banging him in the face as he fought to keep up with Claire's ex. Sean stopped in silence as he reached them and stared down at the sleeping form of his son. "Has he been awake at all?" he eventually said in a hoarse whisper.

"He's been asleep the whole time I've been here. Brenda says he was conscious when they brought him in, though."

"Only briefly, a few minutes at most," said Brenda.

"They ran some tests, he seemed okay," said Claire, "but the scan they did shows some swelling of the brain."

"It is sleep? He's not in a—" His voice was strained, fearful.

"No," said Claire, "no, no. Look, we need to talk, but not here. There's a coffee bar on the ground floor—"

"Yeah, okay, makes sense." He looked at Peterson. "You'll join us, yeah?"

"Yes, of course." He looked at his watch. "I can only spare an hour, though, I'm off shift then and I'll need to hand over to someone else."

"Fair enough," said Claire, "I expect you've had enough of me by now anyway."

"To be honest, I'd prefer to stay on – see it through – but I doubt Chambers will let me."

*

Kate rang just as they had all settled themselves in the canteen. "Claire, where are you? You're supposed to do the Sinclair autopsy this morning? I've got a DS here bending my ear and he's not a happy man. I've put him in your office to give him some privacy, although actually, I just wanted rid. He's already gone through half a packet of biscuits and two cups of coffee. I swear if he asks for any more I'll start charging."

"Christ," said Claire, "I completely forgot. I can't tell you everything now, but Toby almost drowned last night – he's in the hospital; he's here actually, in Addenbrookes."

"Oh, Claire, that's awful. Is he alright? Do you want me to come to you? Which ward are you on?"

"No, no. Not now. I'll ring you back later: they're still doing tests so we should know more later. He seems okay – I don't know Kate, I really don't; I just hope to God he is."

"Okay, I'll be praying for him. If there's anything I can do—"

"No, no, it's fine, don't worry. Can you get rid of the DS for me, though? I can't face doing the autopsy now and in any case, I need to be here for Toby. Who is it, anyway?"

"Hancock – you know, that creep we had two months ago

on the Baker autopsy, the bloke with the ear flaps and the droopy nose. Close relative of Dumbo."

"Okay, just get rid – explain what's happened. Don't want him filing a complaint against me with Ballantyne; I've taken far too much time off already and he's already marked my cards once. Tell Hancock I'll ring later to apologise properly. Hopefully Ballantyne won't find out." She rang off.

"The station might lodge a complaint—" said Sean.

Peterson coughed. "I might be able to help with that, smooth things over with them."

"Would you? That would be really kind if you could," Claire replied. "I'm sorry I abandoned you last night, by the way."

"It's alright, I get it – if it was my son I might have done the same. My fault really for nodding off – Chambers wasn't impressed though, might even end up with a verbal."

"Verbal?" said Sean.

"Verbal reprimand. Worst case, it might be a written warning, but we'll have to see."

"Surely she would understand?" said Claire.

"Not Chambers: she's new, wants to make a mark, show who's boss. Ballantyne's your boss, I suppose?"

"Yes, quite famous actually – wrote the definitive textbook on forensic pathology, did the Moors murders, Dunblane. You name it, he was there."

"Worth reading?"

"Might be a bit dry for you."

"I'll look it out anyway. Imagine I'll cope; you're looking at a man who finds train timetables interesting."

He drained his coffee and got to his feet. "Right, Chambers – need to ring her and sort out my replacement. I'll see if I can find a quiet spot, probably outside might be best. Wish me luck."

"You'll be fine, I'm sure," said Claire.

Peterson grimaced. "I'll be okay. I just hope Toby pulls though."

Claire didn't reply, staring through the windows at the brightening sky. She remembered the livid red of the sunrise as she drove in, the trees silhouetted in black as though a ragged army had risen up to challenge it. Now ominous dark clouds rolled above them, and rain smashed against the glass, the onslaught becoming louder and fiercer as she looked.

Somewhere out there was her nemesis.

CHAPTER FIFTY-THREE

That afternoon Toby woke up. Claire had been sitting beside his bed, half dozing, a magazine lying unread on her lap, when she heard a hoarse whisper. One word. "Mummy." She woke with a start, knocking the magazine to the floor. From across the ward, the girl with the dark curly hair lifted her head from her pillow and looked on with interest.

Claire caressed his cheek. "Toby, Toby, darling, how are you?" she murmured. "How do you feel?"

"Thirsty."

"I'll get you some water." She hurriedly looked round; neither the bedside cabinet nor the wheeled table which would normally hover over a bed had a jug of water or beakers.

"I've got water," said the girl in a clear, high voice. "He can have mine."

Claire walked across, smiled at her, and poured some water into a plastic cup which she then took back to Toby, holding it carefully to his lips. He drank a little, spilling most down his chin and immediately choked. Alarmed, she pulled the cup away. "Sorry, sorry, darling. Are you alright?"

"Yes," he croaked. A pause and then: "Throat hurts. Can I have some more?"

"Yes, of course. Can I lift you up a little? I think it might be easier to drink it if you're sat up a bit."

She put her arms gently under his and pulled. He whimpered with pain. "Hurts – chest hurts."

Tears sprang to her eyes. "Oh, Toby, my poor love, I'm so sorry."

"Don't cry, Mummy. I'm not crying."

She wiped them away with the back of her hand. "No, no, just silly Mummy. You're far too brave for tears. You're so brave, my brave little boy."

He gave a weak smile. "Can I have some more water now?"

She lifted the cup to his lips and this time he managed to swallow some without choking. "I love you, Toby, I love you so much. I love you to the moon and back."

"Love you, Mummy." He sank back into the pillows and his eyes closed again. "Love Mummy," he murmured. "Love…" He was asleep.

The little girl was still staring intensely at them. "Is he going to die?" she said solemnly.

Claire looked round, startled. "No, of course not," she said.

"Would he like some of my chocolate?"

"That's very sweet of you – perhaps later when he wakes up."

"Would you like some of my chocolate?"

Claire laughed. She was immediately reminded of how

hungry she was; it was almost a full day since she had last eaten anything. "Yes, yes, I would – you don't mind sharing?"

"No-oo, I've got *lots*." She opened the drawer of her bedside cabinet and extracted a half-eaten bar of milk chocolate, breaking off some and offering it to Claire. "You can have two pieces," she said.

"You're really kind," smiled Claire. "Hmmn… this is delicious. I think it's the best chocolate I've ever tasted."

"I'm dying," she said solemnly.

"I'm sure you're not," said Claire, shocked.

"I am – I heard Mum talking to one of the doctors. She thought I couldn't hear." The girl had been carefully smoothing the silver foil of the chocolate wrapper, looking down as she talked. Now she gazed directly at Claire.

"Does it hurt?" she said.

"Sorry, does what hurt?"

"Dying – does it hurt?"

"No, I don't think so. It's just like falling asleep, really."

The little girl smiled. "I like my sleep."

"So do I," said Claire. Was this alright? Was she right to describe dying to this child as falling asleep? She knew the importance of telling the truth to children; what if this girl's illness was such that she would suffer horribly before she died? No, no, that was nonsense; they would dose her up with morphine to ensure that didn't happen. It was hard to think straight. She shut her eyes for a second.

"You can sit down, you know," said the girl. You look *ever* so tired."

"Thank you – I am tired." She pulled the chair round next to the bed, so it was facing the girl and sat down.

"I'm tired too," said the girl, and mirroring Claire, also closed her eyes. For the first time Claire noticed the dark rings under them and how pale her skin was. She was desperate to know what was wrong with her, but she could scarcely ask. Perhaps she could ask one of the nurses. She heard the bang of the ward doors and looked up. Kate.

"Thought I'd come and find you; see how you and Toby were. Hope that's okay." She leaned over and kissed Claire lightly on the cheek. "I've been so worried about you both." Claire watched her suddenly catch sight of Toby. She lowered her voice. "God, I'm so sorry, making all this noise; is Toby asleep?"

"Yes."

"How is he?"

"He seems okay," said Claire slowly. She gave a meaningful glance down at the little girl and then looked back at Kate. "We need to talk."

"Are you okay?"

"Yes, just very, very tired."

"I'll bet you are. I finally got rid of that clown Hancock, by the way." She glanced round. "Where's Sean? I thought he'd be here."

"Gone back up north. He's got a meeting with some

clients, said it was for a bid they've been working on for months, so he couldn't get out of it. He's promised to travel back tomorrow."

"Can't be more important than this," said Kate, arching her eyebrows in disbelief.

"You'd think not, no. Still, there it is."

"That policeman outside looks as though he should still be in short trousers. I almost tripped over him coming in."

Claire smiled. Peterson's replacement, Meadows, a young constable who looked to be barely in his twenties. When she had first seen him she had thought that if Turner had suddenly appeared she would probably end up having to defend him rather than the other way round. Brenda had been about to leave to get some rest when he arrived but had immediately changed her mind, saying she would stay after all and it had taken a lot of effort on Claire's part to finally persuade her. "He is a little young," said Claire.

"Young? I've seen newborns older than that," said Kate. "If this was a maternity ward they'd have him in a cot."

Claire smiled. "Look, why don't we grab a coffee, and I can tell you what's happened?"

*

Once they'd settled themselves in the coffee bar Claire took Kate through the night's events. The police officer had insisted on coming down with them, but Claire asked him if he wouldn't mind standing in the main atrium outside to give them some privacy.

"So, what now?" said Kate. "How long will they keep him in for?"

"Not sure. They said a couple of days for observation. The trouble is, I'm frightened of leaving him here on his own. Brenda can cover a bit, I suppose, but I think I'll have to do the night shifts."

"But you won't get any sleep and you're already wrecked. I could do tonight for you, if you like."

"No, no, I couldn't ask you to do that. I'll sleep in a chair, I'll be fine."

"Could they make up a cot for you?"

"I don't know, I'll ask."

"God, what a mess. Surely the police will find this bloke soon. They know who he is; how difficult can it be?"

"I hope so. I wonder why he let Toby go like that?"

"Dunno. Perhaps he decided he'd gone too far, frightened you enough. Perhaps that's the end of it."

"Hmm, somehow I don't think it is. Anyway, I don't think Toby was ever his real target, it's me he wants. I think kidnapping Toby was just his way of sending a message. He always intended to let him go. He'd done his research though; he knew where my aunt lived."

"He's missed his deadline, though."

"Yes, but then he probably wasn't expecting me to have the police camped out at my house. Plus, he wouldn't have allowed for Toby's accident and my rush to the hospital. Perhaps he was hoping that once Brenda had found Toby I would have come over and he could have attacked me then."

"Who knows what goes on in the mind of someone like that."

"It's just so fucking hard, I'm so worried about Toby. I just hope to God he's alright. He seems alright but I just don't know; I mean, if he does have learning difficulties or problems with motor co-ordination it might be weeks before they become apparent, or even months, or—"

Kate placed a hand on top of Claire's. "Claire, stop. He'll be fine, you have to believe that. Don't do this to yourself." Claire looked away, suddenly noticing that two nurses sitting at a table nearby were staring at them. "Let's get out of here," she said. "I need some air."

The rain had stopped, the sky an enfeebled grey. Water pooled in the gutters and on the roadside where the drains had failed to cope. An elderly man, a breathing tube attached just below his nose, sat in a wheelchair just outside the entrance, sucking grimly on a cigarette. Claire forced herself to slow her own breathing, taking deep breaths.

"Are you alright?" said Kate. "You look—"

"I'm fine." She shut her eyes for a moment and reopened them. Still here, the world was still here. When all she wanted was oblivion.

CHAPTER FIFTY-FOUR

She had almost died on the drive home.

It was a second night with almost no sleep. She had again sat propped in a chair beside Toby's bed; a kind nurse had said they could make up a bed for her, but the offer had been made just before dawn, so Claire had waved it away. That had been a mistake.

It was early evening when she finally decided to travel back. Kate had reappeared after work and offered to sit with Toby, so Claire had reluctantly agreed to go home for a few hours to freshen up and catch up on her sleep. Meadows said he would follow her back using his own car.

The A14 was busy as usual with an endless convoy of lorries heading into the Midlands and the North from the ports. She knew she was tired and not really in a fit state to drive so she had left the heater off despite the cold and jammed the driver's window open for good measure. Even so, she could feel her eyes closing as she fought to stay awake and alert. Then, a micro sleep, less than a second. Her eyes shut and she lost consciousness. When she woke up it was to find herself in the outside lane racing towards a stationary line of traffic.

Her heart pumping furiously, she slammed on her brakes and stopped inches from the steel underride guard of a container lorry. She instinctively looked in her rear mirror to make sure nothing was coming up too fast behind her. A car was approaching, but slowly, and with its hazard lights already switched on to warn others. She realised with a start that it was Meadows. Moments later the traffic started off again as the congestion eased.

As she came to a stop on her drive Meadows parked behind her, blocking her car in. He was out of his car first and pulled her door open to allow her to get out. "Are you okay? That was a little hairy back there."

"Sorry, no, I'm fine. I took my eye off the road for a second… realised too late the traffic had stopped."

"Alright, well, luckily, no harm done. Look, I've spoken to Chambers; she's been told to stand me down after tonight, I'm afraid. She argued but…"

"Don't worry, I understand. I can hardly expect you to mount a permanent guard. Are you coming in?"

"No, I've been told to stay outside. I finish my shift tomorrow morning at six and then that's it. There won't be a handover."

"But you can't stay out here all night. That's ridiculous."

Meadows shrugged. For the first time she noticed his monobrow, a dark caterpillar of hair giving him a neolithic air at odds with his obvious charm and intelligence. It immediately aroused her maternal instincts and despite her tiredness it was all she could do to stop herself offering advice on plucking and trimming. She smiled. "Look, I'll bet you're hungry. Come in and eat with us, at least."

"With *us*?"

"My aunt, Brenda, is staying with me. You'll love her, I promise, and she's also an amazing cook."

Meadows looked uncertain, peering out into the darkness as though he expected Chambers to suddenly materialise in front of him. Claire stood up, resting a reassuring hand on his arm. "It'll be fine, honestly; if it's a problem I'll tell Chambers I insisted you come into the house because I felt better protected that way."

Meadows grinned. "Okay, you win; I am starving, if I'm honest, seems like days since I've last eaten."

"You and me both," said Claire.

*

She woke with a start. A horrible dream: when she shut her eyes she could still see its remnants, unfurling slowly in front of her, the stillborn face of her first child morphing into Toby's face, his eyes wide open but unseeing. Other images appeared: a river or a lake, a dark shape rising upwards, a cauldron of bubbles and foam, something breaking the surface. But what? Toby? What was it? Whatever it was had gone. She opened her eyes again. A warning or premonition? No, she had no belief in the power of dreams; scraps of nonsense to entertain an idling brain. But it was unsettling nonetheless.

She reached for her phone from the bedside table. 8.33 AM. Christ. She had been asleep nearly ten hours. How on earth had she forgotten to set an alarm? Then she remembered: the young constable joining them for a meal, a chicken casserole lovingly prepared by her aunt, the third glass of crisp, chilled Sancerre, them both urging her to get some sleep. She got up and lifted back the curtain so she could peer down into the street. The patrol car had gone. She looked again at her phone: two missed calls from Chambers. Her aunt must have put her phone on silent. When she rang back, Chambers picked up immediately.

"Claire, how are you? I'm so sorry about your son; is he alright? What did the hospital say?"

"I don't know, they think he's okay. I hope to God he is, anyway. What about Turner? Have you managed to find him?"

"No, no, he's gone to ground. We will find him, though, Claire, I promise."

Claire felt a surge of anger. Why was it taking so long? It couldn't have been that difficult to track him down. "Why did you remove Meadows then? The threat's not gone away, has it? He's still out there."

"I didn't have a choice with Meadows; it wasn't my decision; I was asked to stand him down. I had a huge row about it. To be honest, Claire, you didn't exactly help your cause by sneaking out on Peterson like that. That was the first thing thrown at me and it was difficult to argue with."

Claire sighed. "Alright, well, what now?"

"I assume you'll be travelling back to the hospital this morning?"

"Yes."

"Right. Well, be careful. Can someone go with you? I don't like the idea of you being on your own, not until we find this bastard, anyway."

"My aunt will probably want to come in with me, but that's to see Toby, not to act as a bodyguard. The poor woman's in her sixties."

"No, I understand. Look, just be very, very careful. I'm worried about you. I'll ring you as soon as I get any more news."

Chambers rang off and for a moment Claire sat on the edge of her bed, staring blankly at the floor. It had been an unsettling phone call. The threat from Turner was obviously a very real one and Chambers' concern had only succeeded in making her own anxiety much worse. Having hurriedly dressed, she found her aunt sitting at the kitchen table nursing a cup of tea.

"How are you, love?" Brenda said. "Are you feeling better?"

"Much better, thanks, although I've never been so tired. You should still have woken me up, though, I need to get back to the hospital. I only meant to come away for a couple of hours."

"You were exhausted and definitely in no fit state to drive. Ollie told me about what happened on the A14; you could have been killed."

"Ollie?"

"Oliver, darling, the policeman who was here last night."

"You two obviously hit it off, then."

"He was a very nice young man. If I was forty years younger…"

Claire said nothing for a moment, staring out into the garden. She remembered the shadow she had seen near the summerhouse. Was that Turner? She looked back at her aunt.

"I should have been with Toby; I shouldn't have left—"

"Claire," said her aunt firmly. "You needed some rest; you'd be no use to Toby if you were dead now, would you?"

"But he was on his own…"

"Kate stayed with him; he was fine."

"She can't have stayed all night—"

"She most certainly did; she rang the house phone just after you'd gone up to see how you were and we had a long conversation. Toby's fine, so don't worry. I gave Kate my mobile number and she texted me this morning."

"You win," said Claire wearily. "Are you sure he's alright?"

"Very. Stop worrying."

"I'm going to give Pete a ring, see if he'll come in with me. Chambers thinks there's still a threat, thinks I need someone."

"Yes, well, that should be their job, shouldn't it? They shouldn't have taken Ollie away."

"Pete's ex-police and he's a friend. To be frank, and notwithstanding your high regard for Ollie, I think he'll do a better job anyway."

"Well, if Pete can't do it, I could go with you."

"No, if he can't do it, I'll go in on my own; I don't want to risk putting you in harm's way."

Brenda stood up and Claire noticed for the first time that she was wearing the same faded blue dressing gown she had worn in the hospital. She had a flashback to her mud-caked pyjamas and an image of the pond suddenly rose up, black, the moon glinting off its surface, her aunt falling to her knees, screaming.

"Are you alright?" said Brenda. "You look—"

"I'm fine, suddenly felt a bit dizzy again."

Her aunt moved closer and slowly stroked her hair. "Are you sure you're able to drive? You still look tired."

"I'll be fine. I'll give Pete a ring; if he is around then I could get him to drive anyway. I'll get him to come here and then we can go in his car."

"Sounds like a plan. Now, let's get some tea down you. I'll put the kettle on. Can I do you some breakfast as well? Toast? Scrambled eggs? That powdered muck you eat with raisins and nuts?"

"Toast is fine, I don't think I can manage anything else, my stomach's too upset really. It's not been right for days."

"Hardly surprising. Hopefully there's some bread left; Ollie must have got through half a loaf."

*

The call to Hamlin went through to voicemail. She left a message for him to ring her and he called back just as she was settling herself into her car.

"Claire? How are you? Sorry, I missed your call, I was in the garden doing battle with an overgrown hedge. Almost fell off the bloody ladder—"

"You do realise how many injuries A&E see each year from pensioners falling off ladders?"

"Not you as well; my wife's already been bending my ear about it."

"Well, she's right, you need to be more careful."

"Point taken. Next time I'll get her to go up the ladder. Now, back to my original question: how are you? I've been worried about you."

"I need a huge favour, Pete, and I hope to God you're free."

"Why? What's happened?"

She hurriedly explained the events of the last few days, Toby's kidnapping by Turner and near drowning, and the offer of round-the-clock protection by the police, now withdrawn.

"I don't know Chambers, but I do know Peterson; he's a decent bloke, good at his job. Look, wait there and I'll come over now – should be with you in half an hour and then we can go in together."

"Thanks, you're a star."

*

Claire had gone back into the house to wait for Hamlin, and it was her aunt who opened the door to him when he arrived. It was her startled cry she heard first.

"Pete, what on earth have you done to yourself?"

"Oh, it's nothing, just a few cuts and bruises."

She hurried into the hallway. Hamlin had grazes across his nose and a deep cut on his lip. Worse, he was holding his hand awkwardly against his side. "Pete, are you alright? What happened?"

"Well," he said ruefully, "when I said 'almost fell' that wasn't entirely accurate. I didn't want to worry you. I'm fine, honestly."

As Claire hugged him he visibly winced with pain. She looked down, noticing for the first time how swollen his hand was. "God, Pete, you have done yourself some damage. Are you sure you're in a fit state to drive? You should have told me; I could have gone in on my own. You didn't need to do this."

"I'm fine, really; look, let's go. I've had a lot worse than this, believe me."

"Show me your hand first; it looks swollen."

Reluctantly, he lifted his arm and, very gently, Claire examined his hand. It was badly swollen, dark bruising having appeared where the blood had haemorrhaged beneath the skin. She turned it over to examine his palm, where bruising was also visible. "Oh, Pete, what have you done? You'll need an x-ray to confirm it, but the bruising on your palm almost certainly means you've broken at least one bone in your hand. You can't possibly drive like this."

"I managed it coming here."

"Well, I'm not going to let you drive to the hospital; we can go in my car."

"But—"

"No, Pete, you can't drive with that hand. I'll take us and when we get there we're going to have to get you sorted out in A&E as well; someone needs to look at that hand. When you fell, you didn't hit your head or anything, did you? Now you've got me worried about concussion as well."

"No, the head's fine; it was my arm and shoulder took most of the blow. Fell on my side. The cuts to my face are from a bloody rose bush. My wife's not too happy about that, either, says I've completely ruined it."

"I doubt that; roses are pretty indestructible. Whereas you—"

"I could drive you," said Brenda. "Neither of you look right to me and I think I'd be happier if I came with you anyway."

"No, it's really kind of you but I'll drive," said Claire. "Better if you stay here and hold the fort."

"Are you sure? I really don't mind—"

"Absolutely."

"I managed to get hold of Peterson, by the way," said Hamlin. "I rang him on the way over."

"And?" said Claire.

"He told me some very interesting stuff about Turner."

"Really? Okay, well, don't tell me now; save it for the journey." She turned, grabbing her car keys from the hall table. "Come on, we need to get moving."

CHAPTER FIFTY-FIVE

"So, what did you find out?"

"In short – he's quite an unpleasant character. Convicted of harassment five years ago against his previous wife, for which he got a suspended twelve-month sentence. Married a second time, and then the RTA accident I told you about which killed his poor wife but which the baby, Alice, survived."

"At the autopsy didn't you say he was something in the City?"

"Yeah, works as a risk analyst at one of the big insurance firms, apparently."

"This conviction – you said it was harassment. What exactly did he do?"

"Psychological abuse, controlling behaviour, the usual, really. Subtle at first, then increasingly nasty. The harassment started once she'd found the courage to leave him and that's when the police finally got involved."

"A real charmer, then."

"Clearly."

*

As she pushed through the ward door, Claire noticed immediately that there had been a significant change since her last visit – Toby was sitting up in bed looking very much awake. Not only that, he was smiling, clearly amused by something Kate had said to him.

"Toby!" cried Claire, almost breaking into a run as she quickened her pace towards him.

"Mummy!"

She bent over him, wanting desperately to pick him up and hug him tightly to her chest. It was her fear of hurting him which stopped her and, kneeling, she contented herself instead with clasping her hand gently behind his head and kissing him lightly on the forehead. "How are you, my darling?" she murmured. "How are you feeling?"

"I want to go home. Can I go home? I don't like it here."

"Yes, of course, of course you can come home… I just need to speak to the doctors first, is that alright?"

"Why do you need to talk to them?"

"I – I just want to make sure you're well enough, darling."

"I am well enough – I had breakfast!" he announced triumphantly.

"Did you? And what did you have for breakfast?"

"Coco Pops."

"Coco Pops – your favourite. They are spoiling you."

"When can I go home?"

Claire turned to Kate. "Have you spoken to anyone? Has the consultant been to see him?"

"Yes, she looked in on him first thing this morning; I think she'd just come on shift. She was nice, I liked her."

"What did she say?"

"Well, I had to push her a little because she wanted to know who I was, but she said he seemed to have made a very good recovery. She asked if you were coming in later and I said you were, so she said she'd pop by again during her rounds to have a chat with you."

"Did she give a time?"

"No, 'fraid not."

"That's okay, I'll ask one of the station nurses, I'm sure they'll know." Claire smiled and stood up.

Hamlin had been standing awkwardly to one side. Kate had clocked his injuries immediately he had walked in, but it was only now she felt able to ask him about them. "Pete, what's happened to your poor face? You look as though you've just done ten rounds with Mike Tyson."

"Rose bush," Hamlin replied. "Fell off a ladder this morning whilst doing some pruning. Thought I'd give the rose bush a closer inspection on the way down."

"Oh Pete, you poor thing. Are you sure you're alright?"

"He needs to go to A&E," said Claire grimly. "I think he's broken a bone in his hand; he really needs an x-ray."

"Can I see it?" said Kate.

Hamlin gingerly raised his arm and Kate carefully took the injured hand in hers. "God, that's really swollen, Pete, I think Claire's right – you've definitely broken something."

"Can I see?" said Toby, peering over anxiously.

"Of course you can," said Hamlin, and held his hand out for Toby to inspect.

"Don't touch it, darling," warned Claire, "because it's very painful and you don't want to hurt him."

"You need a hospital," giggled Toby.

"Lucky I'm here, then," Hamlin replied.

"In all seriousness, Pete, I think you need to get yourself down to A&E and have that looked at," said Claire.

"But I can't leave you – I thought you said…"

"I'm with Kate and nothing's going to happen while I'm here, is it? Look, you get yourself off and just pop back when you're finished," said Claire.

"Have you seen how long the waiting times are in A&E; I'm sure I don't—"

"Come on, Pete, don't be silly, you need to get it seen to – we'll be fine, honestly."

"Well, if you're sure."

"Claire's right, Pete – to be honest, you're not much good like that to us anyway. I think I might do a better job in a fight than you."

"Charming – okay, you win. I'll come back as soon as I'm able. If they let Toby out, can you come and find me before you leave, at least?"

"Yes, of course we will. You'd be stuck here without a car, anyway."

"True enough," he sighed.

Once he had left the ward, Claire turned to Kate. "Have you been here all night?"

"Yes – it wasn't too bad, sleep anywhere, me. One of the nurses took pity on me and brought me a pillow and blanket."

"But you still had to sleep in a chair."

"Well, I thought about giving Toby the chair whilst I took his bed, but he wasn't having any of it."

"You could have had it," said Toby. "I wouldn't have minded."

"That's really sweet of you, but I think you needed it more than me. I also don't think the nurses and doctors would have been impressed with me tipping you out of your bed."

"Do you need to go back and hold the fort?" asked Claire.

"No, I'm fine for a bit. I spoke to Mark and he's promised to cover for us. Your next autopsy isn't until tomorrow anyway."

"Has Ballantyne been around?"

"No, not a sniff."

"Good, let's hope it stays that way."

"Look, you stay here, Claire, with Toby and I'll get us some coffee. Might even stretch to a croissant if they do anything that exotic."

"You should manage it – there's a Costa and a Starbucks downstairs. You could even pop into the M&S outlet and get the croissants there – probably cheaper, too."

"Sounds like a plan. Toby, would you like anything?" said Kate.

"Do they have chocolate?" asked Toby.

"Hmm, not sure. I think so. I'll see what I can dig up. Are you sure you wouldn't prefer a nice piece of fruit? A nice juicy apple, perhaps, or a banana?"

"I want chocolate."

"Course you do," said Kate, winking at Claire.

There was a sound of footsteps in the corridor outside and the door opened: Raynor, followed by two medical students, a young woman with a drawn, anxious face and a man who looked as though he had yet to start shaving, his cheeks decorated with angry pustules of acne and a fine peach fuzz. Both were much taller than Raynor, as was Claire herself. She noticed as Raynor bent over Toby to examine him that her fine, dark hair was threaded with silver and her pink scalp was clearly visible in small patches just above one of her ears and nearer the crown. Alopecia? Poor woman. Self-consciously, she swept a hand through her own hair. It hadn't been washed in days. She couldn't even remember if she had bothered to drag a comb through it that morning before leaving.

"Well, young man, how are you feeling?" smiled Raynor. Toby blushed and grinned back; he was obviously fond of her.

"Can I go home? I'm not sick anymore."

"Let's just have a quick look at you and then we'll see what's possible," replied Raynor. "Lift up your top for me, my lovely, and we'll just have a quick listen to your chest."

My lovely was a quaint phrase, Claire thought. Cornish? There was a distinct lilt to her accent. She suddenly noticed that Toby was wearing his starfish pyjamas, the bright red

314

hair of the Little Mermaid vivid against his chest. Yesterday he had been wearing a shapeless blue hospital gown. Brenda must have brought the pyjamas in for him. *The Little Mermaid*: how many times had she cradled him in her arms as they sat watching endless re-runs? "Again!" Toby would shout. "Again, Mummy, again!" She still knew by heart the lyrics to every song in the film. She closed her eyes momentarily. Tired, she felt so tired.

Kate nudged her. "Are you alright?" she whispered.

Claire opened her eyes. "Yes, fine," she murmured. "Just a little tired."

Raynor had bent Toby forward and was now listening intently to a stethoscope pressed against his back.

"It's cold," said Toby.

"Yes, it is a little, I'm afraid," said Raynor. "Now, take a deep breath for me. Yes, that's great. Can you give a little cough? Perfect. One more time. Yes, that's fine." She stood up. "You're a little bit wheezy still, but nothing really to worry about. There might be a little bit of an infection, so I'll write a script for some antibiotics." She turned to Claire. "Has he had antibiotics before? Do you know if he's allergic at all?"

"No, no, he's not – he had a very bad chest infection when he was a baby, and they gave him penicillin then."

"Good. Right, Toby, I just need to take your temperature." She gently placed a thermometer in his mouth, waited a few seconds, and then withdrew it. "36.4."

Toby beamed. "Is that good?"

Raynor smiled back. "It's better than good – it's perfect."

"I'm perfect, Mummy."

"Absolutely, darling, completely perfect."

"Can I go home now?"

"Do you know, I think you can," said Raynor.

Claire hesitated. "Did you do a second scan?"

"Yes, we did one last night. It was fine, Claire, the swelling we picked up before seems to have gone down and there were no other abnormalities."

Claire felt a wave of relief. "So, I can take him home?"

"Yes. I need to write up a discharge letter but, hopefully, I should be able to give you a copy of that this afternoon."

"But I want to go home now," said Toby.

Claire knelt again by his bedside and covered his small hand with her own. "It won't be long, darling, honestly – just a couple of hours, no time at all, really."

"Right," said Kate, "I'm going to get those coffees." She turned to the doctors. "Since I'm going down anyway, do any of you want anything? Coffee? Tea?"

"No, no, we're fine," Raynor replied. "We'll get something later. It's difficult juggling drinks when you're trying to examine patients."

"Yes, of course. Shouldn't be long, anyway, and I'll also try to remember to get you that chocolate, Toby."

"Yes, please." Then a pause and a sly smile. "Can I have some Haribo as well?"

Claire laughed. "Well, you obviously are feeling a lot better.

You can have chocolate or Haribo, Toby, but not both."

"Toby!" said Kate with mock astonishment. "You couldn't have both – all your teeth will fall out."

"They won't," giggled Toby.

"They will too," said Kate. "I ate too many sweets when I was your age and now all my teeth are gone."

"No, they're not – I can see them in your mouth."

"But these aren't real," said Kate, opening her mouth wide enough for him to see and tapping one of her front teeth with a fingernail. "These are plastic. See, hear that sound? Completely plastic."

Toby laughed. "I don't believe you."

"Well, when we get you home, I'll take them out and show you."

"Eugh!" grimaced Toby.

"Exactly," said Kate. "Completely yuck. So, which is it? Haribo or chocolate?"

"Chocolate! No, Haribo!"

"Haribo it is, then," she said, giving a mock bow. "Sugar heaven. Might even have some myself."

*

It was late afternoon when Toby was finally allowed to leave. Kate had gone back to the office for a few hours to catch up on her work, but re-joined them in the afternoon. Hamlin also reappeared after lunch, having endured a long and tedious wait in A&E waiting to be seen. An x-ray revealed he had indeed broken a bone in his hand. Claire rose to greet him.

"So, there was a break then?" she said. "I see they've given you a cast."

"Apparently it's a scaphoid fracture," said Hamlin. "Very common among the old and infirm and incorrigibly stupid."

"How long will you have to keep it on for? asked Kate.

"Six to twelve sodding weeks, apparently."

"Poor you," said Kate.

"It's not the cast I mind, it's the stick I'm going to get from my wife. I was supposed to make a start on clearing out the loft tomorrow."

"Don't suppose you'll be playing golf for a while either," smiled Claire.

"This retirement lark is starting to get me down," said Hamlin. "I've had more accidents since I retired than during my entire policing career."

Kate grinned. "Obviously a death wish; you've unconsciously already decided to check out."

Hamlin eyed her warily. "Are there any more like you at home?"

"No, 'fraid not – I'm an only child."

"Can't think why," said Hamlin.

"I think you two are worse than children," laughed Claire. "I'm beginning to think Toby is more sensible than the two of you put together."

"Well, that's charming, isn't it, Kate? After all we've done for her," said Hamlin.

"Tell me about it," said Kate. "I think I've broken my back sitting in that chair all night. I'd have been more comfortable sleeping on the pavement."

"Enough already," said Claire. She turned to Toby, still propped up in his bed. "Do you think you feel well enough to walk, Toby?"

He shook his head.

"Don't worry, I'll talk to one of the nurses, see if they can sort something out," said Kate. There was a nurses' station at the far end of the ward and Kate now walked across to it. A nurse looked up from writing her notes as she approached. "Hi," said Kate. "Is there a wheelchair we might use? Sorry, we're just about to leave, but my friend's son is still a little poorly, so he's not really up to walking."

The nurse smiled. "Yes, of course, I'll ring one of the porters and ask them to bring one up. It's Toby, isn't it? He's so sweet. We were all so worried about him when they brought him in, but he's made an amazing recovery. You must be so relieved – I can't begin to imagine how stressful it must have been for you all."

"Yes, it's been pretty grim, I must admit."

A cheerful porter appeared wheeling a small wheelchair especially adapted for children, and with Claire's help they quickly settled Toby into it. It took several minutes to make their way down to the hospital's main entrance and then finally into the cold lobby area of the car park. Claire knew she was far too exhausted to risk driving so, as they stood waiting for the lift, she asked Kate to do the honours. Hamlin wasn't convinced either of them was up to it and offered to drive himself, but his offer was swiftly rejected by both women.

"No, Pete," said Claire firmly. "I think you're still a bit shaky from that accident and I don't fancy watching you driving one-handed, either."

"I'm happy to drive," said Kate. "Pete can keep Toby company in the back."

They were still standing in the dully lit lobby area of the hospital's car park. Claire had left her phone on silent and now she felt it suddenly vibrate. It was a voicemail message from Sean. Sighing heavily, she hit the voicemail icon. His voice sounded clipped, angry.

Claire, please ring me back as soon as you get this. You promised regular updates on how Toby's doing, but so far I've had fuck all from you. I'm stuck up here another day and then I'm driving down. Ring me.

She pressed the "bin" icon.

Fuck… Fuck!

"Are you alright?" said Kate. "You look—"

Claire stared at her. Then she collapsed, her head slamming down hard against the concrete floor.

CHAPTER FIFTY-SIX

Kate screamed. "Claire!"

Hamlin dropped to his knees beside Claire's slumped form. She was lying on her back and he could already see a slowly spreading corona of blood around her head. She was so still. He bent lower, so he could check her breathing. Her breath against his ear was gossamer light, scarcely there at all. He gently rested his index and middle finger against the carotid artery in her neck. There was a very faint pulse. He stood up too quickly and, dizzy, staggered backwards against the car. Alarmed, fearing he too was about to faint, Kate grabbed his arm to try and steady him. Toby had already been installed in the car seat at the rear of the car, the door still half open. He had seen his mother fall and his voice was now one long continuous squeal of terror. Kate climbed into the car beside him and shut the door, hoping the combination of that and her own body was sufficient to block his view. She cradled his body with hers and desperately tried to calm him down, but his choking sobs were now convulsing his entire body. She hugged him more fiercely. "Shush, love, shush, shush, Mummy's fine, Mummy's fine. Don't worry, don't worry, she's fine."

Hamlin groped in the pocket of his jacket for his phone and dialled 999. It was answered immediately: a cool, unhurried, male voice.

"Hello? Emergency services. Which service do you require?"

"I need an ambulance, a friend has fallen and banged her head, she's unconscious."

"Okay, just putting you through now."

There was a brief silence, then a new voice. "Ambulance service – how can we help?"

"A friend has fallen and hit her head badly – she's unconscious so—"

"Have you checked her breathing?"

"Yes, yes, I just did that – she's breathing, I think, and I also checked her pulse. It's very faint, her head's bleeding."

"Right, and how is she lying?"

"On her back, but I can't put her in the recovery position because, well, I'm frightened it will make her worse if I try and move her."

"No, please don't try and move her; with a head injury it's important you keep her head as still as possible. Can you give us your location?"

"We're at the hospital, Addenbrookes, in the main car park, fourth floor."

"Sorry? Did you say you're already at the hospital?"

"Yes, we came in to take her son home. She's fallen in the car park."

"Okay, understood. Look, I'll speak to A&E there and see if they can get someone up to you, but we'll also send an ambulance. Can you give me your number in case we get cut off and I have to ring back?"

"Yes, of course. It's 07700 788436. Do you want me to repeat that?"

"Yes, if you don't mind, sir."

He repeated the number. The call handler told Hamlin he would stay on the phone until help arrived and asked him to check her breathing and pulse again. The results were the same: shallow, barely perceptible breaths and a thin, thready pulse. He was still feeling lightheaded. Adrenalin had kicked in when he saw her fall but now, he was starting to feel increasingly tired. He nodded at Kate through the glass and did a thumbs-up to indicate help was on its way. He gave what he hoped was a reassuring smile, but it failed to reach his eyes. She looked anxiously back at him, her eyes blurred by tears.

Now all they could do was wait, Hamlin's gaze moving between Claire and the entrance doors at the far end of their level each time he heard them bang open. The first time it was a woman with a pushchair, dragging a small reluctant child behind her. Then a man who glanced briefly towards them, hesitated, as though deciding whether he should come across to offer help, but who then, head down, turned off to his left. Hamlin saw him re-emerge moments later from between a bank of cars further down on their row, cross to his own vehicle and then hurriedly drive away. Kate had also seen the man circle round and Hamlin gave her a sour smile, shaking his head in disgust.

Hamlin looked up as he heard the entrance doors bang open again. He felt a wave of relief as he saw two paramedics, wheeling a stretcher trolley between them, hurry towards him.

CHAPTER FIFTY-SEVEN

She woke up. For a moment she struggled to work out where she was. She was in semi-darkness; somewhere in the space around her something was making a strange bleeping noise. There was a soft murmuring of voices, but it was hard to distinguish either its direction or what was being said. As her sight adjusted to the darkness, in the periphery of her vision she could just make out the shapes of two people. Nurses. One sat down at a desk in a partitioned area a little distance away, the other was standing. Whispers. A suppressed giggle. So, a hospital ward. But why? She struggled to think, suddenly aware of a dull pain pulsing just behind her eyes. She tried shifting her head, but the pain increased. Groaning, she stopped, lying still as she waited for it to recede.

She remembered. She had regained consciousness briefly whilst still lying on the ground in the car park. A man she didn't recognise was kneeling at her side. She didn't recognise him, but she did recognise his clothing, a hi-vis green and yellow response jacket. A paramedic. There had been a woman, too. She hadn't seen her face, but she remembered her voice: gentle, reassuring. It must have been her hands cradling her head as her colleague leant over to fit a neck collar. Then what? Nothing. She couldn't remember anything after that. She must have blacked out. Toby? Where was Toby? Her heart raced as she struggled to remember. No, no, it was okay; Kate was there. She'd have looked after him. Pete, too; he had also been there. *Calm down. You need to calm down.* The malignant throbbing in her head ratcheted up again as she continued trying to piece together what had happened. She forced herself to take some deep breaths. The pain in her skull slowly subsided. So, a head injury, but how bad was it? Bad enough for her to have been hospitalised. They must have done an x-ray. Then a scan looking for evidence of brain trauma. She remembered she had been violently sick. Almost choked on her own vomit. They'd had to apply a suction tube to clear her airway. Even now there was a faint taste of bile at the back of her mouth, a rawness in her throat.

She closed her eyes. Rest. She needed to rest.

*

When she woke again it was daylight. Hamlin's was the first face she saw. He was standing looking down, the hint of a smile, his eyes anxious, searching.

"How do you feel?" he murmured.

How *do* I feel? She did a rapid mental checklist. The pain in her head had gone. Her neck felt stiff, but otherwise, she felt fine. Restored. Whole again.

"Better," she said. Her voice a soft croak. "Sorry,

thirsty… my mouth feels like the Sahara Desert. Can you get me some water?"

There was a jug of water on the bedside table, and he poured some from this into a small plastic beaker.

"Are you able to lift your head a little so I can—"

"Yes, I think so. Hold on, I think I might be able to sit up."

She slowly eased herself into a sitting position and held out her hand to take the cup. She took a tentative sip. There was a refreshing coolness at the back of her throat as the liquid slid down. Then she drank greedily, emptying the cup, and handed it back to Hamlin.

"Thanks, I needed that. How long have you been here?"

"Not long, about an hour, I think, long enough to read the paper and complete today's crossword."

"So, what happened? How did I get here?"

"You fainted in the car park, hit your head on the ground. It was quite scary, to be honest; we were worried you'd fractured your skull. You came down with quite a thump and you were bleeding pretty badly from a head wound."

She grimaced. "Sorry to put you through all that. Still, at least it explains the blinding headache when I woke up." She paused. "Who's looking after Toby?"

"Your aunt and Kate – she stayed over at your place last night." He gave her a shrewd, enquiring look. "She's very fond of you, Kate. You too have obviously become quite close."

She looked away, noticed a faded brown spot of blood on the white sheet covering her. Hers or another patient's?

"Kate's an absolute star," she said.

"Yes," said Hamlin. "Yes, she is."

"Is Toby alright? I must have given him quite a scare."

"He's fine. I rang Kate as I was driving in and I could hear him giggling in the background. He saw you fall so it was a bit rough for a while last night. Kate took him home and I stayed here to make sure you were alright."

"You weren't here all last night, were you?"

"No," he smiled. "I'm not that fond of you – I left here around eleven."

"Oh, Pete, you've been so good to me, I don't know what—" Her voice caught. Tears filled her eyes. He reached across and held her hand.

"You mean the world to me, Claire, always have done." He teared up too, and quickly looked away, embarrassed.

"Christ, Pete, I've just remembered – Sean left a voicemail message for me and I didn't get back to him. He'll have been going mental. My phone – where's my phone?"

"I put it in the drawer for you. I put it on silent, though, didn't want you disturbed during the night."

She leaned across, opened the drawer. Her handbag lay on its side and she lifted it out, hurriedly pulling the zip open so she could retrieve her phone. She gazed at it in dismay. Five missed calls from Sean and two more voicemail messages, the last one left not twenty minutes earlier. "Fuck," she said softly. "The bastard's been phoning me all night."

"Leave it, Claire, fuck him. He shouldn't have left Toby and you in the first place. Let him sweat."

"No, I need to ring him. Pete, can you give me some space? I need to…"

"Yeah, of course." He was already getting to his feet. "Look, I'll walk down and get us both some coffee—"

"Thanks, Pete. I don't think I'll be on the phone very long anyway. Hopefully, he won't pick up and I can just leave him a voicemail message."

"That'd be best," said Hamlin. "If he starts acting out, just cut him off." He pointed to his genitals, grinned and walked away. Claire smiled, shaking her head in mock disapproval, and watched as he turned away and, seconds later, disappeared through the ward doors. She didn't bother listening to the voicemail messages. They would be vile anyway and if she did that then she wouldn't find the courage to ring him. She brought up her "Favourites" screen. How ironic he should still be listed there. Even more ironic that he was the first name in the display. She pressed down on his name, lifted the phone to her ear. There was a brief ringing tone as the connection was made, then he picked up.

CHAPTER FIFTY-EIGHT

"Claire, at long *last*. Good of you to phone."

"Fuck off, Sean. You have no idea what I've been through – if you were so concerned you should have stayed here rather than fucking off back to Scotland."

"Nice, very classy, Claire. So, how is he? How is *my* son?"

Her anger rose further; how dare he assume sole proprietorship, reducing her role to that of an unpaid child minder?

"What makes you so sure he's yours?" she hissed.

He gave a short, bitter laugh. "Even classier, Claire. You really are a piece of work, aren't you? Cut the crap – just tell me how he is before I really lose my temper."

She went to hit "end" on the call, her finger poised over the display. She hesitated. He might be a complete bastard, but he still deserved to know how Toby was, she owed him that much. "He's fine," she snapped. He started to reply but this time she did end the call. Shaking with anger, she threw the phone down on the bed. A nurse had been standing further down the ward, ostensibly checking another patient's notes, but clearly a witness to the whole thing. Claire caught her eye, blushing with embarrassment. The nurse walked down towards her.

"Are you okay?"

"Yes – my ex," she said, and gave a rueful smile. She studied the nurse; she looked careworn too, with dark circles under her eyes, her blonde hair pushed back behind her ears.

"No need to explain. I divorced two years ago."

"Do you have children?" asked Claire.

"A girl, Charlotte. She'll be four next week, starts reception in September."

"My son, Toby, is about the same age; well, he's four in October, actually, which means he won't start school until next year." She heard herself say *my* son – wasn't she herself guilty of exactly what she had accused Sean of? No, he knew what he was doing when he used that phrase. For her it was just a figure of speech. Except it wasn't, was it? Toby was her son; she had carried him for nine months in her womb, given birth in a primeval haze of pain and fear, fed him at her breast, nursed him during the night while Sean slept, his only contribution the occasional fart as he tossed and turned. What had he done really? What had any man done? Spilled their seed in a spasm of mindless lust – how did that give them the right to claim ownership, to stake a claim in a child's existence? Women brought new life into the world. All too often, men simply took it away.

She became aware that the nurse was staring at her. "Are you alright? she asked. "You went into a bit of a trance there."

"Sorry, just very tired."

"Understandable. Can I get you anything? A cup of tea or coffee?"

"No, no, I'm fine."

There was a low moan of pain from a patient in a bed at the far end of the ward and they both turned to look. An elderly woman lying on her back, lank grey hair concealing much of her face. The nurse gave Claire an apologetic smile and hurried away. Claire watched as she busied herself at the woman's bed, first talking to her in a low voice and then moving to replace the bag for what she guessed was a saline drip. She sighed, put her phone on silent and, shutting her eyes, curled into a foetal position, dragging the duvet over her face to shut out the light.

CHAPTER FIFTY-NINE

A month had passed since Toby's accident, but still the police had failed to locate or arrest Turner. Chambers said he was managing to elude them by living off-grid; he had stopped using credit cards and his mobile phone was either switched off or he had got rid of it. It would have been relatively simple for him to acquire a new one and a new number. This was not the behaviour of your average criminal, but Turner was undoubtedly intelligent and these days, she said, it only took the briefest of searches on Google to work out precisely what was needed to prevent the police tracking you.

The police's lack of success in finding Turner had ratcheted up Claire's anxiety levels to a point where she found it impossible to live a remotely normal life. As the days morphed into weeks, though, she did finally relax, believing Turner had given up under the pressure of the police pursuit, perhaps even fleeing abroad. She bought a dog, a honey-coloured cockapoo she called Molly, who soon became a devoted companion. Sean hated dogs and with hindsight she felt she should have seen that as a red flag. Her greatest joy now was to take Molly out on Portholme Meadow, a vast expanse of flood meadow and grassland bordered on two sides by the Great Ouse. In winter, such was the volume of water sometimes covering it that it almost resembled an inland sea, waves conjured by the fierce east winds sweeping across it. In the spring and summer, though, it was a dog-walkers' paradise.

She had applied to the court to restrict Sean's access to Toby to a single two-hour supervised visit each week. Recognising the trauma both she and her son had been through and the need to keep him safe, it had readily agreed to this. The court had also noted that Sean was unwilling to move back from Scotland and as such, in practical terms, more frequent access would be difficult in any case.

And so it was that every Saturday, Sean would make the long journey south to spend time with Toby at her aunt's house, with Brenda supervising the visit. Claire wanted nothing to do with him. Any love she once might have felt had been swallowed up in a bitter hatred and it seemed the feeling was mutual. What she hadn't realised was just how deep Sean's hatred really was.

CHAPTER SIXTY

I t was early morning. Dawn had not long broken, and the sunrise had soaked the sky in vivid reds and oranges, grey wisps of cloud tinged with purple. Mist was still rising off the river and there was a magical stillness, only slightly marred by the distant drone of the traffic on the A14, which hummed past on an elevated section of the road bordering the meadow. It was Claire's favourite time of day, a golden hour in which much of the world had yet to stir. She crossed over the lock bridge with Molly at her side and then, as she usually did, began to make her way left along the riverbank. She let Molly off her lead and watched as she raced away towards a pheasant she had spotted walking, wobble-headed, across the grass. In the scrubby ash and buckthorn trees edging the river she could glimpse sparrows nestling in the branches, their grey feathers puffed out against the cold.

Her reverie was suddenly broken by a shout. She turned towards it. Sean. Sean had come though the lock gate and was running towards her. She stopped and waited for him. Molly, alerted by the shout, sat down on her haunches some thirty feet away, looking nervously towards them. Claire had not seen him since her stay in hospital and their final grim phone call. She had blocked his number and insisted through her solicitor that all further contact was mediated through his own lawyer. Now he stood in front of her, unshaven, a wild look in his eyes.

"What do you want, Sean?" she said coldly.

"I want my son back."

She stared back at him, saw the anger in his eyes, his clenched fists. She was frightened, but refused to show it. "You see him every week."

"I want him to live with me, in Scotland."

"Well, he can't, can he? Look, I've got to go, I have to be at work in an hour and—"

She went to move around him, gesturing for Molly to follow, but as she did, he suddenly grabbed her from behind, wrapping his arms around her and lifting her bodily from the ground. Molly launched herself at him, biting down hard on his calf. He howled with pain and shook his leg trying to dislodge her, but Molly clung on, the low rumble of her growling growing ever louder. Then Claire felt herself falling as he reared backwards, twisting at the last moment to land on top of her as she hit the ground. She grunted with pain and tried to get up. He punched her, the blow glancing off the side of her face, her head exploding with an even fiercer pain, a white blinding light. She felt herself being dragged across the ground towards the river on her back, his hands digging hard beneath her armpits. He stopped. His hand clamped down on her forehead and she felt an icy cold sensation as the back of her head was pushed down into the river. She tried to push his hand away, grabbing it around the wrist, but he was too strong. She reached up, trying to claw his face with her nails, but he twisted his head away out of reach. He pushed harder and her head and shoulders were now completely submerged, her lungs burning as she fought the desperate urge to open her mouth and breathe. She could feel herself fading, her strength ebbing away. Almost in a spasm, she brought her knee up, felt it connect with his groin. The pressure of his hand pushing her down suddenly eased and she lunged upwards, gratefully sucking down huge gasps of air as she cleared the water. She scrambled to her feet. Sean was still lying on his side, his hands between his thighs, groaning softly. She kicked him hard in the face and there was a scrunching sound as her boot connected with his nose, blood spilling out across his cheeks and chin. Molly dived towards him and bit down hard on one of his cheeks, Sean yelping with the pain. Claire kicked him again in the belly and then, exhausted, stood bent over trying to get her breath back.

She looked up. Standing a little distance away was a man, a black and white border collie by his side and barking furiously. He was holding the dog by the collar as he tried to restrain it. In his fifties, she guessed, tall, a full head of grey hair, an almost military bearing.

"Are you alright? I saw the whole thing; I saw what he was trying to do… I ran across but… Look, do you want me to phone the police?"

Sean had begun to stir, trying to lift himself onto an elbow. Claire eyed him warily, Molly standing close by, growling, alert for another opportunity to attack. "Yes, yes, please phone the police."

CHAPTER SIXTY-ONE

"Claire? DI Chambers. Can you talk?"

"Yes, of course. I'm at home, still recovering from yesterday. Still feeling a bit shaky, to be honest."

"It's that I want to talk to you about. We didn't get much out of your husband – sorry, your ex – at the interview. He clammed up straightaway and went down the 'I want a solicitor, no comment' route."

"Predictable, I suppose," said Claire.

"Yes, well, we obtained a warrant to search his flat in Edinburgh. Lothian did the search and they found something very interesting."

Claire felt the hairs rise on the back of her neck. "Interesting? What—"

"You remember the temporary grave marker which went missing? Well, it's turned up – it was buried beneath some socks and underwear in a wardrobe in his flat."

She gasped, incredulous. "What? But why would—?"

"Exactly – why would he? We interviewed him again, presented him with the new evidence and finally, realising the game was up, we got a confession out of him."

"So, why?"

"He said he never intended to physically harm you; the hoax was part of a plan to provoke another psychotic episode. He wanted you sectioned again – that way he could persuade the courts to give him custody of Toby."

"That bastard, the complete and utter bastard."

"Yes, not very nice, is it?"

She suddenly remembered. "Wait, my medication went missing when Sean came down, just after Toby was abducted. He must have taken it, hoping it would provoke an episode before I had time to get another prescription."

"Yes, that would make sense."

"But what about Toby's abduction? Was he involved in that as well? Did he conspire with Turner to kidnap Toby?"

"No, no, we don't think so. We put that to him, but he denied it, and to be fair, we haven't been able to find any evidence of any contact between the two. We've searched his laptop, desktop and phone and found nothing, no phone numbers, messages, emails – zilch."

"Okay, but there's something else I don't understand. Sean was away on a golfing trip in Portugal when that funeral card was delivered so how could—?"

"We asked him about that. He came back a day early, which also explains how he managed to remove the grave marker in the gap between you leaving the cemetery and then returning."

"I'm sorry, I still don't understand; I picked him up from

the airport. He couldn't possibly have—"

"It wasn't that difficult. He took a taxi back to the airport so he could then meet up with you. Paid cash to cover his trail."

There was a silence as Claire struggled to take this in. "That bastard. I just can't believe he went to such lengths to deceive me."

"Well, it was useful for him because it also set up a possible alibi."

"But wouldn't it have fallen apart as soon as you started to look into it? His mates would have told you when they all came back and then there would be CCTV footage at the airport. How could he have got away with it?"

"True, but why would anyone have questioned the alibi in the first place? You certainly wouldn't, because you picked him up from the airport and until we found the marker, there was no real reason for us to challenge it either. We thought we were looking at an assault; it was only afterwards we realised what he'd really been up to."

Claire sighed. She felt an enormous weariness descend. So much had happened. How could she ever trust anyone ever again? "Alright," she said slowly, "what happens with Sean now?"

"We're charging him with attempted murder. With luck, and if we can make it stick, he'll get life."

"Will he get bail? Am I still at risk?"

There was a silence before Chambers spoke again. "I'm sorry, Claire, we can try and oppose bail – argue he's a continuing threat – but there's a fair chance it will be granted."

"So, I could be attacked again?"

Another silence. "Look," Chambers said carefully, "I know how difficult all of this is for you… Sean is already facing a charge of attempted murder. Rationally, it would be complete madness for him to compound that with a second attack."

"Yes, but then I wouldn't exactly describe the first attack as rational."

"True. If it was up to me I'd lock the bastard up now and throw away the key."

"Is he in custody now or have you—?"

"He's in custody until the magistrates' hearing on Monday. There'll be an application for bail then, which will probably be granted, and from there the case will go to the Crown Court."

"How long before it goes to trial?"

"Not sure, seems to take longer and longer for cases these days; six to eight months, perhaps more."

"Great. And how do I stop him harassing me in the meantime?"

"If bail is granted, we'll insist that certain conditions apply. He'll have to give up his passport and he won't be allowed to have any contact with either you or your son."

"Are you sure? Can you guarantee that?"

Another silence. "Yes, yes, I think I can guarantee that. Attempted murder is a very serious charge; a judge isn't going to allow contact with the potential victim before the case goes to trial."

Claire could feel her anxiety ramping up despite Chamber's reassurance. "Alright, I'm not happy, but I suppose I just have to suck it up. What about Turner though? Why did he try and kidnap my son?"

"I don't know, Claire. We'll find that out when we find him."

CHAPTER SIXTY-TWO

The night before the magistrates' hearing Claire scarcely slept. It was late afternoon on Monday when Chambers rang again.

"So, how did it go? Did he get bail?"

"Yes, I'm sorry, he did," said Chambers, "but as I predicted, with conditions. He's had to surrender his passport and he's not allowed to have any contact with you or Toby in the period leading up to his trial."

"Well, that's something at least. So, has he been released?"

"Yes, I'm afraid he has."

"And where will he be living?"

Chambers hesitated. "Huntingdon – the address he was staying at when you separated."

"Christ, I thought he wanted to remain in Scotland. It must be a red flag that he now wants to stay down here. It also means I could bump into him just going into town or doing a shop in Sainsbury's. How's that supposed to work?"

"I know. However, if he does make any contact then we can arrest him; he'll end up back in prison on remand until his trial."

Claire sighed. "I'm not happy about this, not happy at all. I may even have to consider moving. I don't want to even glimpse him in a crowd, I just won't feel safe."

"I'm sorry, Claire, I really am, but there's nothing I can do."

"Okay, I understand, it's not your fault and you've been brilliant. This is just so fucked up."

"Yes, it is – completely fucked up."

*

Six days later Chambers rang again, this time with better news. Turner had walked into a police station in Sutton Coldfield and given himself up. Apparently he was simply exhausted and tired of running. He had been kept in a cell overnight and Chambers had driven up with a colleague to interview him the following morning.

"So, why?" said Claire. "Why did he kidnap Toby?"

"He wanted to frighten you, apparently – he wanted revenge after what happened at the trial and then his mum's suicide, but having abducted Toby he immediately realised he'd gone too far. So, he panicked. He knew where your aunt lived because he'd tracked you there before, so he decided to leave him there and run. He wasn't to know Toby was nearly drowned as a result and in fact was horrified when he found out."

Claire sighed. "Okay, I buy that, but what about poor Joan? I still think he was involved in that, despite the fact you've been unable to prove it."

"Ah, well, I do have an update on that. When we interviewed him about it he told us that at the time of the incident he was on a driver awareness course in Birmingham. It was easy to check out – lots of witnesses and his name in the register – so cast-iron really."

"So, we'll never find out what did happen? Whether it was an accident or not? Even if it wasn't him, he could have used an accomplice."

"It's possible, but we think that's very unlikely. London Transport Police carried out a full investigation, but came up blank. The balance of probability is that it was an accident, but we'll never know for certain."

"I still don't get it – if it was an accident, surely the person responsible would have come forward, admitted blame?"

"Not necessarily – might have been too frightened."

"Okay, I give up. Unsolved, then?"

"Yes, unsolved, I'm afraid. Real life tends to be messier than fiction; not everything gets tied up at the end with a neat bow."

From cases Claire had herself been involved with in the past she knew this to be only too true.

"And what happens to Turner now?"

"Kidnap is still a very serious crime and CPS have agreed to prosecute. If convicted, he could get up to twelve years. There are mitigating circumstances though – his mum's suicide, the fact that he only held Toby for a few hours and then let him go. It depends on the judge. It's possible he'll get a suspended sentence, maybe two years suspended, I honestly don't know," said Chambers.

"So, that's it, then?"

"Pretty much."

There was a silence. So much had happened. She closed her eyes, willed herself to speak again. "Thank you for everything you've done. You've been great."

"It's been a pleasure," said Chambers. "An absolute pleasure."

"And I never did find out your first name," said Claire.

"Rosalind, but everyone calls me Ros."

"Rosalind – I like that. Rosalind. I like that a lot."

"I could have been called a lot worse, I suppose. How are you feeling, by the way? I assume you're still anxious about Sean being free."

"Yes, I am, unfortunately. No change there." She hesitated. "I haven't gone into town since we last spoke. I still have to take Molly out for walks, but I've tried to stay as close to the house as possible. I haven't taken poor Molly down to the river since he attacked me, to be honest, and she used to love those walks."

"Yes, well, that's understandable. Look, if you need anything – even if you're just feeling anxious and want to chat – you know I'm here for you."

Claire thanked her and ended the call. It was a Saturday and still early, so she busied herself for a time with humdrum tasks, emptying the dishwasher and hand-washing some of her clothes. Then she settled down with the newspaper and a cup of coffee. She was still feeling tired and, although she tried to concentrate on what she was reading, she found her eyelids getting heavy and closing. She was still holding the cup as she drifted off, and her wrist slackened and turned. Coffee spilled across the newspaper and Claire woke again with a start. She cleaned up as best she could, dumping the soiled remnants of the paper in the bin, and decided to go to bed. Kate was supposed to come round at midday for some lunch. Brenda, bless her, was looking after Toby at her house, having decided to give Claire some 'me' time to recover from her ordeal. She had a free day but now it looked as though most of it would be spent asleep. She texted Kate:

Can we make it two o'clock? Promise I'll cook for us both later. I'm exhausted and need to catnap for a bit. I'll leave the key under the mat.

She added a smiley emoji and pressed send. Moments later, her phone pinged with a response.

No problemo. Get some rest and I'll see you at 2.

Kate accompanied it with an emoji of a bed and some z's spiralling into the air. Smiling to herself, Claire went upstairs, put on pyjamas and climbed into bed. She tried to read a novel she had been looking forward to on her Kindle, but when she found herself repeating the same paragraph for the third time she gave up. Within seconds she was asleep.

When she woke it was to find Kate smiling down at her. "Sorry, I didn't mean to wake you."

"It's fine, I've had a good rest anyway. Just felt so tired."

"Hardly surprising given everything you've been through."

"Chambers rang me by the way – about Turner. He's in custody, gave himself up."

"That's fantastic news – you must be so relieved. So, what are the police saying?"

"That's the thing; he's being prosecuted for kidnap, but because of the circumstances he might just end up with a suspended sentence."

"Sorry, I don't understand; he kidnapped a small child from nursery. Surely that's a custodial sentence?"

"Apparently, there are mitigating circumstances – you know, his mother's suicide, the fact that he only kept Toby for a very short period and then let him go—"

"Almost got him drowned, you mean."

"Yes, but that was an accident. And talking of accidents, the police have decided poor Joan's death was an accident too. There's nothing to link Turner to her death, so that's that as well."

"God. Well, at least it's over."

"Hmm… there's still Sean though, isn't there? It'll be a while before his case goes to trial and in the meantime he's wandering round free as a bird. I'm not going to pretend I'm not frightened, Kate, because I bloody well am."

"I'm so sorry, Claire. I can't believe how awful a time you've had."

"Don't worry, I'll get through it. As they say, whatever doesn't kill you makes you stronger."

"Yeah, but sometimes it just kills you."

Claire laughed. "You're a right little ray of sunshine, aren't you? Come on, the day's a-wasting and I'm starving. Let's see if we can find a nice quiet pub for a meal somewhere. I quite fancy Brampton Mill, actually. Are you up for it?"

"I thought you were a bit wary about going over the meadow?"

"I am – we can drive. We can bring Molly too; it's a nice day so we can sit outside."

"Sounds like a plan."

"One of my better ones," laughed Claire.

CHAPTER SIXTY-THREE

Almost nine months passed before Sean's case finally went to trial and, surprisingly, Claire caught sight of him just once during that period. She had been out for a walk with Toby and her aunt and they were nearing the Chinese Bridge in Godmanchester when Claire suddenly saw him walking towards them, edging round a small knot of adults and children queuing at an ice-cream van. They froze. Toby was still oblivious, chattering away, and Claire hurriedly pulled him into her side, turning him to make sure he couldn't see his father. Sean stood for a long moment staring back, a flurry of emotions passing quickly across his face: anger, then anguish and sorrow and a terrible kind of longing. Then he stepped out into the road, crossed quickly to the other side of the street and disappeared down a side road. Two weeks later, Chambers rang her with news of the trial date. It would start just before Easter, at the end of March.

Claire was asked whether she would prefer to give evidence by video link at the trial, but she instinctively knew her testimony would be far more powerful if she was present. She was determined she would do everything in her power to make sure Sean was convicted; the thought of him being freed and even, perhaps, able to resume contact with Toby was unbearable. As painful as it was, she was also determined to attend every single day of the trial; she needed to be there, to follow every twist and turn, to try to read what the jurors were thinking and feeling, to see how they reacted to the speeches of the prosecuting and defence counsels and to mark every

surreptitious glance they gave Sean as he stood impassively in the dock.

The Law Courts in Huntingdon were housed in a new brick building fronting the ring road and it was rumoured that town planners from other regions would often cite it as an example of exactly how not to lay out a ring road, such was the number of traffic lights which had sprouted up around its circumference.

It was four days into the trial before she finally appeared as a witness. There were two prosecuting barristers, an older man in his late fifties, tall, with a full head of grey hair, and a woman in her mid-thirties who Claire liked immediately. She was plain, with scraped-back dark hair and a no-nonsense air. Her manner belied her looks, though; she had a dry sense of humour, a fierce intelligence and radiated warmth. The presiding judge was also a woman, elderly and undistinguished looking, but with a formidable reputation.

Claire had been thoroughly prepped before appearing by both barristers and it was the young woman who now interrogated Claire on the stand, carefully taking her through the events leading up to the attack, her separation from Sean and the custody battle over Toby. Claire spoke about this as dispassionately as possible, trying neither to look at the jury or Sean standing in the dock. Describing the attack itself was more difficult and she struggled to keep her emotions in check as she relived the horror she had felt when he had first physically struck and then tried to drown her. Tears came to her eyes as she described the sensation of being held down in the river. At one point, her mouth dry with nerves, she forced herself to drink some water, her hand shaking a little as she brought the plastic cup to her lips. At the end of her testimony the judge adjourned the court for lunch. Her real ordeal would begin in the afternoon when defence counsel began their cross-examination.

Sean's defence team also comprised two people, although this time they were both men: a short, stubby barrel of a man matched with a taller, thinner counterpart, a Sancho Panza to his Don Quixote. It was Don Quixote who conducted the cross-examination and there the resemblance ended; instead of the courtly good manners one might have expected from such a figure, what she got instead was a rude brusqueness. It started well enough. He said he was aware of her standing in her profession and aware too that her evidence in several trials as a professional witness had been of critical importance to their outcome. All of this, though, was in fact to get her to lower her guard before the real attack, and she was genuinely taken aback when it started.

"You were sectioned under the Mental Health Act for a period, were you not? For psychosis?"

"Yes, for a very brief time, a number of years ago."

"And what was the diagnosis?"

"I'm bipolar, but it's under control and I receive medication for this."

"So, are you saying you no longer have either manic or depressive episodes?"

"No," said Claire slowly. "I do occasionally still experience both manic and depressive periods, but the difference is they're at a much lower intensity, and for the most part I live an entirely normal life."

"How long did your psychosis last?"

"As I said, a very short time, around three weeks."

"And just so we all have a better understanding of this, what symptoms did you experience?"

Claire knew the lawyer was laying a trap for her, but she was also struggling to see how she might evade it. All she could do was to choose her words as carefully as possible and hope she might yet escape the net. "I had acute insomnia and depression."

"But you also heard voices, didn't you? And there were hallucinations?"

"Yes."

"And what were those voices telling you?"

Claire stayed silent for a moment, her mind a whirl of conflicting thoughts as she struggled with how best to answer. She realised in an instant Sean would have already have shared this with his barrister. If she lied, Don Quixote would tell her exactly what the voices had said, and it was better if she controlled the narrative rather than him. "The voices told me that my husband was evil and that he wanted to destroy me."

There was a collective gasp from the jury as she said this and Claire tried desperately not to look at them.

"You've told us you still have periods of mania and depression, yes?"

"Yes, but at a much lower intensity."

"So, it can't really be said that your disorder is entirely controlled then, can it?"

"No, but—"

The barrister cut across her. "Thank you. Let's turn now to the day of the alleged attack. You say that your husband – the defendant – tried to drown you. Your husband is much stronger than you, wouldn't you agree?"

"Yes, of course."

"He's what, just over six foot, is he not? Around fifteen stone?"

"Yes, about that."

"And how tall are you?"

"Five foot four."

"Five foot four," he repeated. "And what weight?"

"Just under nine stone."

"Thank you. So, to put it bluntly, if he had really wanted

to kill you, to drown you in the river as you've so graphically described, then it seems to me he could have done that with relative ease. But he didn't, did he? So, I put it to you that at most his intention was to frighten you. He lost control of his emotions, was clearly very angry, but there was never any real intention to kill you. You were both angry, words were exchanged, it became physical, which was obviously regrettable, but you cannot, as the prosecution suggests, characterise this as attempted murder. It was an assault prompted by anger, but to call it an attempt to kill you is complete nonsense, isn't it?"

Much as she tried to keep her emotions in check, Claire felt her anger rising and it was impossible to hide it. Her face flushed red. "He tried to kill me... I almost drowned."

"Are we really to believe that? You've already acknowledged he's much stronger than you, a good six stone heavier. He is guilty of assault, but no-one can say, beyond a reasonable doubt – and that's the test we need to apply here – that he attempted to murder you. The charge is excessive and must fall. I have no further questions, Your Honour."

Don Quixote turned away from the witness box and resumed his seat. The judge gave a brief nod towards the defence bench. "Do either of you wish to cross-examine the witness?" The two lawyers whispered together and then the young woman again stood. There was a glint in her eye as she approached Claire.

"Just one question, if I may," she said. "When Sean was

attempting to push your head under the water, how did you finally manage to repel him?"

Claire smiled. "I kneed him in the balls."

A ripple of laughter went round the courtroom and Claire noted that even the judge was smiling.

"And what happened after that?"

"I kicked him hard again a couple of times and then a man who'd seen the whole thing ran across. He then called the police."

"Thank you, Mrs Evans. No further questions, Your Honour."

*

The jury deliberated for five hours before finally delivering a verdict. To Claire's relief their conclusion was that Sean was guilty of attempted murder. The judge said she would reflect on sentencing and reconvene the court the following week. Claire attended this hearing with Kate. Sean expressed no emotion as a sentence of seven years was handed down, the judge taking into account the fact that she did not feel the attempt on Claire's life was premeditated and Sean had previously been of good character. Claire knew that this meant that in all probability Sean would only serve three to four years, but it was enough; she had no wish to punish him unduly. He was still, after all, Toby's father and at some point in the future he and Toby might want to rebuild their relationship. In truth, despite how he had behaved, she felt sorry for him, and she preferred pity to hatred.

Life felt more fragile now, but that fragility made it even more precious.

We are all walking a tightrope, she reflected, but still, we walk on, trying not to look down, knowing that, despite everything, at some point we will slip and fall anyway. For now, though, she could feel the sun on her face. It was enough. More than enough.

WITH THANKS

I hope you enjoyed reading *The Invitation*.

If you did, please feel free to leave a review on the book's Amazon page. Reviews are very important to both readers and authors, alike.

By way of a small 'thank you' for your interest in my writing, here's a taster of another of my novels, *The Faces That You Meet*. This is also available in Kindle and paperback on Amazon.

Patrick MacDonald,
Cambridge, May 2023

PROLOGUE

John hanged himself over the Christmas holidays while staying with his parents. Their house in Caernarfon had spectacular views of the bay and the castle from the front, whilst the back faced on to lush meadows grazed by both sheep and cattle. A short distance away, the meadows were punctuated by a small copse of trees. Ash, sycamores and beech all jostled for space within the wood, but there were also one or two oaks, and it was from one of their branches that he chose to hang himself, his body found the following morning by a neighbour out walking their dog. The dog came across the body first, his excited barking hastening his owner's steps. It was a cold day, but also cloudless, the sky a steely blue, mists still rising slowly from the fields. Crows circled overhead, their rasping cries cutting through the air.

As Sam Clarke approached the tree, the body's back faced him, slowly spinning round as though to greet him. Sam realised with horror that, despite the distorted features, it was someone he knew. Sam had known John for most of his life; Sam's son had been in the same reception class and, later, the same secondary school. Sam had also been close to John's parents. He had been on the PTA with John's mum, Sue, and, for a long time, had nursed secret and unfulfilled fantasies about them becoming lovers.

But the John he knew was very different from the apparition that now greeted him. The face was swollen and almost blue in colour. A fat blue slug, which he realised was John's tongue, protruded from his mouth. The head was also skewed at an angle. There was an unpleasant smell of faeces; looking down, he could see the shoes and trousers were coated with shit.

Sam turned away, his hand flew to his mouth and he vomited, retching until the painful spasms stopped. His dog was hesitant at first, looking suspiciously up at the body, barking nervously, retreating and then immediately circling back. Then, fear overcome, he came nearer to investigate the new smells which had appeared. Sam pushed him away with his hand. He gazed up at the sky; it seemed almost black, so many new crows had appeared. The noise was unbearable. He caught hold of Buddy's collar and clipped him back on to the lead. Then he turned and started to walk back.

Normally, he took a shortcut through a lane which led directly to his own cottage, but this morning he ignored it. John's parents lived in a modern detached executive house in a new development on the edge of the village. As he came up to the house, he saw that Sue was in the garden. She was crouched over, peering at the burgundy flowers of a hellebore which had decided this year to make an unseasonably early debut. As he drew near, she suddenly glanced up.

"Sam, this is a little early for you, isn't it?" she said, smiling. Sam forced a smile.

"It's Buddy. He was scratching at the bedroom door, fit to bust, this morning. Normally he doesn't disturb me until eight at the earliest, but he seems to have made an exception this morning. Sue, I…" He stared at her, hesitating.

There was something in his expression which alarmed her, her throat tightening, a painful cramping in her stomach.

"It's John," he said.

"What about John?"

He looked nervously over her shoulder towards the house.

"Is Paul around?"

"No, you've just missed him. He's gone to work."

"Ah, I see." Another hesitation, and then: "Do you want to go into the house? It might be better if we spoke there."

"What's wrong, Sam? What about John? Has something happened?"

"Sue, I'm so sorry, he's dead."

"Dead? Who's dead?"

"John… John's dead. He's hanged himself, I found him in the woods, the dog, you see—"

"But he can't be. He's in the house – he's still in bed. Look, I'll show you."

She turned, started to hurry back.

"Sue – stop, stop. He's not there. He's dead."

She turned round, staring at him blankly, her face a mixture of disbelief and then rising horror. She gave a piercing, unearthly scream which would haunt Sam until his dying day, sank to the ground and curled herself into a howling ball of anguish. He bent over her, wanting to comfort her, his arm reaching down towards her shoulder. He realised he was too frightened to touch her, felt that if he tried to do this, then her anguish and fear would spill upwards and consume him as well. So, he stood, half crouched, his arm hovering uselessly above her.

CHAPTER ONE

Rachel

3rd July 2012

My last date had looked like a cross between George Clooney and Colin Firth, but, unfortunately, the amalgam was of their worst, rather than their best features. I had sworn this was the last time I would use a dating website. I might have more luck going out into the street with a bag on my head and grabbing the first human being I came across, male or female. But hope springs eternal and here I was again, sitting in a pub opposite a man, who was managing to conduct a conversation which involved at least the pretence of listening to what I had to say, rather than being one long monologue about what a fascinating life he had led. He wasn't particularly good-looking, but as potential arm candy he wasn't that bad either.

Simon was unshaven with an untidy mop of dark hair, so not especially well-groomed, but I like that in a bloke. He was also well-dressed in chinos and a tailored blue shirt and was the perfect height; I'm five foot three and I judged he was about five-ten. I could imagine myself lying snugly against his chest.

"It's just that I think blokes are nicer than women—" he was saying.

What? I had tuned out for a millisecond, but now I was suddenly back. So far, the conversation had followed the usual path, but he had now clearly veered off into the undergrowth.

"What do you mean, 'blokes are nicer than women'?" I said. "Oh, let me think... Pol Pot, Mao Tse-tung, Stalin, Hitler. Yes, you're right, evil bitches, every last one of them."

He looked startled.

"Well, Rachel, there's Maggie Thatcher and, uhm, my mum..."

"Your mum? Anyway, I think you'll find Maggie Thatcher was a bloke. This country has yet to have a woman Prime Minister. What was wrong with her anyway – your mum, I mean?"

Simon hesitated before speaking. "She used to beat me when we were kids... with the wrong end of a broom handle sometimes, or basically with whatever she could lay her hands on – knives, whips, an ice-cream scoop. For a time, I seriously thought she was a witch. I thought she'd kidnapped my real mum and replaced her."

Good God. I felt a little uneasy at this. What sort of mother takes a broomstick to their child? Perhaps, though, she had good reason to thrash him. Perhaps she was psychic and already sensed her son would grow up to become a rampant misogynist. Or maybe he was an evil little sod who even the

Pope might have been tempted to lay into.

He was still single at thirty-five as well, which should have rung at least one alarm bell. On the other hand, why was I still on the shelf myself at twenty-nine and eleven twelfths? Maybe he had just come out of some long, tragic relationship and was making a brief appearance on the shelf himself before being snatched up in the sales.

"The funny thing was," he was saying, "I remember once that she cornered me in the kitchen with the broom handle raised above me ready to strike. I must have been around eight. Anyway, down came the handle. I really can't remember what happened after that. I suppose she must have laid into me and the memory has been wiped because it was too horrible. A bit like Proust's madeleines – I imagine if I bit into the end of a broomstick the memories would come flooding back."

He laughed awkwardly.

"My mum wasn't a witch by the way," he continued. "She was an amazing woman who had a very tough time bringing us up and we were pretty evil kids anyway. We thought nothing of putting a lighted banger through a neighbour's door, ringing the bell and running away."

So, he was a piece of work as a child. I was beginning to think he'd got off lightly being beaten by a broom handle. He did seem to be extremely well read, though. Or, at least, genned up in the bluffer's guide to all things literary.

"Have you read Proust?"

"Only in the French, I'm afraid." Then he laughed. "No –

everyone knows the episode of the madeleine. Have you read Proust?"

"No. Seemed a bit long for me. It's on my list of must-read-before-I-die-books, like *War and Peace* and *Finnegans Wake*. Well, scrub the last one. What was Joyce thinking of? What's the point of writing a book no-one can understand? I bet Nora was impressed. Also, fancy marrying someone called Barnacle – bet they got a lot of limpet jokes."

"Barnacle?"

"His wife was called Nora Barnacle."

Not so well read, then. Definitely beddable, though.

I looked more closely at him. His eyes were a brilliant, piercing blue and the more time I spent with him the more attractive he became. Still, I couldn't sleep with him on the first date. No, that normally had to wait until at least date three. I would console myself tonight with a lingering kiss, perhaps.

Hang on, wake up, he was still chuntering on. I might have missed something important, like the fact that he was seriously rich and adored children.

"Anyway, I hated the City, so I gave it up to become a teacher."

Scratch seriously rich then. "Are you enjoying it?"

"Yes, I absolutely love it. I'm teaching Maths and PE at a secondary school in Hackney. The school badly needs some TLC, but the kids are great. Every day is different and it certainly beats being chained to a desk. I also love any excuse to kick a ball round, to be honest."

"You don't miss the money, then?" I said, hopefully.

"No, not really – I've never been materialistic. I sort of fell into banking because I had a maths degree."

"Which uni did you go to?"

"Aberystwyth," he said. "I think they let you in if you could spell it. I really went there because I had chronic asthma as a child and I thought the sea air might cure it. Strangely enough, it worked – I've never had an asthma attack since. Of course, the fact that both my parents were chronic smokers might also have had something to do with it. The funny thing was, once I left, they both gave up. I once had the horrible thought that perhaps they started smoking in the first place just to get rid of me. What about you? What dark secrets do you have?"

"I went to Sheffield and did English. I got an average degree, but that may have been because I never went to any lectures. I went a bit mad when I first went up. I studied really hard for my A-levels and got a fistful of A grades and, as soon as I arrived at Sheffield, I suddenly realised there were more interesting ways of passing your time. I should have camped out in the library and sucked up to the lecturers. As it was, I managed to antagonise some of them. I remember an Anglo-Saxon class where the lecturer was laboriously taking us through Beowulf, and I said – in a stage whisper – that they must have had a hard time understanding each other, mangling their vowels like that. He wasn't impressed."

"Fancy another drink, Rachel?"

"Yes, why not – could I have a gin and tonic?"

He arched an eyebrow. "Really? Your first drink was sparkling water."

I blushed slightly.

"True, but you've been drinking pints and I feel a need to keep up."

"Any particular brand?"

"Well, Hendrick's and elderflower tonic would be my favourite, but really I'm easy."

"No problem, Hendrick's it is, assuming they've got it, of course. Do you have a second choice, just in case?"

"Plymouth's is fine. If they don't have that then surprise me."

So yes, there was a lingering kiss at the end of the evening, and he tackled the whole thing with sensitivity and flair. In other words, he didn't attempt to give me a tonsillectomy, which is something I've sadly experienced far too often in the past.

All good really, and it was nice to sort out at least one part of my life. I just need to make sure he passes the wet-shirt-in-a-lake test.

I hadn't had much luck with blokes up to that point. Although I was considered attractive and had once been told I looked a bit like Kate Beckinsale, the blokes who came on to me were ironically the type I despised – cocksure (in every sense of the word) and with the emotional depth of a flatworm. The blokes I would have been attracted to seemed to be frankly intimidated by my looks and so didn't even bother to enter the ring.

On the other hand, I wasn't doing too badly job-wise. I had landed a job as a copywriter in an advertising agency and, so far, I was enjoying it.

*

I agreed to meet Simon again, later that week, in the same pub. We thought we might start there and then go on elsewhere to find somewhere to eat. The evening itself was really enjoyable, but something odd happened just at the point I was about to suggest that we moved on.

For some reason, I glanced towards the door. It was just about to close, and I thought I glimpsed someone who looked almost exactly like me. Whoever it was had the same straight black hair and, even stranger, they seemed to be wearing the same dress.

I had wasted a good half-hour agonising over what outfit to wear and in the end had gone for a knee-length black dress from Whistles, which I thought was one the few dresses which flattered my figure. It's funny how it's only the most expensive stuff which seems able to do that, but there it is, go figure.

Simon noticed the startled look on my face, and he turned himself to look at the door.

"Is there a problem, Rachel? You look slightly shocked."

"No, I'm fine, honestly. I just thought I might have seen someone who looked familiar, but I must have been mistaken."

"Old boyfriend?" he said mischievously. "A stalker perhaps

– you look like the sort of girl who would attract reams of stalkers. I might even take it up myself."

"Don't joke about that sort of thing," I said, unnerved. "It's not funny. No, don't worry – I'm sure it was nothing. Where do you fancy eating?"

"I don't really know this area, so I'm happy to be led by you really."

"There's a Pizza Express quite close to here, and at least there you know what you're getting – decent food at a reasonable price. What do you think?"

"Sounds great."

*

At the end of the evening he asked if he could see me again and I resisted the temptation to say, "Yes, why not tomorrow – in fact, why not every day so we could get to the bedroom part a damn sight quicker and sod all this delicate courtship nonsense?" Instead, I took a deep breath, said how much I had enjoyed the evening and suggested that he rang me. This was the time-honoured way for him to show how interested he really was although, let's be frank, also a little risky for yours truly, who would now have to have her mobile phone surgically attached for the next few days until he finally did ring, but life is full of risks, so there you go. And, if he really did fancy me, I guessed he would allow a day to pass and then ring, so let's see, shall we?

I have to confess, I was also a little distracted by what had happened in the pub, but I decided it was nothing worth worrying about. Lots of women had a hair colour and style similar to my own and the dress was a high-street brand, so it shouldn't be too surprising that I should see someone else wearing it.

Simon and I had met up close to King's Cross, so I caught the Metropolitan line to Plaistow and it was then a slightly anxious ten-minute walk to the flat I rented with Alison. I say anxious because the street lighting wasn't great and, to be frank, where I lived was quite an edgy place.

The flat itself was above a slightly seedy dry cleaners, one of the few which hadn't yet been bought up by one of the chains such as Timpsons or Sketchley. There was a narrow door beside the shop and then an equally narrow stairway, at the top of which was the entrance door to our flat. Since it was now just after one in the morning and I didn't want to disturb Alison, I let myself in as quietly as possible and didn't switch on the hall light. The hallway itself was tiny and was littered with boots and shoes and fast-food leaflets that neither of us could be bothered to sort through or pick up.

I noticed the living-room light was still on, which meant, of course, that there was a good chance Alison was still up. I wasn't that surprised, because she was a bit of a night owl and often stayed up late. It would have been rude of me to march straight past, so I pushed the door ajar and peered in.

Alison was sitting on the sofa reading a magazine. There was a half-filled glass of white wine on the coffee table in front of her and she was swathed in a blue dressing gown. She normally wore contact lenses, but ditched these as soon as she got home to give her eyes a rest, so she was now wearing glasses. She sat there peering over the top of them at me.

"How was your date?"

"It was fine. I haven't yet fallen hopelessly in love, so at the moment I'm making do with the faintest glimmer of lust, but, no, seriously, I really like him."

"Good – you clearly had a much better evening than me then and, for that matter, thinking about it, I also had a fairly shit day."

"Why, what happened?"

"I had a review meeting with my arsehole of a supervisor."

"Ah, that would do it."

"He's driving me to drink," she said, waving airily at the glass of wine. "Pretty soon I'll be a fully paid-up member of the AA if this keeps up; either that, or occupying a park bench somewhere."

Alison was having a rough time at work. She was doing a PhD at UCL in physics, and her supervisor was someone called Miles Stafford. I hadn't had the pleasure of meeting him but, apparently, he was someone who could suck all the joy out of a room simply by entering it. In true bully mode, he was also physically overbearing. He was around six-two or three and six-two or three around the middle as well. He also bit his nails in a way which meant that he now had stumps rather than fingers. And when he wasn't biting his nails to the quick, he was making forlorn attempts to resettle his dentures, which meant sticking most of his fist in his mouth for minutes at a time. Alison said that he'd once had voice coaching, but she hadn't noticed any improvement. She said that if he'd asked her, she would have told him he might notice an immediate improvement if he just took his fist out of his mouth. She said he was so fat he didn't so much sit in a chair as temporarily remove it from view, sprawling with his legs apart in a way that would embarrass the most hardened hooker.

"He just keeps overloading me with work. I tried talking to him about it, but he just stares at me. He makes me produce notes of the meeting and then he produces his own notes as well, which he uses to correct my notes. He's driving me mad. I'm seriously wondering how far I would get if I claimed he was sexually harassing me, whether that would actually get rid of him. The problem is, no-one would believe it anyway. I'd have an easier time trying to persuade them he'd tried to roger his filing cabinet."

"Would his filing cabinet be prepared to file a complaint?"

"I very much doubt it, Rachel. Don't suppose you fancy a glass, do you?"

"No, I'm knackered, and I've got an eight o'clock meeting tomorrow so I really need to sleep. I'll see you in the morning, or maybe not since I've got such an early meeting."

I retraced my steps back to my bedroom. This faced on to the noisy main road at the front, but, as a consolation, it was also slightly larger than Alison's room. We had tossed a coin when we first moved in and I'm not sure which of us had really fared better.

Alison was not just a flatmate – I also considered her to be a friend. When I first moved into the flat, I had been sharing with a bloke called Matt. I had found the place through a flat-sharing site on the internet. Matt was very good-looking with strong, masculine features and a head of unruly blond hair. I had fancied him immediately and had entertained vague thoughts that once he got to know me, he would abandon his girlfriend (this despite the fact that they had been going out together for four years) and fall into my arms instead.

What actually happened is that after six months he announced that they were getting married and his parents had given him some money for a deposit on a first house. I pretended to be pleased for him but, in reality, I felt not only disappointed that he was leaving but also dismayed about having to find another flatmate. As it was, Alison's was one of the first responses I received to the advert I had carefully crafted.

I warmed to her immediately. She was funny and self-deprecating. I thought she was attractive, but it was clear she didn't feel that way herself. She had a large birthmark just above her left eyebrow, an ugly irregular mark, purple in colour, which was about the size of a twopence coin. She wore her hair in a fringe to hide it, which she was constantly adjusting. Often, she would reveal the mark by accident, unthinkingly sweeping her hair away from her face and tucking it behind her ear. Realising what she had done, she would then hurriedly bring it back.

When I knew her better, she told me how self-conscious it made her feel. I told her, quite truthfully, that as far as I was concerned, it heightened her attractiveness, rather than disfigured it. I had always found people who had some minor blemish more attractive anyway; it made them more human, somehow. What I struggled with were those godlike creatures with perfect looks who treated the rest of us with mild disdain, as though they were having to slum it a little to have to spend any time at all with us mere mortals.

I found out Alison was also ultra-bright and had pulled off a first-class honours degree in physics. At the same time, she was also very intense and somehow vulnerable, and I quickly came to feel especially protective of her. She told me that at the end of her first year, she had also suffered some sort of mental collapse.

She had been spending insane hours in the library studying for her first-year exams. A friend rang her parents and they immediately rushed across from Cornwall and, within a day, had spirited her back home. She had only sat a few exams before her collapse, but her parents managed to persuade the university to allow her to retake her remaining papers at the end of August. She returned to university in the autumn and, apparently, there had been no further issues.

CHAPTER TWO

11th July 2012

I decided to invite Simon round for a meal so I could show off my culinary expertise in the kitchen and also, to be frank, see what happened from there. Obviously, I wanted to choose an evening when Alison wasn't around. I raised it with her, and she said she was going for a drink the following Wednesday evening with some friends from UCL, so why not invite him round then? She also said that, given the writeup I had given him, she couldn't wait to finally meet him, but she guessed she could contain herself a little longer.

I arranged to meet Simon again after work that Wednesday so we could travel together to the flat. He had bought wine, flowers and chocolates, so either he really knew how to romance a girl, or he'd met a very persuasive and attractive sales assistant. I was impressed, nonetheless.

All was well until we entered the flat. We found Alison in the kitchen making herself a mug of tea.

"Hi – I thought you were seeing some friends this evening?"

"I cancelled. I'm behind on a lab report and Miles has said

he wants it by tomorrow." She shrugged ruefully. "Don't worry," she added. "I'll try and keep out of your way. I'm going to be holed up in my bedroom writing this wretched report anyway."

"No problem," I said. I gestured towards Simon. "Alison, this is Simon – take a good look because once he's sampled my cooking you may never see him again."

"Hi, Alison. Nice to meet you at last."

"And you. Well, I'd better get out of your way."

It was a narrow galley kitchen and I had to move back to allow her to pass. It was only then that I noticed how she was dressed. She was still wearing her contact lenses and was also wearing what she described as her killer jeans, the ones which showed off her figure to its best advantage, the sort of jeans which could only be put on with a lot of tugging and swearing. They were also topped off with a cream blouse showing just a hint of cleavage. In other words, it wasn't an outfit someone would wear who was looking forward to being huddled over a laptop in their bedroom for most of the night. I could see Simon staring in the Pavlovian way most blokes his age did when confronted with a new and attractive female.

"Right," I said, once she'd gone. "Let's get that bottle of wine open."

After much deliberation I had planned what I thought was a foolproof menu. I intended to cook a simple chicken stir-fry (without garlic obviously!) with a lime cheesecake to follow. I had made the cheesecake the previous evening and stored it in the fridge. I opened the fridge to retrieve an onion and peppers and was about to close it again when I noticed that the cheesecake wasn't there. It must be hidden behind something. Perhaps Alison had moved it, to get at something else. But no, it was definitely missing. Perhaps she had taken it out? I went into the living room. Alison was sitting on the threadbare sofa, reading a newspaper.

"Alison, have you seen the cheesecake? I can't seem to find it. It was in the fridge."

She gazed up at me.

"No, 'fraid not. Just as well, really. I might have been tempted to have a piece. What sort was it?"

"Lime."

"One of my favourites, too. Have you looked in the cupboards? Or the cake tin?"

"No, no, I'm sure I wouldn't have been that daft. It had to be chilled. I'll look, but—"

I went back to the kitchen, frowning. The cupboard search was a waste of time and, as expected, the cake tin was empty. Had I made it at all? Had I just imagined it? I glanced at the glass fruit bowl. The limes I had bought in the market at the weekend were gone. So, I must have made it. I looked in the fridge again, hoping it would somehow magically materialise. No, it had definitely gone.

All the time, Simon had been watching me, a look of wry amusement on his face.

"What's happened? You're obviously searching for something."

"I made you a cheesecake, but I can't seem to find it."

"When did you make it?"

"Last night."

"Perhaps you were sleepwalking. Came down in the night and wolfed the lot."

"It's not funny, Simon. Oh, never mind. We'll just have to do without it. I'll knock us up some fruit and ice cream."

"What flavour was it?'

"Pralines and cream, I think."

"No, the cheesecake. What flavour was it?"

"Well, it's a little academic now, isn't it? Lime – lime cheesecake."

"Well, that's a pity – I would have loved that. Never mind, fruit and ice cream is fine."

He nodded towards the wine, which, distracted by the hunt for the cheesecake, I had neglected to open.

"Oh God, I forgot about that. I'll open it now. Can you hand me down two glasses? They're in the top cupboard behind you. Would you mind being my commis chef and cutting up this onion for me? Onions tend to make me cry, I'm afraid, and then my mascara will run."

"Well, we can't have you in tears. Hand me a knife, then."

Suffice to say, dinner, despite the missing cheesecake, was a success. Even the fruit and ice cream worked out okay and it did at least have the advantage of being healthier – well, apart from the ice cream, which I ate too much of. I even sneaked some more when I took the tub back into the kitchen. I'm exactly the sort of girl, who, when the glums descend, ends up slobbing out in front of the telly with a tub of ice cream and a spoon, finishing the lot off over the course of an evening.

We had just retired to the living room with what was left of the wine, when in walked Alison. She looked on the edge of tears and immediately plonked herself down in an armchair facing our sofa.

"I can't do this," she blurted out. "My lab work is rubbish and I'm worried I'm going to get chucked off the course."

"I'm sure that's not true, Alison," I said. I really wanted to strangle her – she was now very successfully wrecking my entire evening. At the same time, though, I felt sorry for her and I could see, as well, that Simon looked concerned.

"No, it is. I'm fine at the theoretical stuff but I'm hopeless in the lab. The simplest mechanical tasks are beyond me and yet all I'm being given at the moment are these wretched experiments and I can't produce the results I've been told should be possible from them. I've rerun these experiments at least a dozen times, and each attempt is taking me two or three days."

I looked at her. "Have you spoken to your supervisor about it?"

"Yes, but I've told you already, he's horrible, and he just keeps telling me how important these experiments are and to keep rerunning them. I just can't do this – I'm going to have to leave."

"Alison, you'll get through this, I'm sure you will. You've

sacrificed too much to give it all up now."

I glanced at Simon and, fortunately, he knew what was expected of him; he knew the evening was ruined and he needed to exit gracefully whilst I carried out emergency repairs on Alison's fragile ego.

"I'd better go," he said. "It was really nice to meet you, Alison. Thanks for a fantastic evening, Rachel. I'll give you a ring tomorrow."

So, that went well, didn't it? Alison had successfully managed to sabotage my entire evening and the worst of it was, I didn't know whether she had done it deliberately, or if it was a genuine cri du coeur. She seemed to be genuinely in crisis, but why would someone that upset go to such lengths to dress up as she had, almost as though she herself had had a date? And what in hell had happened to the cheesecake? Had her arsehole of a supervisor upset her so much, she had felt the need to binge-eat an entire cheesecake? One slice was credible, but not all of it. Maybe she had hidden what was left in her bedroom, too ashamed to admit what she had done? Oh, this was ridiculous. I must have just forgotten to make it – perhaps Simon was right and I had just dreamt I had made it, even dreamt I had bought the limes.

Later, I lay in bed trying to puzzle it through, but only managed to exhaust myself. It was possible she was attracted to Simon herself, of course, but even if that were true, collapsing in tears in front of him seemed an odd way to go about it. Her mascara had definitely been a mess.

Stop, I thought – you're going mad. Take a deep breath. Alison is a friend. She's behaving oddly, it's true, but she's always been a little intense.

I've always thought that the more intelligent you are, the less chance you have of being happy in this life; intelligent people seem to both see and feel too deeply. In fact, I had a friend at university I was really envious of – he wasn't very bright but always seemed incredibly happy, almost as though he floated above the surface of life whereas the rest of us were down in the depths, peering anxiously around for sharks and other hidden perils.

I would love to do that, just skate above the surface of life, moving too quickly to be caught and dragged down into the depths. But no, like J Alfred Prufrock I was doomed to scuttle along the ocean floor – T. S. Eliot in case you're wondering, but don't feel you need to track down the source. Life's too short.

Sometimes, I think consciousness is a curse – why were we saddled with this stuff? I'm sure we'd all be happier if we were reborn as dogs or cats, provided we were placed with the right owners, of course, and were well-loved and looked after. My mum had a cat and, whenever I left the house, it always had a sneering look on its face, as though to say, "Poor you. What a life you lead – not one I could be bothered with, I'm afraid." Yes, quite. Never liked cats. No wonder they're associated with witches.

*

Then things got even odder. I had been desperately worried about Alison being bullied by her supervisor because I knew she was fragile anyway, and I was concerned his treatment of her might trigger another breakdown.

I still remembered the occasion I had found her shaking and crying in the kitchen, curled in a ball on the cold, tiled floor. It had taken me a while to get her to tell me what had upset her and, to my astonishment, she revealed it was because she had tried to open a can of soup, made a mess of it, and spilt half of it on the floor. It was an entirely disproportionate response, but she felt it summed up her complete inadequacy, her failure to come to grips with the simple business of living that everyone else mastered with nonchalant ease.

Small wonder I was now thinking of trying to go and see her supervisor to explain how unhappy Alison was and to make him aware of the effect his behaviour was having on her. I was still uncertain about this, though, because I didn't want to do anything which might damage their relationship even further, and nor was I sure he would even agree to see me – what reason could I give him for wanting to do this? I didn't want to accuse him of bullying her over the phone; at best, I would have to ring and say I needed to talk to him as a friend of Alison's because I had some concerns about her, but would need a meeting with him to explain further.

I was still uncertain this was a good idea, so I decided to google him. I started with the UCL website, which included a profile and photograph of him. Since this was confined to a headshot, it was difficult to form an impression of what he was like physically, so I clicked on Images and immediately a series of photographs of him in different settings emerged – photographs of him at conferences surrounded by colleagues, other photographs of him shaking hands or beaming alongside other worthy eminences in the world of physics.

What was shocking, though, was the fact that he wasn't at all like the creature Alison had described. He was clearly quite small, not bad-looking, and, most striking of all – thin. He looked like someone who ran marathons, not someone who was a threat to every chair he sat on. Of course, it was possible that he had ballooned out and become corpulent as a result of a recently acquired eating disorder, but, looking more closely, I saw that one of the photographs was dated and had been taken within the last year, and there he was, smiling and thin. He didn't look like a bully either – of course, appearances can be deceptive as far as that's concerned, but still.

Now I was worried. Alison had apparently lied about this, but I couldn't work out why. She could simply have described him as a thin bully, and I would have believed her, but she had very deliberately described him as grossly obese.

Now, they say beauty is in the eye of the beholder, and I have noticed a tendency for women who've separated from their partners in acrimonious circumstances to describe with relish how seedy their former lovers have become, and how quickly their looks have deteriorated. I've often been tempted to point out that their partner's looks are probably unchanged, and what has changed is the filter through which they look at them, but that's a fast way to lose friends so, unsurprisingly, I haven't gone there. So, it's possible Alison's loathing of him had distorted the way she saw him. But not to this extent, surely?

What to do, though? I thought about confronting her, but quickly dismissed this. If I said I'd googled her boss, she would want to know why I'd done that and why I was spying on her. She could even claim that I'd confused him with someone else, that I'd got the name wrong and had conflated two people she had talked about. No, it was hopeless. I would have to keep my own counsel and just keep an eye on her to see what else developed.

ACKNOWLEDGEMENTS

I would first like to thank all of the members of the Women's Institute St Neot's book club and the members of the St Neot's book club. Both book clubs were kind enough to read the first draft of the novel and gave me some invaluable advice on where they thought it should be changed.

I would also like to thank Mark Thomas (coverness.com) for his design and typesetting skills and guiding me through the process of getting this novel published. Thanks, as well to Melanie Scott for her brilliant proofreading skills.

Finally, I would like to thank Chrissie Cuming Walters for explaining some of the more arcane points of family law. Any mistakes in interpretation or understanding are entirely my own.

BY THE SAME AUTHOR

Ireland, 1845: The potato crop has failed ushering in a six-year period of famine and disease which will destroy a million lives and compel another million people to flee the country…

A woman cursed by a priest stands alone on a clifftop trying to summon up the courage to jump.

Her brother stands accused of murder and rebellion against the State.

Surrounded by a troop of soldiers a landlord destroys the homes of his tenants leaving them to die on the hillsides.

The British Government responds to the crisis, reshaping Irish society with disastrous results.

Darkness Falling is available now in paperback and for Kindle® from Amazon..

ABOUT THE AUTHOR

Patrick MacDonald is married with two sons and lives near Cambridge.

He has published three novels, *The Faces That You Meet, Darkness Falling* and, now, *The Invitation.* All of these are available in Kindle® and paperback editions on Amazon.

You can stay in contact with Patrick via his website:
www.patrickmacdonald.online

Or via the following social media:
facebook.com/patrickmacdonaldwrites
instagram.com/patrickmacdonaldwrites
twitter.com/patrickmacdonaldwrites

Printed in Great Britain
by Amazon